Cowboy Blessings

Clean & Wholesome Cowboy Romance

Jenna Hendricks

Contents

Books by Jenna Hendricks (Clean & Wholesome Romance)

<u>Triple J Ranch</u> –

Book 0 - Finding Love in Montana (Join my newsletter to get this book for free)

Book 1 - Second Chance Ranch

Book 2 – Cowboy Ranch

Book 3 – Runaway Cowgirl Bride

Book 4 – Faith of a Cowboy

Book 5 – Cowboy Blessings

Book 6 – The Cowboy's Game

<u>Big Sky Christmas</u> –

Book 1 – Her Montana Christmas Cowboy

Book 2 – Her Christmas Rodeo Cowboy

1

Book 3 – Her Mistletoe Cowboy

Book 4 – Her Sleigh Ride Christmas Cowboy

<u>Crooked Arrow Ranch</u> –

Book 0 - Wounded Hearts Ranch (join my newsletter to get this free)

Book 1 – A Broken Heart Mended

Book 2 – Hope's Healing Love

Book 3 - Love's Healing Balm

Book 4 – A Crooked Arrow Christmas

Book 5 – Tripping Over Christmas

<u>Saguaro Bookshop Mysteries</u> –

Book 1 – Saguaro, Snowflakes, and Murder

<u>Standalone Novels</u> –

Christmas Crazy in July

Rebel Hearts Anthology

See these titles and more: https://JennaHendricks.com

Prologue

"With a score of ninety-two, this puts newcomer John Manning way out in the lead today! Let's give him a huge round of applause, folks. John, take a bow for the audience." The announcer sounded like one of those fancy TV sports announcers, and when he said John's name and his score, another shot of adrenaline zinged up his spine.

He couldn't think of a better day in his life. This was the stuff dreams were made of, and he was going to do everything he could to keep this feeling of pride, excitement, and pure joy going. Nothing was ever going to get in his way and keep him from his goal of winning the shiny belt buckle at the PBR championships one day in Vegas.

The fact that this was only John's third time out of the chute with the professional tour made it all that much more surreal. While he was only in his first year of college, John had joined the bull-riding tour and attended rodeos that were less than a six-hour drive from college, as well as only over a weekend. He promised his folks he would graduate from college before joining the tour full-time, but he had never said anything about doing it part-time.

The winnings from today's event would make it possible for him to keep going, at least to the local events. He did promise to finish college, so he would. And he knew that bull riding wasn't a long-term job. If he was blessed he'd get to ride for ten years, maybe a bit longer. Then he would head home to Montana and the Triple J Ranch to work the rest of his life on the family land.

John Manning was on his way to being a legend before he'd even finished his first year of college. Over the summer he had ridden bulls in rodeos that were close to home in Beacon Creek, Montana. He had even won a couple and placed in the top three in all the rest. But none of those winnings were even close to what he had just won. If this kept up, he would be hard-pressed to stay in college and *not* join the rodeo circuit full-time.

Back home, it was easy riding bulls when his family was in the stands supporting him. And he had done quite well. But in Wyoming he knew next to no one, and it wasn't as easy to win when the audience wasn't rooting for him. Well, almost no one.

At the first rodeo in Casper, Wyoming this past November, he had met the rodeo queen who just happened to attend the same college he did—the University of Wyoming. After that, they attended the rodeos together.

While this was only the second rodeo they'd carpooled to, they had gotten very close in the past two months.

Donna Myers was not only a rodeo queen, but she was also a barrel racer. While she had only been riding for a few years, she was on her way up in the rankings. And like John, she wanted to get her degree before she went full-time. She viewed these semi-local races as her chance to get more experience and her name out there before she went full-time.

"Woo-hoo! Go get 'em, Johnny!" Only Donna got away with calling John "Johnny." Not even his family was allowed to call him that. But something about the way Donna said *Johnny* sent his heart fluttering.

She could call him dingleberry and his heart would jump at her melodic voice.

John smiled when he saw her jumping in the stands and waving at him. He waved his arm and winked at her.

Donna blew him a kiss, and he caught it. His eyes lit up every time she did that.

The moment John had seen Donna at that first rodeo in Casper right before Thanksgiving, he was in love. She was in the spotlight, racing around the barrels, her blonde hair flying behind her. Donna didn't win, but she did place third, and that caught his attention even more after he placed third in his bull-riding competition. Then, when he saw her in an evening gown and her rodeo queen crown, he began drooling. There was no coming back from the vision of her in a red gown with shimmering rhinestones adorning the entire dress.

Then, when her leg peeked out from the side slit, he'd tripped over his own feet.

When he looked up, there she stood, smiling down at him. She offered her hand and said, "Hiya, need some help?"

He tried to speak, but his throat dried up and his cheeks felt hot. When he stood up, he just stared into her deep blue eyes that sparkled from all the bling she was wearing.

"Are you alright?" The beautiful ocean-blue eyes crinkled when she looked the cowboy up and down.

"Uh..." Slack-jawed, he stared at the most beautiful woman he'd ever seen and his mind went completely blank. In high school, John had his share of dates and women chasing after him; he was a Manning, after all. But since going off to college he hadn't met anyone who interested him, until now. And he couldn't get his silly mind to work.

Donna's tinkling giggle warmed his body, starting at his toes and moving all the way to his face, when he finally answered. "Yes, thank you."

She had already begun walking away and shaking her head. But when he answered, she stopped and looked over her shoulder and winked at him.

John knew he had blown it, big time. Although, she was probably out of his league anyway. After he stood up on his own, he watched her walk away with two of the princesses in her court and he sighed.

"Dude, that's never gonna happen." Rick Reagan clapped his shoulder and laughed.

"Shut up. You never know what might happen down the road." John kept watching her sashay away until the crowds enclosed her completely and he lost track of her sparkling crown.

At the time, John thought he was the luckiest guy in all the world when he saw her again later that evening. She was being hassled by an older, drunk man in dirty jeans and a wrinkled shirt. This was his chance to show her who he really was, not that simpering fool who literally fell at her feet and couldn't even talk.

"I said leave me alone. I'm not interested." Donna stood to her full height of 5'4", but in her heels she was 5'7". She gave the stranger her evil eye and put her hands on her hips. "If you don't leave me alone, I'll punch you in the nose."

The drunk swayed. "If you don't want my attention, why are you dressed like a hooker?"

Donna gasped, as did a few cowgirls walking by.

John took this as his cue to do something. His momma had raised him to show respect for women and help them when in need. "Sir, there's no reason to disrespect our rodeo queen like that." John got between the belligerent man and Donna. "If you can't say anything nice, then don't say anything at all."

"Who are you? Her handler?" The man poked a finger into John's chest.

John grabbed the man's wrist and bent it back until he cowered on the ground howling. "No, I'm a cowboy."

Those who had stopped to watch the show whistled and clapped.

Two security guards grabbed the man by his arms, pulled him up, and took him away.

"Thank you so much." Donna hugged John when he turned around.

At first he didn't know what to do, but then the fog cleared and he started to wrap her in his arms, though she pulled away too soon. But she was close enough that he'd picked up on her vanilla-and-honey scent. Was that her shampoo? John couldn't be sure, but whatever had caused that scent, he wanted more.

"What's your name, cowboy?" She smiled demurely and looked up at him through her long lashes.

"John Manning, miss?" He wasn't sure if he should call her *Your Highness*, bow, or what. He'd never met a rodeo queen before.

"I'm Donna Myers. It's nice to meet you." She put her hand out, and he took it.

"The pleasure is all mine." John pulled her small hand up to his mouth and kissed it before letting her go.

She giggled. "I guess there are still some gentleman cowboys left."

"My momma raised me right." He looked her up and down and realized her dress was a bit dirty. "Are you alright? He didn't hurt you, did he?"

Donna looked down at her dress and noticed the dirt all along the skirt. "No, he kicked dirt at me when I turned down his offer for us to..." Her cheeks turned pink, and she looked away.

John's nostrils flared. "I see. It's a good thing security has already taken him away. May I escort you back to your friends?" He had noticed she was with a group of girls earlier, all princesses, and thought she shouldn't be out here on her own. Especially with drunk men who didn't know how to act properly around ladies.

She smiled and thanked him. "Yes, I'd like that very much. But I don't know where they've gotten to." Donna looked around but couldn't see her friends anywhere.

"Where are you staying? Maybe I can drive you to your hotel?"

Her eyes widened, and John realized what he had said. With hands in the air, he stumbled through an explanation. "I... Uh... That came out all wrong." He took his hat off and ran a hand through his messy hair. "I only want to help you get safely back to your friends. No funny business. Besides, I need to head back to campus tonight."

"Campus? Are you in college?" Donna relaxed just a bit.

He nodded. "Yup, I attend UW, not too far from here." He put his hat back on his head. "I only ride part-time and on weekends while classes are in session."

"Really? Same with me."

"College? Where do you go?" Hope filled him that this might not be his last chance to see the beautiful rodeo queen.

"Same school as you, University of Wyoming at Laramie." She giggled.

"Well, I'll be." He smiled. "I haven't seen you around, but it is a big campus."

She nodded. "I'm taking business classes. What about you?"

"I'm in the Rangeland Ecology and Watershed Management program." He knew it was a mouthful, but he was proud of his academic accomplishments. It took a lot of high school science classes with straight As to get accepted to this degree program.

She whistled. "Wow, that's mighty fancy."

He toed his boot in the dirt. "My family owns the Triple J Ranch in Beacon Creek, Montana. Everyone does their share to run it."

"And what will be your share?" she wondered aloud.

"We have a lot of little creeks that run through our property, but we don't actually own the water. We have rights to a certain amount. And we also have a lot of trees that use the water. So I want to be able to ensure we keep the land healthy, but also use the water wisely. It's a balancing act with the land, the animals, and the trees."

"You must be very smart."

"As are you, what with going to business school and all." He had never felt so self-conscious before. With Donna, he wanted to impress her, but he didn't want to come off as a dork. John had always been a great student, and he'd even graduated valedictorian. But he wasn't about to share that bit of news. Most people looked at him as though he were some sort of bookworm when he told them. So he had decided to keep it to himself. His grades got him a partial ride to UW, and that was all he needed them for.

Donna's cheeks tinged pink, and he smiled. John figured she was just as smart as he was, and she didn't want everyone to know it, either.

They spent the next hour looking for her friends and getting to know one another. When they found her girlfriends, she programmed her number into his cellphone and waved goodbye.

Over the next six months, John and Donna planned their rodeos so they could ride together. About twice a month they traveled to a different rodeo over the weekends. In February they began to share a room. John knew better, but he agreed with Donna's assessment that they could save a lot of money if they bunked together.

By the end of his second semester, John learned the hard way why it was better to wait for marriage.

Chapter 1

Four and a half years later

"John, you gotta get your head in the game or you're gonna get hurt." Matthew Manning, John's oldest brother, shook his head and helped his little brother pick up the load of wood he had dumped off the back of their ATV.

"I know, sorry Matthew." John shook his head. Lately he'd been having nightmares about Donna and how she'd broken up with him. It had been almost five years since he'd seen her, and yet he couldn't stop thinking about her. He'd get to a point where he thought maybe he could move on, and then the nightmares would start all over again. It was as though the universe was conspiring to keep punishing him and not let him forget what he'd done. And what he'd missed out on.

Matthew took a closer look at John's face. "Are you having nightmares again?" He pointed to his little brother's eyes. "I see the bags, and I gotta say, they're pretty ugly, bro."

John scoffed. "I'm still better looking than you are."

With a chuckle, Matthew patted his brother's back. "Have you talked to anyone about whatever it is that's got you all tied up in knots?"

John shook his head.

"You know, it's not healthy to keep these things all bottled up."

"Yeah, yeah. Dad said the same thing just this morning." John shook off Matthew's attention and walked away.

"Hey, I'm just worried about you. I know there's something big that went down, besides you fallin' off a bull and getting your knee trampled. It's more than that." Matthew pursed his lips and thought about what he would say next. "It has to do with a woman, doesn't it?"

John ignored his brother, went back to the ATV, and began picking up the wood he had dumped when they crested a hill. They were both working on fixing a particular part of fencing that day. The neighbor's bull was back to his old tricks and trying to get into their land to get cozy with a few of the Mannings' cows.

Even when they moved the cattle to the opposite side of the ranch, the old Johnson bull would still sniff out his girlfriends and try to get to them at certain times of the year. Now that it was fall, it was time again.

"I get it, you don't want to talk to me about this. But what about Elizabeth? Or the pastor?" The Mannings were close, but sometimes even Matthew didn't want to share his worries with his family, so he would go to the pastor.

John shook his head. "I can't."

"John."

"Matthew, leave it alone."

The older Manning sighed and brushed his gloved hands off on his jeans. "Alright, but think about what I said. You need to talk to someone. It's very unhealthy to keep it all bottled up inside like this."

John winced. He knew his brother was right, but who could he talk to? Everyone would judge him, and that was the last thing he needed.

"If you're worried..." Matthew tilted his head and considered his words for a moment. "If you think we'll judge you harshly, just remember that none of us are perfect. The Bible says, 'Judge not lest ye be judged.' I've tried to live by that verse."

With a nod, John got back on his ATV and started it up.

"Wait." Matthew put out a hand to stop his brother. "I have a pretty good idea of what went on while you were gone."

John's eyes widened, and he feared that Matthew did in fact know what he had done. But how could he? He never told anyone back home what he had done. Shoot, he hadn't even told Rick about any of it. "How could you?"

"Because I have eyes. I know my little brother. You used to be so happy and outgoing. You always had dates. Since you've been home you've been sullen and so quiet. You rarely even join in with Mark on his practical jokes anymore."

"So, that could just be due to the fact that I won't ride bulls again." John had injured his knee over two years ago while on the pro rodeo circuit, but that didn't mean he could never ride again. He could if he practiced, but deep down he believed that he didn't deserve to be on the circuit again. Not after what he'd done.

John had taken the injury as a sign from God, a punishment. He didn't deserve to be a pro bull rider, winning and living his dream. Not after what he had done.

Matthew shook his head. "No, that was part of it when you came home. But there's much more going on. Your knee is fine. If you really wanted to, you could easily get back on a bull. No, this attitude you have going"—he pointed to John—"it's all about a woman."

John scoffed. "How would you know, Mr. Perfect? Never making a mistake." He gave his machine some gas and took off, leaving his brother in his dust.

"Lord, John really needs your love and mercy right now. Please, help him see that all he has to do is come to you and you'll heal his broken heart. As well as forgive his sins." Matthew sighed and mounted his horse to head back home. Since John had taken off with the supplies to fix the fence, he figured it wasn't going to get done today and he might as well go back to the barn and get some other chores done.

When John finally returned home later that evening, his mom had saved him a plate with two pulled pork sandwiches on Hawaiian bread, potato salad, and a few slices of her homemade dill pickles. The moment he walked into the kitchen, a plate appeared with hot sandwiches slathered in Caleb Manning's famous homemade barbecue sauce.

"Thanks, Ma. This smells good." John's stomach rumbled, and Judith Manning smiled before patting his cheek.

"Now eat up, and then go shower." Judith came back to the table with a tall glass of iced tea. While he was eating, his mother sat down next to him. "John, you know I love you very much, right?"

He sighed, knowing he was in for a tongue-lashing. It was wrong to leave his brother like he did. Especially since the fence didn't get fixed that day, thanks to him taking the supplies with him. "I'm sorry. I'll apologize to Matthew as well, and first thing tomorrow I'll head out to fix the fence line."

"Son, we aren't worried about the chores. We're worried about you. We've given you space, and your father thought for sure that you'd tell us what was going on eventually, but you haven't. And your nightmares have come back." Judith sighed.

"Did Matthew tell you?"

She shook her head. "No, we heard you last night." She gave John a sheepish grin. "You forget, your room is next to ours. When you yell out in your sleep, we can hear it."

John dropped the fork full of potato salad down on the plate with a clink. "You can hear me? How long have you known about the nightmares?" Fear wove its way through his heart. Had he said anything incriminating in sleep?

Judith put a finger to her chin and looked up at the ceiling. "Ever since you got home." She put her hand on his. "Son, it's time to deal with this."

"Ma, you don't understand. I've done something horrible." He hung his head.

"Did you kill someone? Steal a horse?" Judith knew her son. If he had done anything illegal he would have fessed up immediately. He never was good at being bad. So whatever he had done was more on the personal level. Something he probably needed to speak with God about.

His head shot up. "Of course not."

"Then why can't you tell me, or the pastor?"

"You taught me right from wrong, and I screwed up, big time. It's not something I can fix." John rubbed his face and pushed his half-eaten dinner away.

Judith pushed the plate back in front of her son. "You have to eat it all. You know the rules."

John snorted. "And I still broke them."

"Sounds to me like you need to spend some time in prayer and communion with your savior. Maybe even some extra time in the Bible."

John sighed. "I haven't read my Bible since coming home, Ma. And I don't think God wants to hear from me. I made a huge mistake and hurt someone I care a great deal about in the process."

"Can you make it up to her?" Judith and Caleb had discussed John's attitude a lot lately, and they'd agreed it all had to do with a woman.

John looked at his mother. "How did you know it was a woman?"

"Because only a woman could break a man's heart the way yours is." His mom pulled him close and held him tight like she did when he was a little boy and his big brothers left him behind as they went off on one of their adventures.

John didn't normally hug his mom, but tonight he needed it. So, he wrapped her up in his arms and held on tight. Eventually, he let go. "Thanks, Ma."

"You're welcome. Now, about the Bible. I think tonight I want you to read the book of John. Then tomorrow after your chores are all complete, we can talk about forgiveness." Judith stood to leave her son to finish his supper.

John smirked. "Is there any specific reason you chose the book I was named after?"

Judith turned around. "You weren't named after a book in the Bible, you were named after a disciple. The disciple whom Jesus loved. And as for this particular book, you'll have to read it and pay close attention. Tomorrow, we'll discuss it more." She left John to finish his meal.

After he finished one of his favorite dinners, he rinsed off his dishes and put them in the dishwasher. When he noticed it was full, he added soap and turned it on. Then he went upstairs to shower and read his Bible.

John paid close attention to everything he was reading, but he didn't see anything that helped. After reading sixteen chapters, he stopped and prayed for the first time since coming home. Sure, he'd bowed his head at the dinner table and prayed with everyone whenever they prayed. But, he'd not said a prayer on his own since everything went down.

He felt as though he no longer deserved to call on God as his savior. Not after everything he had done wrong. Any time he thought about praying over the past four and a half years, a little voice in the back of his head told him he wasn't worthy. A part of him knew that wasn't the voice of God, it was the voice of the enemy. But he still believed it.

The worst part was that he believed he had to do something before God would forgive him and offer the peace that always came with forgiveness. It didn't matter that the Bible never said that. In fact, there were many passages that said we couldn't do it on our own. Forgiveness was a gift from God, not something we earned or deserved.

So for the first time in almost five years, John got down on his knees and opened his heart to God.

Chapter 2

Lord, I messed up big time. I know I did, and I feel awful. How do I fix this? There's got to be something I can do to make this right. Should I track down Donna? But she married that other guy. Would it make things worse if I did? I'm so sorry, I don't know what to do in order to make things right. Please help me.

John sat there waiting to hear back from God. When he didn't, he sighed and got back in bed to finish reading the book of John. When he got to the final chapter, he sat upright and opened his sleepy eyes. "This is what she wanted me to read."

Earlier in the book of John, he read that Simon Peter, one of the twelve disciples of Jesus, had turned his back on Him in his greatest hour of need and denied knowing him. Now, in chapter twenty-one of the book of John, Jesus had risen from the dead and appeared to Simon Peter, as well the other disciples, and forgiven Peter.

Peter's act of denying Jesus the night before he was to be crucified was one of the greatest sins John could think of. Yet God forgave Peter and established him as one of His own forever. Peter went on to become one of the greatest disciples and helped countless amounts of people come to know the Lord.

If Jesus could forgive a man like Peter, surely He could forgive what John Manning had done, right? This gave him hope. Since Peter did nothing to deserve his forgiveness, John prayed that he would receive forgiveness as well.

John went to sleep with just a little bit of that chip on his shoulder broken off.

In the morning, he smiled when he entered the kitchen. "Good morning, Ma." He walked up to her and bussed a quick kiss on her cheek, something he hadn't done in a very long time.

When he'd woken up, he had felt God's love for him. John couldn't remember the last time he had felt any closeness to God. He realized that God was there all along, just waiting for him to pray and talk to his Lord once more.

Judith Manning smiled at her young son. He was the youngest at home right then, since Roman—the youngest in age of all seven Manning children—was away at college. "Looks like someone had a good night's sleep."

John nodded as he made himself a cup of coffee. "Yes, actually. I think it was the best night of sleep I've had since leaving the pro rodeo circuit two years ago, maybe even since I left college almost four years ago." He turned to look at his mother, who was the only person in the kitchen with him. "Thank you for the suggestion to read the book of John."

"Have you forgiven yourself yet?"

He pursed his lips. "I don't know. I do see the light at the end of the tunnel, and I'm going to spend all of my nights in prayer and reading the Bible. It really did help stave off the nightmares."

"I'm glad to hear it." She took a sip of her cooling coffee. "Your father and I usually do our Bible study in the morning. We like to start our day with God. But a lot of nights we also read the Bible before bed, or spend some time in prayer if there's something on our minds. It does help us to sleep better."

"Do you do this together?" John had seen his parents reading the Bible and praying together over the years, but it wasn't a daily occurrence. Maybe he just wasn't paying enough attention?

She nodded. "Before we leave our room each day we pray together and read. Sometimes we read the same thing, and sometimes we have different devotionals that we work through. But we always do it at the same time and in each other's presence."

"Huh, does that keep you accountable?" Now that he thought about it, it would be nice to have someone nudging him to pray and read when he needed it. His mom did that for him last night and it had helped. John knew he still had a long ways to go, but he would put in the time to pray and read. Hopefully he'd feel God's forgiveness soon.

She nodded. "It does. But it also helps to keep us close to each other and God. One day when you're married, you'll understand what it means to become one with your spouse."

John looked down. He knew what it meant to physically join with a woman. That was the problem. He had done something that God had created for a husband and wife, outside of wedlock, and now he was paying the price.

So was Donna.

As he ate, he wondered what had become of her and her new family. He prayed that they were happy and healthy and he'd one day get to see her again so he could apologize for not being the godly man he was brought up to be.

Guilt began to seep into his bones again, and he thought back to John chapter twenty-one. He had to remind himself that if God could forgive Peter for denying Him, then God could forgive John Manning for adultery.

Just as John finished his breakfast, Matthew walked in dressed in his working Wranglers, a button-up shirt, and his blue, black, and white-checked flannel shirt lined with Sherpa to keep him warm during the cold fall mornings. "Hey there, you ready to get that fence fixed today?"

John chuckled. "You mean am I ready to work and not run off in a huff like a little boy?"

Matthew put up his hands. "Hey now, I didn't say that. You did."

"I know, and I'm sorry. I won't do that again. At least not today." John gave him a cheeky grin, then downed his cup of coffee. "Wait a sec, I do think I'll need more coffee. Hang on while I get a thermos out."

"Did you have more nightmares last night?" Matthew's brow furrowed in worry over his brother.

"Actually"—John poured the rest of the hot coffee into his thermos—"I slept like a baby for the first time in years. I just didn't get enough sleep."

Matthew stared expectantly at his little brother.

Once he had fixed his coffee with enough sugar, he turned around and put the lid on. "I stayed up late reading the Bible and praying."

"Wait, did I hear you correctly?" Matthew put a hand to his ear. "Say that again."

John slapped his brother's shoulder. "Come on, you goofball. Let's get the ATV and head out."

"I think today I'll drive the ATV and you ride a horse." Matthew arched a brow.

With a chuckle, John agreed.

Now that fall had arrived, the days were cooler than summer. But even still, they worked up quite the sweat tearing down the old part of the fence where the bull had obviously charged it and put up a new fence that would hopefully last longer—and stand up to the world's most cantankerous bull.

John took off his hat and wiped his forehead with the sleeve of his shirt. "What say you to heading back for some iced tea?"

Both of the Manning men had shed their lined flannels after only one hour of work. Tearing down old fence lines and putting up new ones wasn't easy work. Since the bull had rammed the fence down, they had to dig new holes for the fence posts and fill in the old ones. It wasn't rocket science. Instead, it was back-breaking work that helped to keep all ranchers in shape and their muscles toned.

"I think that's a might fine suggestion. Lead on, little brother." Matthew put his own hat back on once he was on the ATV and ready to go.

Judith had been waiting for the boys to return. They'd missed lunch and it was close to eighty degrees outside. They had to be hot. The moment she saw them ride in, she prepared two tall glasses of iced tea and set them on the table. Then she pulled out the bread and fixins for sub sandwiches.

When both of her sons headed inside straight for the table, she tutted. "Don't forget to wash up before eating, boys." Behind their backs, she plugged her nose.

Even in his thirties and married, Matthew still felt like a little boy when his mother got in this mood.

Both boys responded in unison, "Yes, Ma." Then they went and washed their faces and arms before sitting down for the feast their ma had prepared for them.

Later that night, after John prepared for bed, he opened up his Bible and began reading the book of Acts after he prayed, asking the Lord to open his eyes to the message He wanted him to see.

With the exception of Judas Iscariot, it looked like Jesus, and God, forgave very easily. All John could remember was the God of the Old Testament, the one who punished the Israelites all the time. The one who got so angry with His own people, he sent them away from the land into captivity. It wasn't that they didn't deserve what they got, because they did. But the God of the New Testament seemed to be so much more forgiving. Or maybe it was that the people in the New Testament were more apt to seek forgiveness and not just expect God to be there to act as their own personal genie.

It wasn't like John was any better than the people of the Old Testament. It was that he had Jesus and the Holy Spirit to guide him, and the Bible to read and learn from. That night, John vowed to read and pray every day. Whether it be at night like he had been doing, or in the morning like his parents, he was going to get closer to God. Because the more he read and prayed, the better he felt. And the closer to God he got.

The next few weeks brought about a lot of changes in John. Not only did he smile more, but he was happier in general. In fact, he planned a little *surprise* for his brother Mark and his new wife, Leah, when they got home from their honeymoon.

Mark was the practical joker in the family, always doing something at the worst possible time. Now it was payback, and all of the Manning brothers wanted in.

Chapter 3

"That was awesome! We've finally done something to rival Mark's pranks." Luke laughed as they left the little apartment above the general store where Mark and Leah would live until Mark could build them a home on the ranch.

I wish we could be here to see their faces when they find all of our little...gifts." Matthew laughed and slapped Luke on the back.

"You know he's gonna seek retribution for this. And Leah will most likely join in," John said as he rubbed his hands together. His smile went from ear to ear, and he couldn't wait for the war that was to come.

"I'd say this is payback for everything he's done to us our entire lives," Luke added.

"If only Roman could have been here to join in." Matthew felt his pocket to ensure he had put his phone back in once they were done showing Roman their handiwork.

"Yeah, but he was the one who suggested the whoopee cushion in the bed." John bent over laughing and slapped his leg.

"I just hope we put it on the right side of the bed!" Matthew exclaimed.

Luke nodded. "Yeah, but Leah does deserve some of this. She's helped Mark out over the years."

"True," John agreed.

Just then the door to the apartment opened, and Logan stood scowling in the doorway. "What's going on in here? I heard a lot of scuffling and giggling like a bunch of schoolgirls."

"Why didn't you come up sooner?" Matthew grinned at his brother-in-law.

"Because we had a store full of customers." He narrowed his eyes at the group of Manning men. "What have you been up to? You said you just wanted to deliver some food for the newlyweds so they wouldn't have to cook when they get home tonight."

John couldn't hold his laugh in anymore. "Sorry, just some payback for our brother." His eyes lit with excitement for what was to come, and his brothers joined in.

Logan scowled. "What? You pulling pranks on my new brother?" He fisted his hands and put them on his hips.

Matthew looked between his friend and his brothers. He had nothing. He put his hands up and shrugged his shoulders.

The scowl on Logan's face started to break, and the edges of his mouth began to turn up. "Why didn't you wait for me? I'd love to get some payback, too."

Again, the brothers broke out howling with laughter.

"Why don't you try and record their reactions when they get home?" Luke suggested. "I'd love to see Mark's face when he enters."

They had set up a netting on the ceiling with shredded paper and a few balloons full of water. When they left the apartment, they were going to rig some rope to pull the netting down once the door was opened. If all went according to plan, the newlyweds would be showered with paper as well as a few water balloons. Nothing too much. They didn't want the floor to leak and water to get into the store below them.

And there were a few other little surprises waiting for them, like food turned upside down in the fridge so that when they went to pull the container out, it would spill all over the place.

An entire case of toilet paper had been used to, uh, *decorate* the small bathroom.

And what John thought was the best part: a recording set up to go off in the middle of the night multiple times and wake them up. That, together with Luke's whoopee cushion, should make for an interesting first night home.

Logan chuckled. "Oh, I'm sure I'll be press-ganged into service. You know they won't feel like bringing their luggage up themselves when they arrive. And when I do, I'll have my phone handy." He grinned.

Matthew looked at his watch. "If I don't hurry up, I won't have time to eat dinner with my wife before I head out to the airport to get the newlyweds." He turned around and headed home.

"Well, I guess that's my cue to head home to my wife as well. She should be off shift by now and waiting for me." Luke waggled his brows and left.

So it was just John and Logan standing in the entrance to the apartment.

"I need to set up the rope, then we can close the door. Just be sure you aren't the one to enter first." John chuckled and finished up the last prank. Or was it really the first one? Oh, if he could be a fly on that wall tonight.

After dinner that night, John hurried up and headed to his room to study his Bible for a while. He knew that if Logan could get video of the newlyweds returning home, he wanted to watch it with his brothers. While Matthew and his wife lived on the property, Luke and Callie lived in town. But they had made plans to Zoom just as soon as they received the video from Logan, Leah's brother.

Sadly, he was so distracted that he hardly got any studying in. "Now I see why my parents start the day with their Bible study instead of end the day with it." He shook his head and decided to head back to the living room where Matthew and Claire were. He'd hang with them until they heard from Logan.

He'd barely said hello to the couple when Matthew's phone rang. He answered it on speaker, and Logan was laughing so hard they couldn't understand what he was trying to say.

"Whoa, slow down there. What happened?" Matthew grinned and looked to his wife and brother.

"Oh, you should have been here. It was classic!" Logan laughed again before he got himself under control. "Get on Zoom and I'll call Luke. I've already sent you both a request. I can't wait to share this video with you."

Matthew hung up, and the three of them went to the laptop that had already been booted up and was waiting for the call. Once Matthew logged into the Zoom link Logan had sent him, they all sat waiting for Luke.

Claire smiled and waved at Logan and Elizabeth. "So, I take it the pranks went off well? How much did you see?"

Elizabeth laughed and nodded. "Oh, yeah. I was there as well to welcome the happy couple home and followed everyone upstairs. I don't want to share the story yet—we have to wait for Luke and Callie. It was priceless! If we shared this on social media, it would go viral in a heartbeat."

Everyone laughed and watched as the other window clicked on, and Luke and Callie greeted everyone.

"Okay, so you all know what the pranks were, right?" Logan asked.

Everyone nodded. A feeling of excitement and anticipation could be felt over the video chat.

John rubbed his hands together, hoping his brother Mark had finally had a good prank pulled on him. But he also hoped Leah would be a good sport about it all.

"Well," Logan began, "we followed the newlyweds upstairs and Mark halted in front of the door. He grinned at Leah and picked her up to carry her across the threshold. She turned the knob after asking me to unlock it." He chuckled.

"Oh no you didn't!" Claire exclaimed.

"Oh, I unlocked the door, but left it closed." Logan laughed again and looked at his wife, who picked up the story.

"Leah gave him a dirty look, and Mark had to lean over so Leah could open the door." Elizabeth, Logan's wife and sister to the Manning brothers, couldn't hold in her laugh. "It was priceless! The second the door was thrown open, the netting collapsed and all sorts of shredded paper blew down on and around them." She looked to her husband.

"They both screamed, and then the water balloons hit them! I couldn't believe they were standing in the exact spot for the most water penetration." Logan busted up laughing, and Elizabeth joined him.

Before anyone could beg for the video, it started. And sure enough, the Mannings watched as the newlyweds bent over to open the door. Leah had on jean capris and a light-pink t-shirt, while Mark had on jeans and a white button-up, short-sleeved shirt. It was obvious they had been in the sun by the warmth of their sun-kissed skin peeking out from their short sleeves.

Mark, holding his new wife in his arms, walked into a snowstorm of paper falling on them. Then they were wet, with bits of colorful balloon in their hair. Paper stuck to their heads as well as their clothes. Mark's white shirt clung to his muscular frame as he let his wife down and turned around to look at Logan, who was recording the entire thing. Leah pulled her soaked t-shirt away from her skin and shook her head. Water and paper flew everywhere.

"*Logan!* I'm gonna get you for this!" Mark bellowed.

Off screen, everyone could hear Elizabeth and Logan busting a gut.

"Oh, this wasn't us," Logan admitted. "We just had to see it for ourselves."

Elizabeth added, "I think you have a group of brothers who decided it was past time to deliver payback."

Leah laughed and began pulling the pieces of paper off her hair and clothes. "I told you a long time ago that one day they'd get you good."

"Me, okay. I can understand." He turned sad eyes to his new wife. "But you? Why would they do this to you?"

John stifled a laugh, knowing exactly why Leah had been included in this prank. He only hoped she didn't get the wrong side of the bed later.

Leah shrugged. "I guess because some of those pranks you pulled when we were in school...well, I helped with a few." She turned to look straight into the camera. "Isn't that right, John? Oh, and Luke, I believe I helped with a few for you as well." She grinned.

The Mannings all laughed and nodded.

"Yup, she did help with a few of Mark's pranks that required a partner," Luke added.

"Well, when one of us wasn't helping him," John admitted.

They all looked at each other and their eyes narrowed.

Matthew spoke first. "You better not come after me. After tonight, I'd say we all got retribution on the ringleader."

John thought about it for a moment. "True. It was always Mark who started any of the pranks."

Claire asked via the video chat, "So, that means I won't wake up tomorrow to any whoopee cushions in my house? Or anything else from you boys?"

"I'd say we're all good, wouldn't you?" Matthew asked.

Callie nodded and added, "I better not find I've been included in any of your pranks." She looked at everyone. "Just remember, I carry weapons all the time." She winked at her husband, Luke.

Everyone leaned back and nodded.

"Don't worry, none of us would mess with a sheriff's deputy." Matthew looked around and noticed all of his brothers agreeing with him.

Logan called them all back to the screen. "Don't miss the next one." He snorted when he laughed. "I gotta say, I was surprised that I got to witness this one."

The video started again, and it showed Mark shaking his head and heading to bathroom, probably to get towels for him and Leah. When he opened the door, his hands went in the air and a loud bellow followed.

John wasn't sure what his brother said, but it probably wasn't good.

Mark turned around, his face red. "What in the world do you dingleberries think you're doing? Do you know how expensive toilet paper is these days?"

Logan walked closer to the bathroom and angled his phone to see the inside. It looked like a winter wonderland. The entire room was white from the paper, and not a single bit of surface showed.

Everyone could hear Logan laughing as he recorded it, but also again from the Zoom call. "Oh, this was priceless!"

"Did we use up all of his toilet paper?" John asked.

Logan nodded. "Yup, I had to go downstairs and get them a package of Charmin. Leah refused to use anything that had already been used or touched by other people."

Claire sat up straight and tried to hide her laugh behind her hand. "I don't blame her. I wouldn't want to use that stuff, either."

From the video, everyone heard Logan laughing. Then Mark accusing him.

"No man, I was working downstairs when they were doing this. I did hear their laughing and feet scuffling, but we were swamped. By the time I was able to get away, they had already finished."

"What else did they do?" Leah's exasperated sigh came through clearly on the video.

They couldn't see Logan, but everyone heard his reply. "I honestly don't know. The only thing I knew about was the paper set to launch when you opened the door."

Leah narrowed her eyes and put her hands on her wet capris. "Is that why you refused to open the door when I asked you to?"

A chuckle came through from who John surmised was Logan. "Yup. I wasn't going to have that stuff come down on me. This was your payback for all of those pranks."

"Ha, ha. You guys got us good. But just remember, I've now got a full-time partner to help me mete out justice." Mark grinned into the camera, showing off his pearly whites.

"Uh-oh, I think we're gonna have to watch our backs. Doesn't matter that we still owe him a ton of pay-back—he isn't going to see it that way." Luke grinned and looked to his brothers. "I say we plan for more payback if he does anything else."

Matthew held up a hand. "Hold on." He looked at Logan on the screen, then Luke. "Remember when you first got home from your honeymoon?"

The married men all stared off into space with dreamy looks on their faces.

"Yeah," Luke replied.

"Mark just got home from his. He has a new bride. Do you really think he's gonna have time, or the energy, to come up with more pranks? And then actually put them into effect?" Matthew arched a brow, waiting for his brothers to come back to Earth.

Logan waved his hands. "Yeah, okay. I can see your point."

Luke took his wife's hand and squeezed it. Callie winked back at him.

Matthew kissed Claire's cheek and whispered something in her ear that no one else could hear.

John lifted a hand. "Uh, does this mean that since I'm the only single man left in the house, I'll have time to plan and implement Operation Payback?" He grinned.

While he was getting out of his two-year funk, he wasn't anywhere near ready to even consider dating a woman, let alone finding a wife. Which meant he just might get up to some interesting trouble.

Chapter 4

The next morning, John arose and opened his Bible before he even got out of bed. Beginning his day with a Bible study and prayer had started to change something inside him. He wasn't the only one to notice, either.

When he went down to grab a cup of coffee before heading out for morning chores, his father was at the coffee pot doing the same thing. "John, good to see you looking so bright and chipper."

John grabbed a travel mug, filled it with coffee, and smiled at his father. "I feel good this morning. Are you ready to move the cattle to another pasture after breakfast?"

Caleb eyed his son warily. "What has you so happy?"

John put his mug down and looked into his father's eyes. "God does." When his father arched a brow, he continued, "Mom told me about how you both do Bible studies and pray together every morning before you start your day. I've been doing that on my own and I can see why you're always ready to begin your day."

With a sip of coffee, Caleb nodded. "Does this mean you've begun to get over whatever it was that had you down these past two years?"

John knew he was going to have to tell his family something. He wasn't quite ready to spill the beans on what he'd done, but he was ready to think about what he'd done and maybe even speak to the pastor about it. He took a shaky breath. "I made some big mistakes. Things I thought were too big for God to forgive." He shook his head.

"Son, nothing is too big for God to forgive. All you have to do is ask." Caleb put a reassuring hand on his son's shoulder.

He nodded. "I'm coming to believe that. The thing is, I want to made amends, but I don't know how to go about doing it."

Caleb took another sip of his coffee. "Are you praying and asking God to show you how to do this, or if you even need to make amends?"

"Yes, and I know I must do something. I just don't know what, or how to go about doing it."

"Mmmm. The first thing is to find out the *what*, then the *how* will work itself out." Caleb put his mug down and turned his head when the doorbell rang.

John turned his head, too. It was too early for visitors. The sun had barely risen.

Georgia, a former homeless woman who lived in a cabin on their property, walked into the kitchen with a woman carrying a little girl. "Excuse the interruption, but I was coming in to help Judith start breakfast and found this woman on the porch." She motioned toward the woman with auburn hair that looked like it hadn't seen a brush in a while who held a wiggling young girl in her arms. The little girl had strawberry blonde hair and was wearing pink fuzzy pajamas with puppies all over them.

The squirming child was smiling at John and holding her arms out for him to take her. He wiggled his finger in her direction and smiled. The little girl gurgled a laugh and jumped in her momma's arms so hard that she had a difficult time keeping her from falling.

"Daisy, calm down." The woman winced and tried to hold the little girl tighter against her chest. "Sorry, she's just really excited to meet you all. I've never seen a toddler more social than this one."

Caleb smiled and took hold of the little girl's hand. "I'm Caleb Manning. How can I help you?"

Daisy giggled and looked to John before calling out, "Daddy!"

Everyone laughed, except the auburn-haired woman.

John laughed and looked at the little girl. "Hi, Daisy. I'm John." He figured she probably called all men daddy.

The stranger cleared her throat and a cute pink hue covered her cheeks. "I'm River Cassidy, and this here is Daisy..."—she cleared her throat again—"Myers."

John's head popped up, and he stared daggers at River. "As in Donna Myers?"

River licked her lips. "Yes. Do you remember her?"

"Of course I do. Where is she?" John's piercing gaze sent shivers of fear up River's spine.

"Uh, I think I'll go to the pantry and start to gather the items we'll need this morning." Georgia looked between Caleb and John and scurried out faster than a rat running from a cat in the barn.

"Why don't we go into the living room?" Caleb directed the small group away from the kitchen that would be bustling with family very soon.

John looked at Daisy, then back at River. "What's going on?" he demanded, and stood in front of the frightened woman.

Daisy looked up to John and smiled. When he noticed her sweet face and the cute dimples in each cheek, he took a deep breath and calmed down. Then he took a seat across the room from River and Daisy.

River looked at Caleb, then back to John. "Um, I'm afraid I have some bad news." She pulled Daisy close to her chest before continuing. "Donna died over three years ago."

"What?" John burst out as he stood up and ran both his hands over his face. "She couldn't have. Donna was so vivacious and healthy. You must have the wrong person."

She shook her head. "I'm sorry, but I was there with her through it all."

John took a closer look at the newcomer. In addition to her needing to brush her hair, she also needed to change her clothes. Her light-colored blue jeans had food stains on them, as did her wrinkled short-sleeved t-shirt that sported a unicorn proudly holding a coffee mug in its front hoof. Come to think of it, she did smell like coffee and chocolate when he was standing close to her in the kitchen.

Caleb stood up and put a hand on his son's chest. "John, sit down. Calm down and let River tell us what's going on." He looked at the little girl in River's arms and then back at John, recognition showing on his face.

Judith walked in and looked at the room. "Is everything all right?" When she noticed the little girl on the stranger's lap, she clapped her hands and smiled from ear to ear. "Oh, isn't she pretty."

River looked tentatively at Judith and smiled.

Daisy looked up, and her dimples made another appearance as she put her hands out to Judith.

"Hi, I'm Judith Manning, Caleb's wife and John's mother." She walked closer and took one of Daisy's hands and shook it. "Aren't you just a little angel."

River winced. "I'm River Cassidy, and this here is my foster daughter, Daisy Myers."

"Oh, can I hold her?" Judith asked.

Daisy looked to Judith and said, "Juice?"

"I think she's thirsty. I have a sippy cup in my tote bag. Can I trouble you for some juice or milk?" River looked into Judith's smiling face.

"Of course, why don't you let me hold little Daisy while you make the sippy cup? And if you don't mind, I can feed her. It'll be good practice for when I'm a grandmother." Judith beamed at her husband. Elizabeth, one of their twin daughters, was going to have a baby soon. It would be Judith's first grandchild.

"Are you sure?" River asked.

"Of course. You're here for some business, I assume? I can watch Daisy while you finish up." Judith looked to Caleb and John for confirmation.

Both men nodded their heads.

River stood. "Alright." She handed Daisy off to Judith. Then she picked up the tote bag and followed the nice woman to the kitchen to make the sippy cup.

Once River was in the kitchen, she noticed a couple drinking coffee and discussing horses.

"Matthew, Claire, this here is River and Daisy." Judith pointed to each.

"Oh, what a little cutie-pie!" Claire exclaimed.

Matthew chuckled. "Nice to meet you." He looked at Daisy, then did a double-take.

River, not having noticed, prepared the sippy cup and gave it to Judith, who handed it to Daisy. She grabbed hold of it and began drinking in earnest.

"Well, I guess someone was thirsty." Judith chuckled. "Has she had breakfast yet?"

River shook her head. "No, we haven't had a chance to stop and eat yet."

"I can make her some oatmeal," Claire offered.

"Uh, okay. If it's not too much trouble." River looked around the room and relaxed her shoulders. The family seemed nice and wanted to help her, so she would allow it while she was talking to John. "Could I trouble you for a glass of water?"

"How about some coffee? It's still very early—you must need caffeine?" Judith offered. "Or we have tea, too."

River sighed. "Coffee would be wonderful. Thank you. Cream and sugar?"

"How about you go back in and discuss your business and I'll bring in a tray for everyone." Judith got to work brewing a fresh pot of coffee and pulling out some scones from the pantry to go with the coffee.

River thanked the nice woman and headed back to John. Before she entered the room, she stood tall and took in a deep breath. *You got this. He's just shocked. He's not a mean man. He couldn't be, not after how Donna spoke about him.*

After her mental pep-talk, she entered the room displaying more confidence than she actually felt.

Both cowboys stood when she entered.

John cleared his throat. "River, I'm sorry I was so, uh...difficult when you first arrived. But"—he threw his hands in the air and turned in a circle—"I'm just so confused as to what's going on."

River sighed. "I know. It is very confusing." She sat down, and the men followed suit.

"Maybe you can start from the beginning?" John asked. "What happed to Donna and her husband?"

River gulped and looked anxiously between the two men in the room. "Actually, Donna never married Andrew."

John's mouth opened and closed, and his eyes widened. So many questions rumbled around in his head. Why didn't they marry? Was Daisy Andrew's kid, or someone else's? Could it be possible? He also needed to know what had happened to Donna. "Why?"

She bit her lower lip and began Donna's story. "You know she was a party girl, right?"

John rubbed a hand across his face. "I did see her at one party, but I've never been big on parties or drinking. Not really my thing, so whenever Donna asked me to go with her, I always declined. And I asked her to skip them as well." He sighed and looked to his dad. "But she always had some excuse as to why she needed to attend."

With a pained expression, River looked at John. For the life of her, she couldn't understand why Donna would have wanted anyone else. The man was handsome, and from what Donna said, a total gentleman. "I think she needed the spotlight. Being with you would have dulled the light she had shining on her at parties. At college, at least. But in the rodeo she was always in the spotlight."

"Yeah." John nodded. "I did wonder about that. It seemed like my attention was never enough. Barrel racing and entering a lot of the rodeo queen competitions, at least the ones close enough that she could drive over from college when they had mid-week events, kept her so busy when we were at school I didn't see much of her there." He had wondered what she did at those parties, but he never thought she was seeing anyone else.

When he learned that Donna had been seeing Andrew at the same time as she was seeing him, he was devastated. Not only had his pride taken a hit, but it started him down a path that had him wondering if he was enough for any woman. Why couldn't Donna be happy with just him? He'd doted on her, given her everything he had.

River fidgeted in her seat. "Donna was not only my best friend, she was also my foster sister."

Caleb raised a brow, but continued to sit in silence.

Judith walked in with a tray of coffee and scones. "In case you're feeling a bit peckish. We're making breakfast, and I hope you can join us, River." The older woman began to pour coffee for everyone in the room, beginning with their guest. "How do you like your coffee?"

"Two creams and two sugars, please." River smiled at Judith. There was something calming about the woman. She was definitely warmer than John was. She had yet to get a feel for Caleb Manning; he'd been pretty quiet so far. How would he react when River told him the rest?

Once everyone had been served, Judith left. The room was so quiet you could hear the coffee mugs settle on the table and the forks scrape the plates as the occupants ate in silence.

"Did your mom make the scones?" River looked to John for confirmation.

"Yes, she did. I'm blessed to have such a great cook in the house." John had calmed down a bit with some food in his stomach and time to begin processing what he'd heard so far. For the first time since she'd opened her mouth, John smiled at her.

River felt something in her stomach move when John smiled, and she wasn't sure what to make of it. Feeling a bit awkward, she took another sip of her coffee and sighed. It was so much better than truck-stop coffee, which was all she could afford on the drive here.

After John set his plate on the coffee table, he picked up his mug and held it for comfort. The warmth of the mug settled his soul, and he sent up a quick prayer asking for wisdom and patience. Then he asked, "Can you tell me why Donna and Andrew didn't marry?"

River took another drink of her coffee and watched Caleb over the rim of her mug. She wasn't sure if John wanted his dad to know all of this. From the looks of things this was a tight-knit family, but she was going to be getting very personal with Donna's story.

She turned her gaze back to John. "Are you sure you want him to hear this?" The visitor tilted her head toward the patriarch of the Manning family.

John considered her words and his history with Donna, then nodded. "Yes, I think it's time my dad knew the truth." He wasn't exactly sure what the truth was now, but he knew his dad would support him, and it sounded like he was going to need it.

"Well..." River stopped and took a fortifying breath. "As you know, Donna was also seeing Andrew when you two met." She gulped loudly. "And..."

Before she could continue, Matthew came running into the room. "Mr. Johnson just called. His bull rammed down another fence and has made his way into the middle of our herd."

"Sorry, we gotta go." John jumped up, followed quickly by his father, and they ran outside.

River sat there stunned, not sure what all that meant.

Judith came in with Daisy in her arms. The little girl reached toward River. "River, River!"

River smiled at Daisy and stood to take the little girl in her arms. "How's my sweet thing? Are you all full now?" She poked the little girl's belly, and Daisy giggled. Then she yawned.

"Do you have a place where Daisy can take a nap? I'm afraid we were up all night long driving here." River yawned and held Daisy close.

"Oh, dear. Why don't you both take a nap? The men will be busy for a while. That darn bull from next door." Judith shook her head. "When he gets"—she looked at Daisy—"frisky, he doesn't let our fences get in his way."

River chuckled. "Doesn't he have his own cows to uh"—she cleared her throat—"visit?"

With a short laugh, Judith nodded her head. "He does. But we have a few who seem to be his particular favorites." She led them to the guest room and helped them get situated for a nap. "Sorry, but we don't have a playpen or crib."

"Don't worry, Daisy can sleep on the bed with me." River yawned again, and Daisy's eyes drooped.

Chapter 5

The Manning men ran to the barn and quickly saddled their horses, all grateful that they had fed the animals in the barn already.

"What has gotten into that ol' bull? Doesn't he know he can't keep breaking down fences?" John huffed. This was the last thing he wanted to deal with. River and Daisy were so much more important at that moment. However, he also knew that the Johnson bull tended to mow his way through the herd, looking for his girlfriends. The last time he did that, several of the cows ended up injuring themselves. Thankfully, none had to be put down.

Sometimes, John was very grateful his sister was the local veterinarian.

"Apparently, he can." Matthew grinned. "But what's with that woman and her little girl?"

"Daisy isn't her little girl, not really. River is foster mom to the little girl." John wasn't sure exactly what was going on, but he had an idea where this was headed. However, he needed to keep his mind on the task at hand. If he was distracted he could get injured, or the cattle could.

It didn't take long to find the bull. The cows were all mooing and upset. It was a good thing they weren't dairy cows, or their milk might have turned sour. Although, if they were dairy cows they would have been close to the barn for morning milking. And the ol' Johnson bull probably wouldn't be interested in them, as he wouldn't ever have much of a chance to see them.

"You know, Mr. Johnson really should get rid of his old bull. The thing just runs through the pasture scaring his cattle and fighting the younger bulls for dominance. What does he still need this old one for?" John had never liked the bull. For as long as he could remember, it was the meanest, nastiest thing he'd ever seen.

Caleb finally entered the conversation. "This old bull used to be for breeding and teaching the young bulls about dominance. But you're right, he's not useful for anything these days. However"—he looked pointedly at his young son—"we never put an animal down once they've outlived their usefulness. We let them graze and enjoy their retirement. Even if they are old codgers."

Matthew laughed. "At least he keeps us on our toes." He pulled up on the reins when he found the old bull next to one of his girlfriends.

"Alright." Caleb sighed. "Let's get the rest of the herd moved into the next pasture and leave the lovebirds alone. Maybe if we let the Johnson bull spend the day with his girls, he'll be happy and leave our herd alone."

John agreed it was worth a try. They'd tried everything else they could think of. Even when they reinforced the fence line, the bull still rammed his way through. Many times he had hurt himself in the process, but he seemed to not notice when he was bleeding. The bull continued on like a moth to a flame.

A few hours later, after they had moved the herd to a different pasture and left the ol' Romeo to his girls, the men headed back to the barn where they gave their horses extra feed and brushed them down.

Once the horses were put away, John gave his horse an apple and offered to give treats to the other horses. A part of him was nervous. He wanted River and Donna's story, but he was also a little leery to move forward. His heart skipped a few beats when he thought about River. Not like when he remembered Donna, but in a way that still disconcerted him. He wasn't sure what to think about the pretty woman.

John finally got the courage up to head inside. But once he was in the kitchen, his mother put a finger to her lips. "Shh, our guests are napping. They drove all night to get here."

With a furrowed brow, John got a fresh mug of coffee. "Do you know why they drove all night?"

Judith scowled and shook her head. "No, but I don't like it. With a little one like Daisy, she should have waited for the morning."

"Agreed." John's stomach rumbled.

His mother smiled. "Sit down. Georgia and I waited to make breakfast until you all came home, so it's fresh and waiting."

River woke to the scent of bacon and coffee. Her stomach rumbled. The scone she had earlier was the only thing she'd eaten since breakfast the day before. The day had been too stressful, and she wasn't hungry. Now, well, that was a different story.

The scent of homemade breakfast also woke Daisy. "Yum yums! I hungry."

River chuckled. "Of course, we'll go see what Mrs. Manning has made for breakfast." She quickly ran a brush through her hair, realizing it was a rats' nest and full of bristles. Then she put it up in a ponytail. Finally she brushed Daisy's hair, who squealed with joy. The little girl was *all girl*. She loved wearing dresses and tights. And any chance she got for someone to do her hair, she jumped at it.

"I want to wear my dress." Daisy turned pleading eyes on River.

"Aren't you hungry?" River sure was. Even with the scone earlier, her stomach told her just how hungry she really was.

Daisy had eaten a bowl of oatmeal when they arrived, and had eaten three meals plus a couple of snacks on the trip to Beacon Creek. Her stomach wasn't grumbling. "I wanna be pretty."

River knew it was a losing battle. The little girl would find a way to rip open their luggage without her help and change herself. Then, she'd make a mess in the process and cause havoc. River had learned it was best to help the little girl change her clothes when she demanded it.

When both girls entered the kitchen, everyone at the table stopped talking and looked up.

John smiled. "Please, take a seat. Are you hungry?"

Daisy reached for John. "Yes!"

He chuckled and pulled out two seats next to him. One held a booster chair that someone had found in the attic and cleaned up that morning.

Instead of sitting in the booster chair, Daisy climbed into John's lap.

"Well, I guess we know she has good taste." John grinned and kissed the top of the little girl's head.

Everyone but River chuckled. Instead, she nervously took the other open seat and watched Daisy. "Um, maybe I should take her."

"Nah." John waved a dismissive hand. "I got her. This will be good practice for my future nieces and nephews." He looked to Matthew and winked.

Matthew coughed and spluttered. "Whoa now, it's a bit too soon for us."

John shrugged. "Well, we know Lizzie is due in a couple of months. I'm sure you and Luke won't be too far behind her."

"What about Mark?" Matthew gave his brother an indignant look.

"What about Mark?" The man himself walked in and greeted everyone at the table, but stopped short when he saw John with River and Daisy. "I know I was gone for a few weeks, but I couldn't have missed something this big, could I?" He pointed between the three of them.

River blushed and ducked her head.

John snorted.

Daisy squealed, then put her arms around John's neck.

The entire room quieted, and Mark raised questioning brows.

John raised his hands. "Whoa, I just met River and Daisy this morning."

The returning newlywed took a closer look at the little girl in John's lap, then at his brother. His brows furrowed and he shook his head. "Uh-huh." But then he looked at River and back at Daisy and tilted his head. Try as he might, he couldn't see any resemblance between the two. "Uh, someone want to tell me what's going on?"

John looked at his brother sheepishly. "Surprise! Would you believe it's another prank?"

"Nope." Mark took the last open seat, near his dad. He turned to Caleb and arched a brow, not unlike his dad did in times of confusion. "We're gonna have a discussion about what's appropriate to do to a newlywed's bed and what isn't."

Everyone who was in on the whoopee-cushion prank laughed, while the rest of the table looked on in confusion.

Mark waved his hand. "A story for another time. I wanna hear this story."

"We're all waiting for this story. But it seems Daisy is the daughter of an old, uh"—Caleb cleared his throat—"college friend of John's."

"And this young lady?" Mark nodded toward River.

"I'm the foster mom to Daisy, and foster sister of Donna, Daisy's mom." She quickly glanced at Mark and turned her gaze to Daisy instead.

"And your name?"

"Oh, sorry. I'm River Cassidy." She took a sip of her coffee, then added another scoop of sugar and stirred it.

"Nice to meet you. I'm Mark Manning." He nodded toward River.

"Mark has just returned from his honeymoon with Leah," John offered.

"Well, now that everyone has been introduced, what say you we finish up breakfast so everyone can get back to their chores?" Caleb's booming voice filled the room, and Daisy's bottom lip quivered.

"Hey, it's alright little princess," John cooed. "He's just a loud ogre."

A tear was hanging off one of Daisy's lashes, and John reached up to wipe it away. He looked into her eyes and felt a zing of recognition. While John now had brown hair, he did have blonde hair as a young child. And Daisy's blue eyes made him feel like he was looking at a picture of himself at that age. He turned questioning eyes on River.

She mouthed, *Later*.

Was it possible? This little girl was almost four years old. Counting back in his head, he realized that it was possible. He needed to know when, exactly, Daisy's birthday was.

Meanwhile, Daisy calmed down and ate her breakfast of scrambled eggs, fresh-squeezed orange juice, hash browns, and toast with jam.

River watched as Daisy enjoyed her breakfast. "I've never gotten her to eat eggs before. I'm surprised she's eating this. Normally she turns her nose up at adult food."

Judith smiled. "I think Daisy noticed what we were all eating and decided she wanted to be a big girl like the rest of us." She put a fork full of eggs in her mouth and smiled at the little girl, who grabbed a handful of eggs and stuffed them into her mouth.

River giggled and then tried to stifle her laugh.

John laughed out loud. "Don't worry, we aren't too strict about table manners for kids." He looked down at Daisy and couldn't hold back his smile. "She really is adorable."

River sighed. "Yes, she is."

Once everyone was finished with breakfast, Judith suggested Caleb, John, and River get fresh mugs of coffee and go back into the living room to finish discussing their business. She started to clean away the plates, and Georgia helped her. "Oh, lunch will be a little bit later since breakfast was so late. How about one o'clock?"

Multiple heads nodded their understanding.

John led the way to the living room, feeling anxious. Daisy was left to the care of Claire and Georgia, who both gushed over the little girl. The remaining men went outside to check on the stock and ensure they were all fine after the encounter with the Johnson bull.

"Can we address the elephant in the room?" Caleb asked when he took his normal chair.

River's eyes widened, and she looked between both men.

John nodded. "When was Daisy born?"

"Ah." River sucked in her lips. "She'll be four years old come October twenty-first."

At first, John held his breath. Then after doing some quick mental calculations, he deflated and slumped in his chair. He couldn't be Daisy's dad. The timing didn't match up to their first time sharing a bed.

"Why are you here?" John was beginning to get suspicious. If he couldn't be Daisy's dad, even though she looked like the spittin' image of him at four, what could River want with him? Surely it wasn't just to tell him that Donna had died so long ago, was it?

"I know how this might look, but I think you could be Daisy's dad..." River was about to explain why when John interrupted.

"Nope. Not possible. Donna and I..." He looked to his father, then felt his cheeks grow warm. "We didn't, um... We weren't together when Daisy would have been conceived."

River shook her head.

John threw up his hands. "Well, we were together, but not *together*, together. If you know what I mean?"

River's lips quirked up on one side, and she nodded. "But Daisy came early. There were complications, which eventually is what took Donna away from us."

John felt a burning sensation in his nose and behind his eyes. He put two fingers to his nose and breathed deeply before asking anything else. "What..."—he cleared his throat—"complications do you mean?"

"Donna had preeclampsia. It was really bad, and with the rotten free insurance, her doctor didn't catch it in time. They almost lost Daisy, too." Tears began to stream down River's face.

The tears John hoped to keep at bay in his own eyes ran down his face. "I'm so sorry. If I had known, I would have been there." He wiped his face. "But she told me she was going to marry Andrew, Daisy's dad. What happened?"

She took a moment to collect herself. "He walked out on her before they could marry."

The doorbell rang again, and John rolled his eyes. "What is this, Grand Central Station?"

Caleb put out a hand as he stood. "You stay here, I'll go see who it is."

John heard his dad's voice welcoming the sheriff.

River paled and bolted upright.

"Whoa, it's alright. The sheriff's our friend." Silently, John wondered if River had done something to get herself in trouble with the law.

Chapter 6

"Caleb, I'm here to see Georgia, but"—the sheriff scratched his balding head—"I noticed a car outside with Wyoming plates. We have a BOLO out from Wyoming, so I ran these plates and..."

"And you need to speak with River." Caleb nodded and waved for the sheriff to follow him to the living room.

John smiled and welcomed the sheriff.

Sheriff Roscoe held his hat in this hand and looked at the young woman sitting frightened on the couch. "Miss River Cassidy?"

She stood. "Yes, sir."

"Where is Daisy?" Roscoe looked around the room but couldn't see any signs of a toddler.

Georgia walked into the room smiling. "Roscoe, you're early." She kissed his cheek before she noticed the tension in the room. "What's wrong?"

His eyes danced with love when he looked at Georgia. "Sorry Georgia dear, but I'm here on official business right now."

She took a step back and put a hand to her throat. Georgia had been homeless not too long ago and wrapped up in a gang of thieves run by Big Bart. But for the last few months, everything had been going smoothly. She prayed Bart wasn't causing trouble again. "Is it..." She left off Bart's name, knowing Roscoe would know who she was asking about.

"No, sweetheart. This has nothing to do with you or that other situation." He smiled at her and lightly touched her elbow.

"He's here about me and Daisy." River stood tall and raised her chin defiantly. "I have custody of Daisy. He can't have her. He has no claim to my little girl."

"I think you should come with me." Roscoe looked around. "Where's the baby?"

Judith walked in carrying Daisy. "She's not a baby, Roscoe. What's going on?"

The lawman nodded at his old friend. "Mrs. Manning, can you take care of the little girl while I bring River in for questioning?"

Daisy looked between Roscoe and River. She held her arms out for River. "River?" Her lower lip quivered and she tried to get to her foster mom, the only mom she'd ever really known.

River went to her. "Don't worry, I'll be fine. I just need to talk to this lawman. You stay here with the Mannings. You'll be safe, sweetie." She kissed Daisy's forehead and cupped her cheek, then turned to look at John. "She needs your protection."

"Mine?" John pointed to his chest.

River nodded and followed the sheriff outside.

Daisy fisted her little hand and hit Roscoe as he walked by her. She puckered her lips and said, "Don't take my momma!"

Roscoe's shoulders drooped. He felt like a louse. "Honey, I'll bring her back. And I promise I won't hurt her. We just need to ask her some questions, that's all."

Even though Daisy was still in Judith's arms, she put one fisted hand on her hip and the other in the air. "I'm gonna bop you one if you lie to me!"

Judith pulled the squirming girl closer to her chest. "Shhh, don't worry sweet thing. River is going to be just fine."

John walked over, and when Daisy saw him she reached for him. He took her in his arms, and she wrapped her arms around his neck and buried her face in him. Before long, her body was wracked with sobs.

"Oh, little darlin', you're safe here with me. And River will be safe with Sheriff Roscoe. Don't you worry. You'll see, she'll be back here soon." John rubbed the little girl's back until she wore herself out and fell asleep in his arms.

While he was comforting Daisy he sat on the couch, his family surrounding him with no one talking.

Claire pulled out her phone and did an internet search on River Cassidy. When nothing but an old social media account came up, she tried Donna Myers. She found a lot of hits on Donna when she added Wyoming to the search term. She clicked on one news article and read it to herself. Then she went through several others before she found the obituary.

When she handed the phone to her husband, Matthew furrowed his brows. "What's this?"

"There's a lot of older news articles on a Donna Myers who had once been a rodeo queen and up-and-coming barrel racer," Claire answered quietly so as not to wake up Daisy.

He read the articles. Most spoke about her accomplishments and the hopes everyone had for her. But the obituary was sad. It mentioned her foster family and how devastated everyone was, as well as her newborn baby girl who almost didn't survive. Matthew put the phone down and sighed. "Looks like River's been telling the truth, if this is the same Donna you knew."

John looked at his brother, confusion evident on his face until a picture of a pretty blonde filled the screen. "Yes," he said softly, "that's my Donna."

Matthew went back to the article and pushed the phone closer to John so he could read it without letting Daisy go.

Not for the first time that day, John cried tears of sorrow and loss. The only woman he had ever loved had died. If only he could have been there for her.

Judith blew out a breath. "Does anyone know what's going on?"

They all looked to John, who shook his head.

Caleb stood and motioned for the family to follow him. "Let's go talk in the other room so we don't wake Daisy. I think she's had an awful few days."

Once they were out of earshot of Daisy, Matthew looked to his father. "What in tarnation is going on here? That little girl is the spittin' image of John at that age."

Caleb held up a hand. "I know, I know. I don't know why Roscoe took River in, but it is looking like Daisy might be John's. Although, he said the dates were off. He couldn't be her father."

"Oh my!" Judith exclaimed. "I think she might be."

Claire watched her new family and stood up. "Alright, we're the Mannings, and we fight for each other, right?"

They all looked her way and nodded.

"Then let's make sure Daisy is safe and find out what's going on with River and the sheriff. She's Daisy's legal guardian, right?" Claire looked to Caleb, who nodded. "Then she's family, too. We have to help her."

"I agree." John walked into the room without Daisy.

"Where's Daisy?" asked his mom.

"She's sleeping on the couch in the other room. I was thinking I could leave her here with you, Ma, and Dad and I can go into town and find out why River asked me to protect Daisy, and why in the world Roscoe took her in to the station instead of talking to her here." He nodded and turned around. When no one followed him, he looked back over his shoulder at his father. "Well, you comin'?"

Caleb nodded and kissed his wife on the cheek. "Matthew, I'd prefer if one of you boys stayed inside with

Daisy. Somethin's not right here, and I want to make sure the little girl has plenty of protectors around her."

"Of course. Claire and I will keep a close eye on her." Matthew put an arm around his wife.

Luke walked into the room with furrowed brows. "What's going on?" His wife Callie, better known as Deputy Manning, had the morning off and the two of them had breakfast together at Rosie's Diner before she went into work and he headed out to the ranch to start his day.

"I'll explain, but don't wake the little girl. She's had a very rough day already," Judith explained. "Maybe someone can put her in John's bed so she can sleep longer?"

"I got her," Claire offered.

Caleb and John grabbed their hats and coats before getting into John's old Ford pickup. The drive into town was quiet as both men thought about the day so far, and what it could all mean.

When John parked outside the sheriff's station, he turned off the engine and looked to his dad. "Dad, do you think Daisy's mine?"

Caleb rubbed his chin and looked out the window. "I don't know exactly what went down with you and Donna, but it sounds like you two could have created a baby. That little girl"—he pointed back toward their ranch—"is the spittin' image of you at her age. And I'm not the only one to notice."

"But the dates don't add up. And besides"—he looked down at his hands still on the steering wheel—"it was only a few times."

"Son, all it takes is once." His dad stared at him.

John gulped and nodded. "Right, that's not important right now. Helping River is what we're here for."

"Exactly."

Both men exited the vehicle and walked into the station as though they owned the joint.

"I want to see River and the sheriff," Caleb called out the moment he entered the station and didn't see either inside.

Chapter 7

C allie stood up from her desk and looked at her father-in-law and brother-in-law. Since she had married Luke Manning, these two had become family. But she was also a sheriff's deputy, and she took her job seriously. "I'm sorry, Caleb. You'll have to take a seat and wait for the sheriff to finish his questioning."

"Where are they?" John asked.

"In the back breakroom. Roscoe thought it would be better to sit back there and drink coffee while they talked." Luke's wife took her chair and waited expectantly for Caleb and John to follow suit.

Once John took his seat across from Callie, he asked, "Do you know what's going on here?"

She shook her head. "No, today I had the morning off, and when I came in they were walking to the back. Sheila told me that Roscoe wanted to discuss something with River, the lady in the back room, over coffee." Callie looked between the two. "Who is she?"

John looked to his father, who nodded. "She's the foster sister of my old college girlfriend." He went on to tell her about the visit that morning, and Daisy. But he kept the part about the little girl possibly being his quiet. Until he knew exactly what was happening, he didn't want the sheriff's deputy to know. Although, his brother Luke would probably spill the beans when he got home later that night.

Callie took it all in and looked at John. "If this River chick has custody of Daisy, why is she here to see you?"

He shrugged. "We didn't get that far before Roscoe came and took her away. All I know is River asked me to protect Daisy."

She sat back in her chair and it squeaked. "I see." Then she smirked. "How about a cup of coffee?"

John was about to wave off her suggestion when it hit him. "Yes, I'd love a cup. Thank you."

"Why don't you both follow me and we can get you each a fresh cup of coffee from the back?" She winked at her brother-in-law.

All three headed to the back as though they weren't up to anything.

When Callie entered the room followed by the two Manning men, the sheriff shook his head. "I wondered how long it would take you to make your way back here."

River's eyes widened. "Where's Daisy? Who's protecting her?"

John put up his hands. "Don't worry, my entire family is watching out for her. She'll be safe." He wanted to add that they were more worried about her safety, but he didn't.

"Roscoe, did River do anything wrong?" Caleb asked his old friend.

"That's what I'm tryin' to discover. It seems that the baby's father has filed a missing person's report. But according to social services, River here is the only custodian of the little girl. So I'm not sure how a..."—Roscoe looked at his notes—"Andrew Ryan would have had the ability to file a missing person's report on a kid he didn't have legal custody of."

River scoffed. "His father plays golf with the chief of police back in Cheyenne. I'm sure it was his dad who called in a favor. You know the rich and entitled." She rolled her eyes.

"I thought you said Andrew wasn't Daisy's father?" Caleb narrowed his eyes at the woman sitting across from the sheriff.

"He's not. I don't know why he's all of a sudden claiming to be. He hasn't had a thing to do with Daisy since she was born." She crossed her arms over her chest.

"I'm going to look into this further, but for now I need to know what your plans are, Miss Cassidy." The sheriff gathered his file and began straightening the papers.

"She's going to stay out at the ranch with us, along with Daisy." John looked to his father. "Isn't that right?"

He nodded. "Of course. We have plenty of room, and plenty of women who will dote all over that little girl."

Roscoe chuckled. "I don't doubt that." He looked from River to John, and then to Caleb. "Alright, I'll release her on one condition."

They all asked, "What's that?"

"River, you and Daisy must stay here. You can't leave Beacon Creek until we get this all settled. While you technically have custody of Daisy, it appears the baby's father is suing you for custody."

"What?" River jumped up. "Andrew can't do that. He's not even the father. There was a paternity test and everything."

"Like I said, I'm looking into matters and you have to agree to stay here. You and Daisy will be safe at the ranch." The sheriff eyed her and waited for agreement.

"Alright. If the Mannings will agree to put us up until this nightmare is resolved, I'll stay here." She sank back into her chair, tired. Tired of the rich always getting what they wanted, and tired of poor Daisy being treated like a possession and not a little girl.

Everyone always spoke about Daisy in the third person when River was trying to get custody. No one treated her like a baby who had just lost her mother. She was a burden on the system. And if River hadn't had a video of Donna saying she wanted River to care for her baby should something happen to her, River knew that the little girl would have been thrown into the system without a backward glance or a care as to what would have been best for her.

River had been in the system and knew how bad it was. It wasn't that the social workers were cruel; for the most part it was that they were overworked and under-paid. They had lost their heart and ability to empathize with the kids.

River had one great social worker who got fired for caring too much. The woman had helped her get to the Hanson Ranch, where she met Donna. Apparently she went too far when she approached the Hansons, who were very happy to have her. But the social worker's boss didn't like that River ended up going there.

Secretly, River believed that her social worker, Betty, was fired because Betty's boss wanted to place someone else there. Someone she had been having difficulty plac-ing. But without proof, Betty wasn't able to prove her case and she got fired. Didn't matter that a lot of other foster kids and their parents came to support her. River was shocked when she learned how cutthroat it was in the social work business.

If only social workers were allowed to actually care about their charges and work to do what was best for the kids, and not the *system*. That was why River fought so hard to make sure she got custody of Daisy. There was no way she was going to let such a beautiful and innocent baby go through any of the garbage she and Donna had to endure before they'd ended up with the Hansons.

Speaking of which, River needed to find a way to send them flowers.

Just one more regret, and failure, for River to deal with.

Now she was going to do what was best for Daisy, no matter what. And if that meant accepting charity, then she'd do it. It was time for River to throw aside her pride and accept help. Shoot, she could see that the Mannings were already getting attached to Daisy. They'd probably offer to help the little girl without River even asking.

As soon as the three of them got into John's truck, he asked, "What's going on? Why is Andrew all of a sudden coming after you and Daisy?"

River shook her head. "I don't really understand it, either. He never wanted anything to do with Daisy, even when he thought she might be his. The second he found out she wasn't, he was out the door and never once checked in with Donna."

John pounded the steering wheel. "Then why didn't Donna call me? If Andrew wasn't the dad, it must have been me, right?" He turned stern eyes on River.

She shrank back in her seat. "Um, not exactly."

Caleb, seated in the back of the quad cab, decided he needed to step in. "John, let's wait until we get home to finish this. I don't want you distracted. An accident is the last thing Daisy needs right now."

The mention of Daisy calmed John's nerves, and he focused on his driving and didn't ask another question the entire ride home.

"Did the sheriff treat you well?" Caleb didn't want another silent trip, and with the tension so thick it could be easily cut with a pocketknife, he decided to get to know River a bit better.

She nodded. "Um-hm."

"Where did you say you lived?" John joined the lighter conversation, hoping he could get something out of the woman to help him understand this confounding situation.

"Daisy and I lived in the same apartment I shared with Donna after she left college." River sighed. "I had worked for a diner for years and was just promoted to manager last year. But, it had to close its doors. We just weren't getting enough business."

"Does this mean you're out of a job now?" John kept his eyes on the road and his temper in check.

"Yes. I've been looking for another job, but nothing has come up yet." She fidgeted in her seat. "I thought I had one last week, and then all of a sudden they rescinded the offer. I think I'm gonna have to move elsewhere to find work."

"We have a diner here. I doubt they need a manager, but you might be able to get some shifts serving while you're here. And who knows, maybe they can even use you full-time. With spring coming and all the various events hosted in the area, Rosie's gets very busy." Caleb chuckled.

Hope filled River's heart. "Do you think I could? Really?"

"I'll talk to Rosie and see if she can use another hand. Someone with your experience will probably be needed very soon." Caleb looked at John through the rearview mirror.

John gave a slight nod.

"We have a lot of fairs and carnivals when the weather warms up, not to mention our little town hosts two rodeos a year in the summer and fall. Even if Rosie's isn't hiring, there will be plenty of other places offering part-time employment. We never seem to have enough people during this season who need work."

"That would be wonderful." River considered the offer and looked to John. "Would you mind if Daisy and I stayed in the area?"

John's nostrils flared. "I think it's best you stay here until this is all figured out. And if Daisy is who I think she is, she'll need you close by." He wasn't sure how he felt about River staying, but he had already decided that if Daisy really was his, he'd do whatever he needed to in order to keep the little girl. And if that meant ensuring River stayed close by, he'd deal with her.

"Besides," Caleb added, "you can't leave town until this situation with Andrew is concluded. If this man is insisting he's the father, then it's going to take a while to get the legalities all sorted. Both you and Daisy will have a home with us for as long as you want."

"If I get a job, who'll watch Daisy? Back in Cheyenne, Daisy stayed with one of my neighbors. Mrs. Metz was retired and sweet as pie. She loved caring for Daisy when I worked, and I think Daisy saw her as a grandmotherly figure." River chewed on her lower lip, not really sure what to do. She didn't have money for a sitter. Mrs. Metz didn't charge her. Instead, she accepted dinner from River along with apple pie, or coconut cream pie from the diner every day that she watched the little girl.

"Don't worry about that. We have plenty of people at the ranch all day who can watch Daisy. We never had sitters or caregivers for our kids when they were growing up." Caleb reached over the back of River's seat and patted her shoulder.

"But, aren't all hands on a ranch busy all day long? Daisy is sweet, but she loves to play and needs constant supervision." River worried that her little girl might get hurt on a ranch if not properly supervised.

John pulled into the ranch's drive and all talk about Daisy stopped.

In the front yard, the little girl was kicking a ball around with Georgia, Matthew, and Claire.

The moment the truck stopped, River jumped out of her seat and ran to Daisy. "Oh, my little girl. Are you alright?" She scooped up Daisy in her arms and held her tight.

"Aunt River! You're back." Daisy wrapped her arms around her foster mom's neck and shrieked.

John chuckled as he watched the pair interact. "She really does love River, doesn't she?"

Matthew and Claire had walked up next to him.

"Yes, she kept asking about her Aunt River while you were gone and wanted to know what was happening." Claire turned her head and stared at John. "She also kept asking for you. Why is she so attached to you after one morning?"

John shook his head. "I don't know. Not unless River told her about me. But I don't think she's said much about me to Daisy. Although, I could be wrong." He took his hat off and scratched his head.

He wasn't sure what to think about Daisy. Not yet. Though she sure did look like him. But if Andrew was claiming he was the natural father, then why did the paternity test all those years ago say he wasn't? "I think we need to get a paternity test as soon as possible."

"I'll call Harper and see if she can set it all up right away." Matthew scratched his chin. "I think the sooner we know for sure, the better."

"Agreed." John looked at the little girl who had instantly taken his heart.

Chapter 8

John paced the little room at the clinic where he'd met up with Nurse Harper Bensen to discuss the situation. "What do you mean we can't take a sample from Daisy? If River agrees, why can't we? She's the little girl's guardian."

"The sheriff thought you might try this, and he's been ordered by a court in Cheyenne to not allow a DNA sample to be taken from Daisy until the court orders it." Harper threw her hands up in the air. "I don't like this. Something smells rotten here. I've never heard of a court *not* allowing a DNA test if the legal guardian agrees to it."

River and Daisy were out in the waiting room while John and Harper discussed the situation.

"They're both here right now. Can we do the test on the down-low? Just so I know if I should be fighting or not?" John stopped his pacing and turned pleading eyes to the nurse who had been a friend to the Manning family for as long as he could remember.

She shook her head. "I wish I could, but we'd be in hot water if we did it." Harper looked around and motioned for him to come closer. "If you happen to have some hairs that just appear in your house one day and you take them to another lab—say in Idaho—and ask them to be compared, I wouldn't say a word."

Realization dawned on him. It wouldn't hold up in a court of law if he did this, but it would help him to know if he should go to the courts for the right to discover the truth. If Daisy was his, he had to know for certain.

A still small voice told him he was on the right path. He'd keep following that voice since he knew who it came from. God wouldn't lead him astray.

"I'm not recommending this, but if it were me I'd brush the person's hair with the same brush repeatedly for a few days. Then put said brush into a Ziploc baggie to take to the lab. A cheek swab is the best way to go about this, but if someone did that, they could be in a lot of trouble. Taking a brush from your own house with hairs in it might not get you into hot water." Harper shrugged and tapped the side of her nose.

John nodded, but didn't say a word.

Since bringing River back from the sheriff's office two days ago, he hadn't had a chance to get the entire story from her. No one wanted to discuss any of this in front of Daisy, and the little girl had been glued to John's side, as well as River's, ever since they got back.

Daisy refused to be without one or the other. Caleb had offered to take River aside while John distracted Daisy later that night in order to get some questions answered. He was going to play dress-up with the girl and be sure to brush her hair, a lot, over the coming days.

They had a friend with a ranch in Coeur d'Alene, Idaho. Maybe John could come up with an excuse to visit said friend and then find out from the Masons where he could go for this DNA test on the down-low. Now to find a valid reason for leaving Daisy and heading to Idaho. He wasn't one of the Mannings who was close to the Masons.

But Mark was.

A plan was beginning to develop in John's mind. All of those practical jokes had honed his imagination, and now it would be helpful. Mark might even be able to help John tweak his plan in such a way that it would keep everyone on their toes.

Caleb called an impromptu family dinner and meeting for that night. Not everyone had met River and Daisy yet, so it was the perfect excuse. The fact that Deputy Callie Manning had the night shift had nothing to do with the exact date of the family gathering.

During lunch that day, John smirked when he saw River walk in wearing another ironic coffee t-shirt. She seemed to have several of them. His favorite was the one with a little green alien reaching out for the human girl's coffee mug that had the typical green alien head with huge gray eyes on it. And the alien looked like it might be the model for the coffee mug.

"River, can you take a walk with us?" Caleb and Judith asked the young woman after Caleb decided a change in plans for the night was needed.

They had just finished lunch, and John agreed that the afternoon chores could be done without him and his dad.

"Daisy, how about we go play while your Aunt River takes a walk with my parents?" John knelt to her level and hugged the little girl.

"Is Aunt River in trouble?" Big, worried eyes looked between River and John.

John pulled back. "No, sweetie. She's not." He smiled down into Daisy's angelic face. "I just wanted to spend some time with you. Is that alright?"

Daisy grinned and nodded enthusiastically. "Yes, please." She clapped her hands, ran toward the room she was sharing with River, and pulled out a princess dress from her little suitcase.

"Oh, this is pretty." John held out the white, blue, and purple shimmering dress and noticed how worn it was. He wondered if she had just worn it out, or if it was a second-hand dress. He doubted River had much money to spend on pretty new dresses for Daisy.

Not that there was anything wrong with second-hand clothes, but John knew they could afford to treat the little girl. Maybe on his trip he'd come back with something cute and fun. Making a mental note of the size, he helped Daisy dress up as Princess Daisy.

"My princess," John said in a mock servant's voice, "should I do your hair for you?"

The little girl squealed and grabbed her hairbrush and a Ziploc baggie with a few pins and ribbons in it. "Yes, please!"

By the time River walked back into their room, John was ready for a nap. "I tell ya, keeping up with a little girl is more work than helping to run a large ranch." When he stood up, his knees almost gave out on him. "I'm almost twenty-three years old and I think I need knee replacement surgery already."

River chuckled. "Your body will get used to being on the ground if you keep playing with Princess Daisy. She tends to love it when her *servants* bow and get on their knees to play at her level."

"Hmm, sounds like someone needs some friends her own age. This Sunday we'll have to introduce Daisy to some of the other ranch kids her age. Maybe even set up some opportunities for her to play with them." John rubbed his knees. They felt like they were going to permanently ache from the hardwood floor.

"I, uh. I don't know about that." River fidgeted with her hands. "I mean, I don't know that I'm comfortable with her going to strangers' houses."

"Don't worry, we can have the kids over here to play with Daisy until you're comfortable with their parents." John thought back to when he was a kid. "We usually hosted the gatherings when I was growing up, anyways."

He chuckled when he remembered some of the trouble he got into as a little boy. Then he frowned. "Yes, I think it would be best to have the kids come here and we can keep a close eye on them. Make sure Daisy doesn't get hurt."

The memory of climbing the Johnson tree when he was five—and falling out after only getting to the second branch—had entered his mind. Daisy was too young to be climbing trees, especially if she'd never done it before. No, he was going to keep a close eye on her and make sure she didn't hurt herself.

A ranch could be a wonderful place for kids to play, but it could also be very dangerous.

When Luke walked into the house later that night, his father stopped him. "Son, I'll understand if you don't feel comfortable keeping a secret from your wife. But everything discussed tonight is confidential and can't be shared with Callie. It would put her in an awkward situation at work."

Luke held up a hand. "Pa, Callie and I have already spoken about the, ah, *situation*. She wants to help the little girl. She's already told me to keep family secrets secret." Luke grinned. "In fact, she told me she wanted to know nothing about tonight."

Caleb chuckled. "You married a very smart, and wise, woman." He took his son's hat and coat and put them on the rack. "Come on in. Everyone else is already here."

Luke looked at his watch. "I'm on time. Did everyone else just get in early?" He turned confused eyes on his father.

"Ah, no." Caleb shook his head. "I told you to come out here thirty minutes later than everyone else. We needed to talk about a few things, like how to handle the fact that your wife is a sheriff's deputy and duty-bound to report certain things to the sheriff." He arched a brow.

"Ah." Luke held up a hand. "Say no more. I totally understand. You know, we don't tell each other *everything*. We can't."

Judith walked up to her son. "I know she can't tell you certain things about her job, but your job doesn't require confidentiality. We don't want to get between you and your wife. She's a part of this family just like Logan, Leah, and Claire are. And we wouldn't want to cause any strife for any of our children and their spouses."

"We understand, Ma. Don't worry. Callie told me to keep tonight secret. She understands that sometimes her job will get in the way. As long as we don't do anything to hurt anyone else, she's fine with us keeping secrets." Luke considered his statement. "Well, I can only keep Manning family secrets from her when it's absolutely necessary. I can't keep any personal secrets from her." He chuckled.

John walked up to greet his brother. "Luke, I understand if you won't want to be a part of this, or even know what's going on. I won't be hurt or disappointed if you feel the need to bow out."

"Not at all. If Callie weren't on the force, she'd be here helping us plan whatever it is that's going down. She wants us to do what we need to, within reason." Luke added the clarification more for his own sake than anyone else's. He knew that his family wouldn't do anything to truly cross a line. But they would skirt that line in order to protect their own.

With pursed lips, John took a second to consider his brother's situation. "Alright. But if you feel uncomfortable at any time, please stop us so you can leave. None of us will hold it against you, or Callie. I already love her like a sister, so don't worry."

Luke grinned at his little brother and clapped a hand on his shoulder. "Brother, I'm here for you. And Callie is too, in spirit. So no worries. The only thing that would stop me is if you were to plan on hurting or killing someone. Then I'd have to bow out for my own conscience, not just because of my wife."

Since none of the Manning family would ever try to hurt anyone, unless it were in self-defense, no one was worried about Luke's clarification.

Everyone chuckled and went into the dining room, where dinner was ready. Daisy and River were at the table, seated next to John, so no discussion of battle plans was shared yet.

And Caleb hadn't had a chance to tell John about his and Judith's discussion with River. Instead, everyone was just waiting for Daisy to eat and go to bed.

Chapter 9

Conversation flowed easily at dinner, and both of the newcomers were included where possible. All the while, John was counting down the seconds until Daisy went to bed. Then chiding himself for wishing she weren't at the dinner table with his family. He just wanted to get going with the planning and get to the bottom of everything.

The truth will set you free, but in this case, it was gonna drive John nuts. At least trying to get to the truth.

"Daisy, what do you think of horses?" Claire smiled at the little girl from across the table.

Multiple conversations had been going on, but everyone quieted and waited to hear what Daisy had to say.

The little girl giggled and looked at everyone watching her. She took John's hand and held it under the table.

He squeezed it, urging her to speak up.

"Well, I love the pony I saw at the Christmas carnival. But big horses scare me." She shivered and made a sour face before turning uncertain eyes to John. "Will you get me a pony?"

He chuckled. "We'll have to see about that." John wanted to get her anything she wanted. In a few short days this little girl had stolen his heart, and he never wanted it back. If she proved to be his, he would get her an entire stable full of ponies if that's what she wanted.

"I think we need to get a pony to visit us this week." Judith's eyes sparkled, and she looked at her husband. "I think we should ask one of our neighbors if we can rent a pony, don't you, Caleb?"

Before he could answer, John spoke up. "I know the Masons have several ponies. I bet we could borrow one from them."

"The breeders in Idaho?" Mark set his fork down on his plate and looked at John.

The conversation was turning exactly the way John needed. It couldn't have been better even if he'd planned this out with Claire. This must be a God thing. He'd almost forgotten how God could weave plans to fit His desires. It had been so long since John had felt God working in his life. It felt good. Actually, more than good. It felt...*right*.

"Yes, I was just thinking we haven't seen them in a while, and they do breed ponies as well as various other breeds of horse. How about we drive over there in a couple of days and see what they've got?" John's mind was working a mile a minute now. "When was the last time you spoke to, or saw, Stu Mason?"

Stu Mason, or Stewart Mason, was Mark's age. They had met one summer when the Masons came by to sell them a few horses. Mark and Stu became fast friends, and the rest was history.

"Well, the Masons were here for the wedding, but Stu and I really didn't get a chance to catch up." Mark chuckled. "I was a little bit busy."

"Exactly. And how long before that?" John inquired.

Mark expelled a breath. "Oh, way too long. I think you might be right—it's time to go see my old friend. And now's the perfect time. Leah's going to be closing for the next few weeks as they prepare for inventory." Mark narrowed his gaze at his brother-in-law. "Personally, I think it's payback for taking such a long honeymoon."

Leah tilted her head and grabbed her husband's hand. "Now cowboy, we've discussed this."

Logan chuckled and put his hands behind his head.

Elizabeth sighed. "I'm sorry, Mark. It's my fault." She put her hands on her protruding belly. "I'm having a tough time right now, and the doctor doesn't want me home alone at night."

Logan erased the look of triumph from his face, and worry creased it. "Darlin', don't worry. Leah and Mark understand, they're just complaining since they're new-lyweds."

Elizabeth sighed. "Leah, I'll owe you when you get pregnant."

Leah chuckled. "No worries. I understand." She grinned at her brother. "It just means that Logan gets to handle the entire inventory on his own."

Her brother sat up straight. "Hey, we never agreed on that."

"Oh yes we did." Leah crossed her arms over her chest in victory. "Remember when we discussed what the closer would and would *not* do?" She arched a brow.

Deflated, Logan sat back against his chair. "The closer works the floor while the other person handles the inventory."

"Cheer up, bro. We've got more help this year, so you won't be stuck doing it *all* by yourself." Leah winked at Mark.

"I'll give Stu a call tomorrow after morning chores and see if he can put us up for a day or two. And if he has any ponies he can loan us." Mark winked at Daisy.

The little girl clapped, and the gravy on her hands splattered all over River and John. "Uh-oh." Daisy sank in her chair and sucked her thumb.

"Daisy, it's alright." River looked up at Judith, then to John. "It is alright, isn't it?"

John chuckled. "Yes, these things happen. Especially when little girls get overly excited. I think a bath is in order." He looked to River. "What do you say, Aunt River?"

She took the hint and nodded. "Sure, but..." River licked her lips. "Can we have dessert first? I saw that your mom made a homemade chocolate bundt cake today."

"Oh, please? Please, please, please, Uncle John?" Daisy pleaded, and even stuck out her lower lip just like her mother did when she really wanted something.

The sight of Daisy looking at him like her mother used to hit him right in the heart. Tears pricked at the corners of his eyes, and his nose burned. Taking a moment to collect himself, he picked up his napkin and wiped away the non-existent gravy from his face. Then he did wipe off actual gravy from his hands. After clearing his throat, he said, "Of course. No little girl should miss chocolate cake."

"Yeah! Thank you, Uncle John." Daisy wrapped her tiny arms around John as much as she could, transferring more gravy to him.

He chuckled. "Looks like I'm going to need a shower as well." He looked to his mom. "How about you save me a piece of that cake and I'll go clean up now and come right back?"

She nodded, and he kissed the top of Daisy's head.

Uncle John? Since when did Daisy think of him as her uncle? John wondered as he cleaned up if it was wise to let her call him that, just in case he really was her father. He had always wanted to be called "Pa." Would the little girl easily be able to change up the name if need be?

When John had cleaned up and went back downstairs, River and Daisy had left the table. A large slice of decadent chocolate cake sat at his spot along with a fresh cup of coffee. "Thanks, I think I'm gonna need this. Is this the gluten-free cake?"

"Of course it is." Judith harumphed.

It wasn't that anyone there needed to be gluten-free. But when she made a cake from a box, she just hated to add in the damaging chemicals the food producers added, like gluten. And to be honest, this particular box cake was better than any homemade cake or other boxed cake any of them had had.

The family—all but Chloe, her boyfriend, and Callie—were still sitting at the dinner table. The dishes had been cleared away, and now everyone else was drinking coffee.

When John sat at his seat, all eyes turned to him. "Well, what do we know?" He looked down the long table to his father.

Caleb finished off his mug of coffee, and Judith got up to pour him another cup.

"We spoke with River earlier. That girl really does love Daisy. I think if she hadn't come across some hard times, she wouldn't have come looking for you, John." Judith handed Caleb a fresh cup and then smiled at her son.

"Is there a chance Daisy is mine?" That was all John cared about at the moment. The rest could be discussed later.

Caleb cleared his throat. "Ah, Daisy was conceived in March of your freshman year in college."

John's brows furrowed. "But she was born in October."

"It seems that Donna had a very rough time of it. She ended up getting preeclampsia and almost died, along with Daisy."

John's fork clanked to the plate and he sat back. "I never should have walked away from her. I should have fought for her. I loved her." He had heard this part earlier, but it still got him in his gut, and heart. He'd probably kick himself forever for leaving the woman he loved and not looking back.

His mother walked over and put a comforting arm across his shoulder. "We know you did, son. And I'm sorry."

"So, that's what killed her? She died in childbirth?" Tears formed in John's eyes, and not a single eye at that table was dry, either.

Elizabeth and Logan put protective hands on her belly and looked in each other's eyes.

Judith noticed. "Elizabeth, you don't have anything to worry about. Your doctor is fantastic."

"But Ma, I'm having such a hard time with this pregnancy." Tears began to fall down Elizabeth's cheeks.

John looked at his sister. "Is that what happened to Donna? Do you have the same symptoms?"

Elizabeth wiped her cheeks. "If she had preeclampsia, then there were obvious signs that her doctor missed. Like swollen ankles and elevated blood pressure." She looked to her husband and a small smile was on his face.

"She doesn't have cankles. At least not like what Donna must have had. And her blood pressure is fine. Her issues have more to do with upset stomach. Very different situation. But we are monitoring her vitals every day, and I've looked into preeclampsia. Our doctor says Lizzie doesn't have those symptoms." Logan rubbed his wife's belly and kissed her cheek. "We know that Lizzie and the baby are fine, but whenever someone mentions pregnancy issues, we just get nervous."

Judith reached across the table and took Elizabeth's hand. "It's natural to be nervous about your first baby. All is fine. Just put on your medical hat and you'll see that there isn't anything truly wrong, mostly just indigestion and fatigue. Both are absolutely natural."

"You're right. Thanks, Ma." Elizabeth looked to John. "Please, do go on. We'll be fine."

"Where was I? Oh yeah. March." John cleared his throat. "Is it getting hot in here?" He pulled his shirt away from his chest and fanned himself.

"No, it's not. And we'll discuss what you did later, let's just get on with it. Is it possible?" Caleb's gruff voice caused everyone to sit back in their seats.

John sighed and nodded. "Yes, it is. That's when we first"—he looked up with regret covering his face—"we, uh began our, uh...*relationship* in March. And I swear, it only went on for a few months. Not even that many times."

"John, how many times did I tell you it only takes once?" Caleb stood up and ran a hand through his hair. "But it doesn't matter now. One look at that adorable little girl and I could see she was yours. I doubt anyone would think otherwise if they saw your pictures at that age."

"Honey, even I can see the resemblance now." Judith sat down next to her husband. "The question is, what do we do next?"

John pursed his lips. "I have a plan, and I don't want any of you to get in trouble on my account. Just know that I need to travel to Idaho with Mark in a few days. I'll get proof. It may not hold up in court, but it will be damaging for Andrew if it comes back positive. And it will make any sane judge not on the take order another paternity test and question the validity of Andrew's claim, especially since his original paternity test came back negative."

Mark stood up. "I'm in."

Leah joined him. "Whatever you need, you can count on us, John."

Everyone else at the table, including Luke, stood up and agreed.

"Thanks, guys. I really appreciate the support." John looked at his father. "What did kill Donna if she survived childbirth?"

"Her heart gave out." Caleb ran a shaky hand over his face. "The trauma of the birth weakened her heart. She may have had a pre-existing heart condition, but they don't know for sure. She lived for two months and then went to sleep one night to never wake up."

Again, tears flowed freely down John's face. "At least she went in her sleep. I hope she didn't feel anything."

Elizabeth shook her head. "Most likely she didn't."

River walked in. "Sorry, I didn't mean to eavesdrop, but the doctors said that Donna felt no pain. It was too quick and she probably never even woke up."

John stood up and looked around her. "Where's Daisy?"

"She fell asleep right away. I think all of the chaos lately has worn her down." River winced.

"Or maybe it's just trying to keep up with the adults on a ranch. It's pretty crazy here, and it's not something a kid can keep up with," Claire added.

"I think tomorrow I'll let Daisy watch some TV. Do you even have cable out here?" River laughed nervously.

John chuckled. "Yes, we have satellite TV out here in the boonies."

"And we even have several kids' channels." Judith smiled and stood up to get River a cup of decaf coffee. "Normally I'm not a big fan of letting kids sit in front of the television for long periods of time, but with everything going on it might be relaxing for her to have a jammies day."

"Oh"—Elizabeth looked out into the distance—"a day on the couch in my PJs and the remote would be wonderful." She looked to her husband. "Do you mind if I do that this Saturday?"

Logan chuckled. "Lizzie, I've been trying to get you to do that for weeks now. Please do. It might help you to catch up on the rest you need."

Judith raised a hand. "That's probably my fault. We rarely, if ever, let our kids veg out in front of the TV when they were growing up."

"Well, we did when we were sick." Mark considered. "But that was pretty rare. None of us got sick very often."

"What about when Mark brought home chicken pox?" John grinned at his brother.

The entire Manning clan groaned.

"Please, don't remind us." Caleb slapped a hand to his forehead. "That had to be the worst spring in the history of springs."

Claire looked to River, and both women frowned.

Leah said, "Just about the entire town of Beacon Creek got chicken pox. They even closed the school for a few days. It was awful."

"Yeah, but all of us got to sit in front of the TV with pink splotches all over our bodies. We were so sick that I don't think anyone complained when their turn to choose the show switched to someone else." Elizabeth stuck her tongue out. "The itchiness that went with chicken pox was worse than the fever."

They spent the next few minutes reminiscing over the TV and how often they fought over it, which is partly why Judith didn't let them watch it much while they were growing up. It was also because they had homework and chores to do around the ranch. And she firmly believed that if they could play outside, they should. For heaven knew there were plenty of days during the winter where they'd be stuck inside.

For the next few days John played with Daisy as much as possible, which included brushing her hair and ensuring as many hair follicles as possible were left on the princess brush.

While River noticed, she said nothing to John about what he was up to. She too wanted the truth to finally be known.

Chapter 10

The morning that John and Mark were scheduled to leave, John said goodbye to Daisy, who in turn threw a fit.

"Daisy, sweetheart"—John put a hand to his heart—"you're going to make me cry."

The little girl sniffled and wiped her eyes. "Why do you have to leave, Uncle John?"

It still sent a thrill through John when she called him that. But for the life of him, he didn't understand why the girl called him uncle, or how she could have become so attached to him so quickly. He couldn't leave a room without her following him. Someone had to distract her in order for him to get away.

John bent down on her level. "Daisy, I'm going to see a friend who has ponies. I thought I'd see if he would let me borrow one for you. Will that be alright?"

She hugged his neck. "Oh, yes. I can come with you and pick one out." When Daisy pulled back, she was all smiles and giddiness.

River cleared her throat. "Uh, Daisy, we can't go with John right now. It's important that we stay here on the ranch." She got down on her knees. "I have to get a job if we want to stay here, and you can't leave me. Not now."

The little girl hung her head. "But I want to go and pick out a pony." She stomped her foot.

While John had seen her sad, he had never seen her throw an actual temper tantrum. "Now Daisy, is this any way to act when I'm going off to get you a present?" He gave her his sternest look. Although he wasn't accustomed to giving kids a parental look, he figured he needed to nip this sort of action in the bud before she grew accustomed to getting her way, or became too much of a drama queen like her momma.

One lone tear dropped from her eyelashes before she shook her head. "No, I guess not."

"That's my girl. Now you be nice and stay with your Aunt River." John stood up and smiled at his mother, who had stood by watching the entire encounter quietly.

Judith walked up to the little girl. "How about we make some cookies today? Would you like to help me frost sugar cookies?"

That got Daisy to perk up. "Really? Can I?" She turned excited eyes to River and waited for her answer.

With a chuckle, River agreed.

When Judith walked Daisy inside, John and Mark took that moment to leave so that the little girl didn't see them drive away.

Mark tuned the radio to a local country music station, but changed it when he got tired of the pop music blaring from the speakers instead of true country. "What's this world coming to when country music sounds just like Justin Timberlake or Katy Perry?" He shook his head and searched for a station that played classic country hits.

John chuckled. "Oh, I don't know. I kinda like 'Dark Horse.'"

"Sure, that's a great song, but it isn't country and it was never billed as being a country song." Mark finally found a station he liked and sat back.

"At least Taylor Swift officially changed to pop music. I have to respect her for realizing the difference between the two formats and calling it out," John added. "Although, I'm not really a fan of her newer stuff."

Mark scrunched his nose. "Yeah, I give her props for changing over officially to pop, but you're right, the newer stuff doesn't do it for me."

"This from the guy who had once practically wallpapered his room with Taylor Swift posters?" John lightly punched his brother's shoulder, then put his hand back on the steering wheel.

"Ha, ha. You know that was ages ago." Mark sat up straighter. "Besides, I'm a very happily married man now. I don't need posters of Taylor or anyone else on my walls."

John snorted. "Yeah, and remind me. Your room at the ranch—didn't you ask for more Taylor Swift posters for Christmas last year?"

This time it was Mark's turn to playfully punch his brother.

"Hey, not while I'm driving." John eyed his brother from the side. "You do want to get home to your posters...I mean your new wife, right?" He chuckled and slapped the steering wheel.

"Humph. I don't think I like this happier version of you. All you've done since I got home is tease and prank me. What's gotten into you?" The serious look in Mark's eyes sobered the men in the cab of the truck.

John coughed into his arm. He figured his brother would see his new morning routine on this trip and decided he shouldn't be keeping it a secret anymore. "I've been reading my Bible every morning lately. And praying for direction in my life."

Mark's mouth fell open, and his eyes widened. "You, reading your Bible lately? And praying? Mr. I Don't Want To Pray This Time?" Mark regularly prayed before his meals, and had asked John repeatedly to pray, but the younger brother never wanted to. Which was strange, since before he left for college John regularly prayed before meals.

"Yeah, yeah. Yuck it up." John shook his head and smiled. "It's really made a difference in my life and my outlook. I still have a long ways to go, but I'm starting to realize that God forgave me of my sins." He quickly looked at his brother. "Of which everyone now knows about."

"So that's what had you in a funk these past two years? Donna and Daisy?" Mark always suspected his brother had woman troubles, but he never thought his little brother would have slept with a woman outside of marriage. And he certainly never thought he'd have a kid. Especially at such a young age.

"Yes." He nodded, then shook his head. "No. I didn't know Daisy might be mine. When Donna told me she was pregnant, she assured me it was Andrew's baby and not mine."

John sighed. "Although if I'm honest, I did wish the baby would have been mine. I would have married her in a heartbeat and been the happiest man on Earth. Instead, I dropped out of college at the end of my sopho-more year and joined the rodeo. At least while on the circuit I was too busy to think much of Donna." He glanced at his brother out of the corner of his eye. "But the night of my fall, the one that ended my career, I was distracted."

"By what?" Mark asked.

The memory still haunted John. He grabbed ahold of the steering wheel so hard, he figured he'd leave marks on the wheel. "The rodeo queen that week." He blew a breath out. "She wore a red dress almost identical to the one Donna wore the night I met her. I couldn't stop thinking about her and her baby. I wondered about them and if they were alright." He turned his head to look out his side window for a moment before continuing. "And

I wondered what it would have been like if I was the baby's father instead."

"I see. So does this mean you're praying that Daisy turns out to be yours?" Mark could see the resemblance between the two and was pretty confident that Daisy was his niece, but until the test results came in, he wasn't going to get his hopes up. Especially now that this Andrew character was trying to get custody of the cutest little girl ever.

"How could I not hope she's mine?" John pictured the little girl with her strawberry blonde hair, blue eyes that looked like a sunny summer sky, and those dimples in her cheeks. Not to mention how much she looked like him when he was three, almost four. He also noticed that Daisy's birthday was the same day as his, October twenty-first. When he'd first heard her birthday, he knew it was a sign from God.

"If I'm being honest"—Mark shrugged his shoulders—"I kinda hope she's yours as well."

The rest of the drive they spoke about country music stars who actually sang country songs, and the last time each of them had seen the Masons. Both cowboys were looking forward to spending time with their old friends.

Trees lines the drive all the way up to the house from the street. There was a split wooden railed fence that lined the long road. It had a sort of movie majestic feel to it. John could see this drive in a movie with some big celebrity like John Wayne or Kevin Costner owning this ranch. He pictured one of them on a tall, brown horse ambling down the road with a piece of hay in his mouth and a ten-gallon hat on his head.

The Mason's walked outside and met them when they parked the truck. While John didn't know them well, he was glad to be there and see them again.

After getting all settled, John pulled Stu aside to discuss why he was really there. "Hey, man. I do need a pony like we discussed over the phone, but there's something even more important I need your help with."

"Shoot. Whatever you need, I'm your man." Stu pointed to himself and grinned. He liked to think he was the kind of man who could deliver on a promise. He was also usually the go-to guy amongst his friends.

John looked around to make sure no one else was in hearing range. The last thing he needed was someone with loose lips who would run to the local sheriff and turn him in. Then he'd never find a way to get the truth. "I need to quietly have a DNA test done and see if the two samples are from people who are related. Do you know anyone who can perform a test like that?"

Stu chuckled. "Don't tell me some little lady is claiming you fathered her love child?"

John's face flushed. "Something like that."

The cowboy's eyes widened in understanding, and after taking a moment to get his breathing under control, he looked around just like John had done. "My girlfriend is an assistant in our local lab. She might be able to help. Or point you in the right direction." He scratched the stubble on his chin. "She's at work now. I can call her and see what she says."

John nodded. "Alright, but it can't be linked back to me. Is there any way to keep the names off the samples?" He didn't feel like telling his friend the reason behind his strange request. That might keep him from helping, or at least keep his girlfriend from helping.

"Sure thing. I'll call her now." Stu pulled out his cellphone and dialed his girlfriend. Once he had finished the call, he smiled at his old friend. "You're in luck. We can go over now if you have the sample from the other, uh, person?"

"I do." John nodded and went to get his suitcase out of the back of his truck. He put the baggie with the brush and hair in his messenger bag and followed Stu to where he'd parked his own truck.

Stu introduced John to his girlfriend, who was tall, lean, and quite pretty with a long black ponytail hanging down to her lower back. It stood out starkly against the white lab coat she wore over her camouflage scrubs.

After John's mouth had been swabbed, he asked, "How long will it take to get the results?"

Indigo, Stu's girlfriend, looked up from the paperwork she was filling out. "We're a little busy right now, but it shouldn't take longer than a week. How can I reach you when I have the results?"

He hadn't thought that far ahead.

Stu put up a hand. "Why don't you just tell me the results and then I can get them to my friend here? That way he stays anonymous."

She nodded. "Good idea. I don't want to be tied to this. Something tells me you don't have permission to be testing this other source?" She quirked a brow.

"Actually, I do have permission. But, uh..." John scratched his head.

Indigo held up a hand. "No, please don't. I don't need any more information than that you have permission for me to test what appears to be a little girl's hairbrush."

"Good call." John grinned and thanked the lab tech again before heading outside to wait for Stu.

Chapter 10

J ohn leaned against Stu's Ford F-250 Lariat white-and-silver truck, waiting for his friend to come outside. What a day he was having. Technically he wasn't breaking any laws; River had given permission for the DNA test. Sheriff Roscoe only told Harper Bensen that she couldn't do the DNA test. Well, her facility couldn't do it. He wondered if those were the specific words used, or if he'd just imagined that even Roscoe was trying to find a way to help the Manning family.

"Hey, since we've got some time before dinner, do you want to go do some shopping? I need to stop by the tractor supply store for an order I placed online." Stu clicked the lock on his truck and both cowboys hopped in.

"Sure, I could actually use the chance to pick up something for Daisy." John wanted to get the little girl a few new dresses and some cowgirl clothes for when she rode the pony. But he'd wait until he could take her down to the store for a proper fitting on the cowgirl boots.

Once they were in the store and John was looking at the frilly country dresses for little girls, he felt a small twinge in his gut. He missed her already? But he hardly knew her, and there was a chance she wasn't his. Who was he kidding? She was most obviously his little girl.

After picking out enough clothes to open his own store for little girls, he stopped at a rack of funny t-shirts. When he saw the coffee shirt, he smiled and thought of River. Would she like a shirt with BB-8 holding a cup of coffee and an Ewok pointing his little arrow at it? The saying was what made him go ahead and pick up a medium shirt in heather gray. *Give me coffee and no one gets hurt.* Some days that sentiment was exactly how he felt.

A slow smile spread across John's face as he thought about the various funny t-shirts River had worn since arriving. Matthew would probably roll his eyes at John for contributing to her strange quirk, but John thought it just made River unique. But when an ache in his chest began, he couldn't believe he might be missing her as well. It couldn't be. There had to be something else going on in his heart. It was most likely that he associated River with Daisy, and he knew he was already missing Daisy.

Yeah, he'd just tell himself that was all it was. Then he'd sell himself a bridge.

Early the next morning, John got up and looked outside his window. The sun was rising over the tops of the trees blanketing the ranch. The Mason ranch was about twenty miles off the I-90 highway, and it backed up to the Coeur D'Alene National Forest.

After living in Wyoming and heading out to the various rodeos there, and now being in Idaho, he knew Montana was home. His entire being wanted nothing more than to be back home on his family ranch with his family. And that family just might now include a cute little strawberry blonde girl and her "aunt" with auburn hair and hazel eyes. Eyes that had his stomach bucking like a bronc trying to remove a rider.

John shook his head and hoped those emotions weren't what he feared. River was going to move on, wasn't she? No one had said it, but John thought she was there to give him Daisy if he proved to be her pa. But something about that didn't sit right with him.

Daisy was almost four years old. River hadn't tried to contact him at all during all this time she had Daisy, or even when Donna was dying. A memory in the back of his mind wiggled to the forefront. He didn't want to think about the possibilities. There were so many other reasons why River had only come to him now. Surely it had something to do with Andrew? But she seemed so confused about why Andrew was after custody of Daisy.

All he knew what that he needed to get home, and fast. Visiting with old friends was nice, but not when there was something more pressing to handle. He didn't need to stay in town until the results came in; Stu said he'd get them and forward them on. No, he and Mark had to head home today after they chose the pony. If they ended up bringing it back for some reason, they could extend their visit then.

Chapter 11

John was anxious to leave, and was quite surprised to find that Mark was as well. Maybe the whole newly-wed thing really had changed his brother for the better. But when it came time to leave the Mason ranch, he was surprised at how much he hated saying goodbye to his friends. "We have to get together more often. Maybe next time you can come out and visit us for more than a wedding visit."

Stu chuckled. When Mark got married, it was only him and his sister, Lola, who came to Beacon Creek. And they were only there for two nights. "You got it. Maybe I can come and pick up Pickles when you're ready to send her back?" Pickles was the pony that John chose to rent from the Mason ranch for Daisy.

John had been serious about getting the little girl a pony. The fact that it covered his original reason for going to Idaho was just a bonus.

"We can have a big family barbecue and everything." Then Mark added, "As long as you promise to stay for at least four days."

"I think something might be arranged as long as your dad makes the sauce, and not Mark." Stu raised a brow before chuckling.

Mark raised his hands in the air. "Hey now, I make just as good sauce as my dad does. Leah even admitted to it when we were on our honeymoon."

"Riiiight." John exaggerated his nod.

"And pigs fly," Stu added.

Lola interjected, "I thought Leah had better taste than that?"

"Well, she did marry him." Stu pointed to Mark.

The group laughed, and all said their goodbyes before John and Mark took off in John's truck, hauling the pony down the drive in their trailer.

They made great time on the drive home, and in less than seven hours they were unloaded and inside getting hot coffee served to them by Judith and Caleb.

"Where is everyone?" John asked, specifically wondering where River and Daisy were.

"The boys are still out doing chores. They'll be back in about an hour." Judith poured Mark a cup of coffee.

"And River is napping with Daisy." Caleb took a drink of his coffee. "The little girl's missed you, but she's overly excited about getting to ride a pony."

John chuckled. "I hope she realizes she won't be going anywhere on her own, and I doubt she'll even get out of the paddock while she's here."

Judith tilted her head. "Do you think they'll be leaving soon?"

"I think that once they're allowed, River will take Daisy far away from here." With a furrowed brow, John ground his teeth at the through of never seeing Daisy again. No matter who her father was.

Caleb covered his smile by holding his mug up to his mouth. "I take it you aren't too keen on them leaving town?"

"No, I'm not. I want to be there for Daisy as she grows up. I don't want to miss out on any more of my little girl's life." John set his mug down too hard, and little bit of coffee slushed over the side.

"What if she's not yours?" Again, River had been eavesdropping. She felt guilty, but only a little bit. She and John really needed some time alone to talk about everything, but whenever she tried, someone always interrupted. She had no idea if it was all just accidents or if John had asked that they never be left alone.

He took a steadying breath. "Then I'll cross that bridge when I come to it. But even you have to believe she's mine. Why else would you come here?"

River took a seat across from John after getting a mug of coffee. "There were others."

John's forehead crinkled in confusion. "Others?"

"Yeah." River bit her bottom lip. "Donna put together a list of possible"—she looked around, ensuring that Daisy hadn't gotten up from her nap and found her—"baby daddies."

"Uh..." John's heart sank. "How many others?"

"She wrote out a list, and you were on the bottom." River cringed. As Donna's best friend and foster sister, she had known each and every name of the men her sister had been seeing when she first met John. But she also knew that Donna was falling in love with John. A fact that River had yet to share with the cowboy.

Any time she thought about telling him, she cringed and hated the idea of Donna and John being together. When Donna would tell her all about her time with John on the road, River fantasized about what it would be like to have someone of her own who treated her like John treated Donna. Well, minus the sharing-a-bed part. Donna told her stories of how John opened doors for her, literally. He held her chair out when they sat down to eat. He even paid for most of their meals. John was a complete gentleman.

River had never wanted to have kids. She had seen too much while in the foster system, and she had zero desire to have a kid that she'd probably not be able to care for on her own. She learned at a young age that most men took off and left the woman to care for the kids on her own. That wasn't fair to the mom, and most especially it was cruel to do that to kids.

That was until Daisy came along. Once Daisy was in her care, River knew she would do whatever it took to care for Daisy. She was so busy working and caring for the little baby that she no longer even had time to *think* about men, let alone date one. But now? No, now she needed to keep the walls up around her heart. There was too much uncertainty still. Maybe, just maybe, she would think about dating again once this whole Andrew situation was settled. Right now, the most important thing was to ensure Daisy's safety.

Finding her biological father would help with that.

John sat back, face white as a ghost. He must not have considered that there could be more men in Donna's life than him and Andrew. River felt sorry for the guy; he must have really been in love with Donna.

"She was with more than me and…Andrew?" He turned sad eyes to River, waiting for her response.

Hurting him was not what she wanted, but keeping secrets had already hurt so many people. This was why dating was wrong for women like Donna—and her. They weren't the sort who were lucky enough to find love and have it work out. Plus, River knew she wasn't the type men loved, anyway. She was the sort they ignored. Donna was the one who always grabbed men's attention. River was the sidekick, the wingman. Or was it wing-woman?

"Um…" River looked to the rest in the room, then back at John. "I'm sorry, but yes."

"How many more?"

"During her time in college, up until she met you, there were four other guys." River cringed. She knew she was making her best friend and sister sound bad.

John hung his head. "This can't be happening. It's too much."

Judith went to her son and put a comforting arm around him. "Shh, we know Daisy is yours. Just keep thinking about that little girl sleeping in the other room right now. She'll give you the drive to keep fighting."

All heads in the room turned to Caleb when he spoke in a commanding voice. "Why are you here now, after all this time? Why didn't you come to John right after Donna passed?"

A little squeak escaped River's lips. Caleb intimidated her when he stood up and spoke like a drill sergeant. He reminded her of one of her worst placements. The husband had been kicked out of the Army for inappropriate behavior toward a recruit, and he'd taken his anger out on her. Thankfully, she was moved within a few days of his court-martial. The minute the social worker had heard what happened, she drove down to get River and moved her to a group home until she could find another situation for her.

"Dad, take it easy." Matthew stood up and put a calming hand on Caleb's shoulder. "She's here now. That's all that matters."

"I would have come sooner, but John's name was on the bottom of the list," River whispered.

"What do you mean?" Claire asked.

"It took a while to get custody of Daisy. I knew if I told social services about the list, they'd take Daisy and put her who knew where. Donna didn't want that. She wanted me to get custody first, then go looking for the father."

John looked up as River continued.

"I started at the top of the list. The first guy was difficult to locate, but when I did, he didn't believe me. After a few conversations, he agreed to take a paternity test." River grinned. "I'd never seen anyone so happy to have a negative test before. You'd think he won the lottery or something the way he jumped in the air and hooted and hollered."

"Sounds like it was a blessing he wasn't the dad." John scowled. Something inside of him hated that guy for no good reason.

River chuckled, finally sitting back in her chair after Caleb sat down and stopped frowning at her. "I took my time looking for the next guy, and I was the one who thought she'd won the lottery when he tested negative." She scrunched her nose. "He lived in a tiny room full of empty beer bottles that probably hadn't been cleaned since the day he moved in. There was no way I was going to give Daisy to that guy."

"What in the world did Donna see in him?" Judith mused.

River shrugged. "I honestly don't know. If there's an afterlife, I'm gonna ask her that, right after I ask her what she was thinking..." She stopped herself quickly; she'd almost said *breaking up with John*. If it had been River instead of Donna living that life, she would have stayed with John, prayed he was the father, and forgotten all about the other idiots in her life.

"I got discouraged, and busy. Life just got in the way. Donna never even once considered that John could be the father." When River looked to John, she shrank back.

He was furious. Not with River, but with the situation. "If I couldn't have been the father, then why did all of the other guys test negative?"

"I wondered that myself. Then I thought that maybe one of the tests was wrong." River sighed. "If you turn out to be Daisy's dad, I'm really sorry for not coming to you sooner."

"Why did you come to me now?" John had been wondering this for days, but never had the chance to ask until now.

John's ears perked when he heard the front door open and close.

Georgia called out, "It's us, me and the sheriff."

She never called out her arrival—she just always walked in. Georgia lived on the property and was like family now. There was no need for her to announce herself or ring the bell, even though she had done that when River showed up.

John's nerves were on edge. Something was wrong.

Chapter 12

When Sheriff Roscoe entered the room, he had his hands on his belt and his hat still on. He always took his hat off when he came by for a visit. He only left his hat on when it was an official visit.

Georgia stood behind him and to the side, worry on her face and her hands fidgeting in front of her.

"Caleb"—the sheriff nodded to the head of the Manning family—"I'm afraid I'm here on official business."

"No, you can't take her!" River jumped up from her chair and pointed at the sheriff.

John stood up and moved to her side. "What's going on, Sheriff?"

Roscoe sighed and removed his hat, but held it in his hands. "I'm afraid Andrew Ryan has a court order to see his daughter."

All color left River's face, and she fell back into the chair behind her.

When realization dawned, John thudded into the chair next to River. He couldn't lose Daisy, not now. And there was no way Andrew was the father. *He* was Daisy's pa.

Judith sucked in a breath, and her eyes widened when a little girl entered the room rubbing the sleep from her eyes.

"What's going on?" Daisy looked from River to John. "Uncle John, you're home! Where's my pony?" She instantly perked up when she saw John and ran to him.

He picked her up and sat her on his lap. After John kissed her warm cheek, he hugged her tight.

The sheriff rubbed a hand over his face that looked as though it hadn't seen a razor in a few days. The stubble was rough and not the least bit tidy. "I'm sorry. I've tried to stall long enough to give you time."

John turned to River. "Why don't you take Daisy into the other room?"

"No, I want to stay with you." Daisy held on to his neck, not letting go. "I missed you, Uncle John."

"I'm staying right here." River sniffed.

With another chunk of his heart breaking, John held her tighter. "I missed you, too."

Caleb asked the question that no one else in the room seemed able to. "Roscoe, how long do we have?"

He couldn't bring himself to look anyone in the eyes, so Sheriff Roscoe looked at the floor. "He's in town, waiting for me to come back with her."

"Don't you mean the both of us?" River wasn't about to let Daisy out of her sight. She was still Daisy's legal guardian. There hadn't been a court date set yet, at least not one she had been told about.

"Right, since you're the legal guardian, you are of course welcome to come, too." Roscoe cleared his throat. "But no one else will be allowed in the room."

John knew what Roscoe was saying: he'd follow them and sit outside the room to ensure Daisy and River's safety. The sheriff's hands may be tied, but John's weren't.

"I'm coming, too." John held his hands up. "I know what you just said. I'll wait close by."

Without a word, the sheriff turned around. When he saw Georgia and the look of compassion filling her face, he reached out a hand to her. She grasped it, sending strength through their connection.

John watched the two and realized that this had to be on hard on the sheriff. He was just doing his duty. But that only meant that John had to ensure he did his duty to keep Daisy safe.

Once they were outside, John pulled out his keys. "We'll follow you into town, Sheriff. I want this time with my girls."

One side of Roscoe's lips quirked up, and he nodded before getting into his official sheriff's SUV.

The ride into town was quiet, except for Daisy asking about the pony. John really wanted to be excited about showing her the pony, but he was nervous about what Andrew might do. Would he be able to take Daisy now? Was he serving River papers? For surely she had to be served with papers, and confirmed that she was served, before a hearing could take place. Right? He wasn't sure what was going to happen, only that he was going to be there and he would be the one to make sure that both River and Daisy were safe.

River couldn't believe Andrew had come all this way to see Daisy. She thought for sure that by coming here, he'd give up. The louse had always been lazy and never worked for anything. Why was he working so hard to get near Daisy? He must have some ulterior motive, but what?

Until he revealed what he was up to, River would have to be on her guard. She never did understand what it was about Andrew Ryan that had attracted Donna in the first place.

Well, okay, he was gorgeous. She'd give him that. And his family was rich. Not that River cared about wealth, but Donna did. Looking back at Andrew from Donna's perspective, she could see it. The Ryan family had a lot of connections in town and throughout the state. A foster kid would probably see that as something to strive for. But not River.

No, River knew she wasn't good enough for that lifestyle, so she never even wanted it. But Donna, she most likely thought that by being near that type of person, the wealth would rub off on her. Plus, the spotlight. Donna loved the attention. The wealthy and influential always had the limelight.

Donna had been one of the early internet influencers. Her time in the rodeo, even as short as it was, helped her to gain lots of followers. Had she not gotten pregnant, she probably would have ended her freshman year with over a million followers between all of her social media accounts.

River *hated* social media. She thought it rotted the brain, like TV and video games did to kids. She had seen too many adults lose their jobs and relationships because of stupid comments on social media platforms. Comments that were things most people should keep to themselves, not share all over the information highway.

In fact, she didn't have any social media accounts. Well, she did have one that she used for the sole purpose of communicating—the chat app that was included on her phone was pretty useful. And her foster parents had used it, so she did. And of course, Donna had it as well. And the handful of friends she had were all on it and they communicated on occasion. She didn't think she'd posted a single picture or meme her entire life. Why do it? It never made any sense to her. If River went her entire life without having to use any social media apps, she'd be totally happy.

That's not to say she didn't have a smart phone, for she did. The weather app was probably her best friend in the winter. And she might like a couple mind-bender games, like Sudoku and Words with Friends. But even those didn't take up much of her time. No, she was happy with how she viewed apps and social media. Even if Donna did always tease her about her attitude.

Thinking back to Andrew, she could see why Donna would like the man. But he was someone she would never consider. Now, John Manning? That was a whole different universe of man. Sure, he could be gruff, but if she put herself in his shoes she could understand why he had been mean a few times since they'd met.

But for him to go all the way to Idaho and get Daisy a pony, as well as find a way around the sheriff's proclamation that no one in town could test Daisy's DNA? That was out-of-this-world sweetness. Donna was a fool to let him go.

When they pulled up outside the sheriff's station, River scoffed.

"What?" John's brows furrowed, and he looked in River's direction.

"I bet that's Andrew's Hummer. He never did anything normal." River shook her head and turned to look at Daisy in the back seat. "Sweetie, we're going to meet an old friend of your momma's. I haven't seen him since you were born, but he's really excited to meet you."

Daisy shrank back in her seat. "Do I have to? I wanna ride my pony." For most of the ride into town, the little girl had laughed and giggled and played with a toy version of a pony that John had bought her before he'd left Idaho. It seemed to appease her when she wanted to ride the pony he'd brought back with him.

"How about tomorrow we saddle up Pickles and get you started learning how to ride?" John's eyes sparkled with mischief. "But first, you gotta be nice to the man. And then...guess what we'll do?"

Daisy put her pony on her lap and stared intently at John. "What?"

A grin spread from ear to ear on John's face. "We'll see about getting you some real cowgirl boots to go with the new clothes I got you in Idaho." He knew that would get the little girl's attention.

She squealed. "Cowgirl, cowgirl, cowgirl." Daisy clapped her hands and jumped as much as she was able to in her car seat.

River chuckled. "Now you've done it. We better make sure that no matter what, we can take her to the general store before they close tonight. She won't let you rest if you don't get her those boots today."

"No worries. I know the owners." He winked at River and got out of the truck. He headed around to River's side to help her and Daisy out of the truck.

River took Daisy in her arms. "Sorry, but I feel the need to be close to her right now."

John nodded. "I understand." He put a hand on Daisy's back as they walked inside the sheriff's station.

The sheriff arrived at the station before they did, so Andrew was standing at the doorway, anxiously waiting for their arrival. River wasn't sure what she expected, but this version of the man she'd met almost five years ago wasn't it. He was clean-shaven, dressed nice in pressed jeans, a light-blue button-up collared shirt, and loafers. He hadn't aged, but he did look as though he'd had some work done, as he appeared a few years younger than she remembered. Although, it could have just been her imagination. Maybe the nicer clothes helped?

Andrew Ryan's hair was cut and styled like someone who actually cared about his appearance. His brown hair did appear windblown, but it looked as though it was on purpose, not as though he'd been driving all day with the windows down and didn't bother to run a hand through it. No, this man's meticulously styled unkempt look was planned, and had probably cost a fortune like his clothes.

The nervous smile crossing his handsome features caught River off guard. "Hi, River. It's good to see you again."

With her stomach tied all up in knots, she accepted his handshake. "Long time no see." She couldn't say it was good to see him, that would be a lie. But she also didn't want to start their conversation out with something snarky, no matter how much she wanted to reply with, *No, it isn't.* She'd be nice. Maybe he had changed. And maybe aliens were real.

The sheriff cleared his throat. "Why don't we take this to my office?" He ignored John, as did Andrew.

River couldn't help but feel John's presence directly behind her, giving her the strength to move forward. While John wouldn't be allowed in the room, she knew he'd be close by. And that knowledge was enough to do what she had to.

Andrew licked his lips. "Is this my little girl?" He tentatively smiled at Daisy, who frowned at him.

"Daisy, this is the man I told you about. His name is Andrew Ryan and he was friends with your momma when she was in college." River's calm words belied the storm brewing inside. If she was a praying woman, she would have said a prayer right then and there. But she knew God wasn't on her side. How could he be when he'd taken the closest thing she had to family away, after taking away her original family?

No, she was on her own and she knew it. But that didn't mean Daisy would be on her own. River was going to be the advocate and family that Daisy no longer had. The type of caregiver River had always wanted.

And if there was a God out there, she dared him to help her out.

"Do you have a pony?" The simple words spoken by a naïve little girl cut the tension in the room, and the adults chuckled before taking their seats. Daisy sat in River's lap.

"No, I don't. Do you?" Andrew smirked at River as though he knew there was no way she could have one.

Daisy nodded. "Uncle John got me one today." She showed Andrew the toy pony she hadn't let go of since John gave it to her.

"Oh, that is nice." Again, Andrew smirked. "How would you like a real pony?"

Daisy perked up. "Oh, I have one of those, too. Uncle John brought it back from the 'tato ranch."

River's brow furrowed before she smiled. "Idaho is a state, Daisy. John brought you a pony from a ranch *in* Idaho state."

Daisy concentrated and looked from her pony to River. "Like Montna and Wyomim?"

"Yes"—River smiled and ran a hand down the length of Daisy's blonde hair—"like Montana and Wyoming."

She stressed the correct pronunciation of the two states Daisy had been in.

"That's what I said, Montna and Wyomim." Daisy nodded once to signal the end of that conversation. Then she turned to Andrew. "You have a real pony, too?"

Andrew put a hand out to see the toy pony. Daisy let him take it, and he looked closely. "I think my pony looked a lot like this one. Does she have a name?"

"Pickles. Like the one John got me." She turned her head around to look at River and frowned. "I haven't seen da real Pickles, have you?"

"Not yet, but tomorrow we will all see Pickles when we go for our ride together." River purposely kept her gaze from meeting Andrew's. She did not want him to think he was invited to join them, for he most certainly was not.

"Ah, that might not be possible." Andrew looked to the sheriff and then back at River. "I have the right to spend a few days with Daisy." He pulled out a manila file from the backpack he carried, then handed her the documents.

"What's this?" Frustration filled her chest, and she frowned. When she opened the file, her heart dropped. It contained court documents with her name on them, along with Daisy's and Andrew's.

"The court back home has given me visitation rights until this is all sorted." He pushed aside the top documents. "And you'll see here that there is also a summons to appear next month before a judge in family court."

River looked to the sheriff. "Did you know about this?"

He hung his head. "I just found out this morning, before headin' out to see you. I'm sorry, River, but the visitation can be supervised."

"What's that mean?"

"It means that if you want, you can stay with Andrew and Daisy all day long. But you get to keep her at the ranch with you at night. Or if you don't want to be around, I can assign one of my deputies to keep an eye on them." The sheriff glared at Andrew.

"No, I'll be with them the entire time. I don't think Daisy will take too well to me leaving her." River kissed the top of Daisy's head. Even if the little girl took to Andrew like she did to John, River wasn't ready to be apart from her little cowgirl.

River looked through the papers and began reading the one that discussed his temporary rights.

"I'd like to know what Daisy's schedule is like..." Andrew started to clarify his question, but River held up a hand.

"Give me a chance to read this document first." She wasn't about to take his word, or even the sheriff's word, regarding the *rights* Andrew had. River was going to read the court order herself.

Chapter 13

John sat on a hard wooden chair outside the sheriff's office. His nerves were going to kill him. As he sat there, his mind wandered to the worst possible outcomes and his right knee wouldn't stop bobbing up and down.

So he stood and paced the room with his hands behind his back. But that didn't help his nerves, either.

Callie came over. "John, you've gotta stop. Your nervous energy is making me nervous. How about a chamomile tea?"

He scrunched his nose. "Gross. How about you go get us some of that good coffee from Rosie's instead?"

Callie put her hands on her hips. "What? Our coffee isn't good enough for your refined palate?"

He tilted his head. "Really? After all that good coffee Chloe has sent us from her friend in Frenchtown, you can really stomach the burnt coffee here?"

"Actually"—it was Callie's turn to scrunch her nose—"I have a single-pod coffee maker at my desk." She put her finger to her lips. "Shh, don't tell anyone or I'll never get to use it."

John almost chuckled. For the first time since River went into the sheriff's office, he smiled. "Whatcha got?"

"How about some of that Sumatra blend you liked so well the last time we went into Bozeman?" Callie and John had to go into the city to get some supplies, and they'd stopped in a local coffee shop. After a wonderful cup of fresh-brewed coffee, they both picked up a pound of ground Sumatra. But what John didn't know was that Callie had ordered some pods and more ground coffee online when she got home.

As the coffee brewed, the scent of earth and spice permeated John's senses and he relaxed just a bit. The caffeine might make him more nervous, but the taste of the bold coffee would counteract any unwanted caffeine effects.

"Mmmm, this is wonderful. Thank you." John took another sip of the hot coffee with sugar. "Exactly what I needed to get me through the rest of this long day." Since he had been up at the crack of dawn and had driven back from Idaho only that day, he was exhausted. Adding on the stress of Andrew showing up out of the blue and not knowing what was going on in the other room only made it even more so.

John looked at his watch; they'd missed dinner, and most likely everything was all cleaned up by now. He hoped Daisy had at least been given a snack. "What's taking so long? It feels like they've been in there all day long."

"It's only been a little over an hour. If Andrew has visitation, then this could take longer. Why don't I go pick up something from Rosie's for all of us?" Callie stood and pulled out her wallet from her desk drawer.

"I'll pay. Here." John handed her his credit card, then wrote down on a slip of paper what he and Daisy would like. The little girl was easy—chicken nuggets and fries with a chocolate milk. He was going to have the BBQ ranch burger. "What do you think River will want?"

"I'll get her a chicken salad. I've seen her eat them before, so I know she'll enjoy it." Callie left John all alone after calling in their order.

While he had been drinking coffee with Callie, his sister-in-law, the rest of the deputies, and even the receptionist had left for the day. John felt guilty not offering to pick up the food since Callie probably needed to man the building while the sheriff was busy. But to be honest, not much happened in Beacon Creek. He doubted there would be a need for any more deputies while Callie was out. And there was no way he would leave River and Daisy with Andrew.

Turned out to be a good thing Callie only got a salad for River; they didn't come out of the office until after both she and John had finished their dinner and John called home to let everyone know he was still waiting.

Finally, after eight o'clock they all came out.

Daisy was asleep in River's arms, and the woman looked about ready to fall asleep herself.

John stood up and went to them. "Here, I'll take her from you." He reached for Daisy, but Andrew put a hand up to stop him.

"Who are you?" Andrew demanded.

River blew her bangs out of her eyes. "He's John Manning. The one Daisy calls Uncle John."

Andrew looked John up and down and sneered. "Is he family?"

"Yes," John said while staring the intruder down.

Andrew moved his hand, and River handed her over. "How are you related to River?" Andrew's narrowed eyes took in how easy it was for John to hold Daisy while she slept. He also didn't miss the fact that Daisy put one arm around his neck as though she subconsciously knew the best way to fit in his arms.

River got in between them and gave John a firm look. "Actually, he's not a relative, but more of an old family friend that Daisy took an instant liking to."

John wasn't sure what River was up to, but he didn't want to hide the fact that he was Daisy's dad. There was no way this dark-haired man could be related to Daisy. Even his blue eyes didn't look like Daisy's.

"Callie got you a salad, and we need to get going if we're gonna meet up with Logan and Leah." John almost said what they were going to do, but he didn't want Andrew tagging along.

"Sounds good." River turned to Andrew. "I'll meet you in town tomorrow for lunch with Daisy. We can meet up at Rosie's diner, say twelve-thirty? That should give Daisy plenty of time to take her morning nap."

"Fine. I'm staying at the B&B close to the highway. Call me if you need anything." He turned soft eyes to Daisy. "And if she needs anything, please let me know."

River nodded.

Andrew scowled at John when he passed him before exiting the building.

It didn't take long to get over to the general store. The moment John walked in, he said, "Close the door and put up the closed sign. I don't want Andrew following us in here."

Logan's eyes widened, and Leah's mouth dropped open. Both had decided to wait for John once he texted them the plan. Even Mark was in the store waiting. He scowled as he looked through the front window at a shadow off to the left.

Leah did as John suggested and closed up the store. It was a bit early, but not too much. And besides, this was family. Family would always come first.

John took Daisy to the back corner where the shoes were displayed and woke up Daisy. "Hey there, sweetie pie. Wanna get your cowgirl boots?" He hoped she wouldn't wake up cranky. It was way past her bedtime. If he got the chance, John would give Andrew a talking to about bedtimes for little girls. Although, he wasn't being much better.

"We're at the store and you can pick out any pair of boots you want." John didn't care how much they cost. He only wanted to make sure that Daisy had what she wanted, and needed.

As she woke up, a little smile spread across her face. "Uncle John, you kept your promeese." Her words slurred a little as she wiped the sleep away from her angelic face.

"Of course I did. Do you want to look at these ropers with pink flowers on them?" John pulled down the most girly display boot they had in her size.

"Ohhhhh, pwretty!" Daisy got down off of John's lap and took the boot in her hands. Then she took off her own shoes and tried to put the boot on, but had trouble. Her bottom lip immediately stuck out.

From somewhere behind him, John heard, "Aww, how cute," from Leah, and he almost lost it. This little girl had gone from stranger to his daughter in such a short period of time, he wasn't sure what he would do if Andrew managed to take her away from him.

"Here baby, let me help you. I think the size might be wrong on this one boot." He looked at the inside of her black patent leather shoe to get a size, then went looking for the boot boxes that matched the one in Daisy's hand. When he found the right size, he pulled the box out.

Daisy tried to put the boot on herself, but couldn't get it over the heel of her foot.

Before that cute little pout showed back up, John leaned down. "Here, let me help." He was able to get the boot on, and before he knew it her other shoe had flown across the carpeted area and slapped against the wall. He couldn't help but chuckle. "It seems someone is in a hurry to get her new boots on."

Her dramatic nod with wide eyes caused him to stop and stare at the little girl. It didn't matter if she ended up being the biggest drama queen in the entire world, he'd never stop loving her. And he'd never stop fighting for her, either.

Once the boots were on, Daisy strutted to the full-length mirror and walked around as though she was a boot model on a runway in New York.

"She is so adorable," River said when she grabbed John's arm.

"She is."

"But those boots are too expensive. We can't afford them." River worried at her bottom lip.

"It's all part of my gift to her." John watched his little girl and smiled. But when he looked to River, his voice hitched. "Ah, don't worry about cost. I've got it covered."

"No, we've got it covered," Logan said when he and Leah joined them.

"Thank you, but I can afford this," John assured them.

"I know you can. But this is our gift to Daisy." Then more quietly, he added, "She's the first niece in the family. Let us spoil her a bit before everyone starts having kids."

Mark and John both chuckled.

"Don't you mean before you start having children?" Leah added.

"Just don't tell Elizabeth, or she'll buy out the catalogs shopping for Daisy." With a finger to his lips, Logan winked.

"Uncle John, I love you." Daisy ran to him and put her arms around his legs and held on as tight as she could.

He finally understood why the little girl in the Grinch story was able to cause the crusty ol' curmudgeon's heart to grow three sizes. Tears of joy ran down his face, and John wasn't the least bit ashamed for all to see.

Chapter 14

The ol' feisty rooster on the Triple J Ranch must have known that Daisy needed to be up early that day, for he was outside her window and crowing up a storm before her normal wake-up time. If John didn't know any better, he would have sworn that ol' bird was singing to Daisy and telling her how much fun she was going to have, for she was up and ready to go with a smile on. Normally it was like pulling teeth to get her to wake up.

With her new boots on and one of her new pairs of little-girl Wranglers and a pink cowgirl button-up shirt with daisies on it, Daisy was ready to ride. "I'll eat later." She waved to Judith as she walked out back as though she owned the ranch and did this every day.

John ran after her. "Oh, no you don't. Breakfast before a ride—that's a rule for cowpokes everywhere."

He picked her up and kissed her cheek before turning around and bringing her back inside.

"Aw, do I have to? I'm not hungrwey." That adorable pout made another appearance and just about had John ready to cave.

"Daisy, what did we say about following the rules?" River arched a brow in the little cowgirl's direction.

Daisy took her seat and bowed her head. "Yes, Aunt River."

Before he sat down, John kissed the top of Daisy's head. "That's my little cowgirl. We'll eat breakfast and then head out to the barn to meet Pickles properly. Then after you get to know her, we'll saddle her up."

Bright eyes turned to John. "Can I help saddle 'er up?"

John thought about it and put a finger to his chin. "Hmmm, how about you watch the first time and then next time you can help?"

"Okay," the chipper little voice agreed, and then dug into her breakfast as soon as the plate of hotcakes was placed in front of her.

"Whoa, little lady. Slow down or you'll give yourself a tummy ache," John warned.

With her mouth full, Daisy replied, "but I want to ride Pickles faster."

Hiding his smile behind his coffee mug, John said, "You gotta wait for River and me to finish our breakfast before we can all go out there together." He sipped his coffee and then oh so slowly picked up his fork and knife and cut a tiny piece of pancake. Then he took a break before inching the fork up to his mouth. Before he could put the fork in his mouth, he looked to his mom and asked her, "Are these chocolate chip pancakes?"

Her mother took the bait and went into a long story of how she'd prepared them. All the while John kept his first forkful of pancake next to his mouth, never eating it.

Daisy palmed her face. "Ugh! We're never gonna ride at this rate."

River chuckled at the grown-up sentiment displayed by her little charge. "Daisy, he's teasing you. I bet if you eat your food properly, John will start eating just like he normally does."

Over Daisy's head, John winked at River. Who in turn turned a pretty shade of pink.

Ever since his trip to Idaho, John had been thinking about River differently. And when she blushed, he couldn't help but hope something was happening between them.

"Alright, who's ready to ride?" Caleb's loud voice broke the mood that was rising between River and John.

John blinked a few times and cleared his throat. "Once we finish breakfast, we'll be ready to go." He finally put his first bite in his mouth and followed it up with more, not really tasting the sweet goodness. Instead, he couldn't seem to get his mind off the pretty newcomer sitting on the other side of Daisy.

As John ate, he noticed the different strands of red and brown weaving their way through her long braid. She had braided her hair back, but she still had bangs that went to just above her sparkling hazel eyes. He had never noticed the flecks of gold and all the green in her eyes. He had thought her eyes were brown. There was definitely brown in her eyes, but today they almost looked all green.

Then he noticed her shirt. It was a green-and-black buffalo-checked, button-up blouse. Her eyes must have picked up the green hues from her shirt.

"John, hey John." A voice in the distance called him, but he couldn't place it. Then a pat on his back caused him to jump in his chair, and he spilled the cup of coffee that was in his hands on what was left of his plate of pancakes.

"What?" John looked down at the mess he had created and thanked God it hadn't spilled into his lap.

Matthew chuckled and shook his head. "Looks like someone was off in the back forty."

He accepted the napkins his mother handed him, and John answered, "Yeah, I guess I was somewhere else. What's up?" He finished cleaning off his hands and reached to the center of the table for the coffee carafe to refill his mug.

"We all thought we'd join you this morning for Daisy's first ride." The oldest Manning brother grinned from ear to ear and looked around the room at all of his brothers present.

John paused with his coffee mug halfway to his lips. His eyes burned, and he set his mug down. The fact that his brothers all wanted to support him and Daisy in this monumental moment hit him—hard. His stomach clenched, and he hoped he wouldn't cry again. He'd been way too teary lately. If he didn't get a handle on his emotions, he'd be kicked out of the cowboy club for being too soft.

"Thanks, I appreciate your support. It really means a lot to me." John brought his coffee mug up much like a toast and then took a drink.

"Hey, we aren't here for you," Mark teased. "We're here to see the newest Manning cowgirl ride."

John noticed River tearing up, and he put a hand on her shoulder. "Hey, are you alright?"

She nodded. "It's just"—River wiped a lone tear from her cheek—"growing up, I never had support like your family. Y'all are just like a TV sitcom from the sixties or something."

"Yeah, we are pretty awesome, aren't we?" Luke stated proudly.

Ignoring his family, John leaned in closer to River. "You and Daisy can be a part of this, too." He wasn't sure how River would fit in, but he wasn't about to kick her out of Daisy's life. She had raised the little girl to this point, and he knew how important she was to Daisy. And how much River loved his little cowgirl. He was not about to break up this little family. Not for all the belt buckles in the rodeo.

"Daisy"—John led the little girl by her hand and slowly walked to the stall—"this is Pickles." He held his hand out palm up for Pickles to sniff. "When you approach a new horse, always let them smell you with your palm out flat."

He held her little hand in his and brought it up to the pony's muzzle. Pickles snuffled their hands and nodded his head. Daisy snickered and then put her other hand over her mouth. John had explained how important it was to be calm and quiet around a horse. Especially one that didn't know her. She couldn't squeal or laugh out loud, at least not yet.

"Sorry." Daisy cringed.

"It's alright. When a horse nuzzles your hand, it can tickle a little." John pulled their hands back. Then he pulled over a step stool and placed Daisy on it. "You can pet her forelock, like this." John demonstrated how to pet the hair that came down over the horse's head and into her face.

Daisy ran her hand down the hair, then scrunched her face. "It's not wery swoft, is it?"

John chuckled and noticed she didn't pronounce some of her words quite right. He had noticed it before, and now he wondered if she did that when she was nervous. "Are you alright?"

She nodded.

"A horse, or pony, doesn't always have soft hair. A horse's mane might be soft, depending on the breed. However, their tails are usually coarse, as is their fur." John hoped his explanation made sense.

Daisy focused on the pony's mane and slowly moved her hand to it. "Can I pet her mane?"

John was impressed that Daisy already knew what the mane was, but if she watched any horse shows, then she would know at least what the mane and tail were. "Sure, just remember they can feel it. So be gentle and don't pull the hairs."

With a smile and a light in her eyes, Daisy ran her hand down Pickles' mane. She repeated the action over and over until Pickles nuzzled her head against Daisy. The little girl giggled and started to step back, almost falling off the stool, but John got behind her and steadied her.

"Easy, Pickles." John rubbed her forelock while Daisy reached for her mane again. "Daisy, do you think you're ready to sit on her?" John's old pony saddle had been pulled out the night before and oiled just for Daisy to use. It was sitting astride the fence next to the little pony.

While trying to hold in her excitement, Daisy pulled her hands back to her body and clenched her fists against her chest. "Yes, please." She also clenched her jaw from what appeared to be an effort to keep from squealing like she normally did when excited.

John laughed. "River, why don't you take her outside so she can jump and scream out some of her excitement while I saddle Pickles? I'll meet you in the small paddock to the left."

Daisy jumped down off the step stool and ran outside with River and Claire trailing her.

The Manning brothers watched with big grins on their faces.

John looked to Matthew. "I would guess your wife won't be too far behind Elizabeth. You might want to be prepared for this yourself."

Matthew's face blanched, and he wiped sweat from his brow. "It's way too soon for kids. I'm not ready."

John chuckled. "And you think I was?"

A slow smile spread over Matthew's face. "You still aren't ready."

The boys all started teasing each other and razzing the married ones about when they would have kids.

Caleb stood back by the entrance of the barn, smiling at his boys.

When Luke noticed his dad just watching, he asked, "What are you doing?"

"Just grateful that I'm going to get to see so many of my sons get married and have kids." He blinked. "I think I'm already a grandpa. How did that happen so fast?" Caleb shook his head and joined his sons.

Once Pickles was saddled, John led her out to the fenced-in area where River and Daisy waited. Daisy had been running in circles, laughing and calling out Pickles' name. When she saw the little pony coming toward her she began to squeal, but stopped herself and jumped up and down in place with both hands over her mouth.

John stopped. "Now Daisy, before you come near you need to calm down. Horses can sense your emotions. If you're too excited, they get excited and might run or stomp on you by accident. Pickles is a sweet pony and would never want to harm you, but you have to remember that they aren't humans and can't control themselves as well as you can."

Without a word, and with her hands still covering her mouth, Daisy nodded emphatically. After a few moments of her nostrils flaring, she removed her hands and took a few deep breaths. "Okay, I'm calm."

Behind him, John heard a few snickers. "Alright, slowly walk toward me."

Daisy complied, and when she got close enough to touch Pickles, she stopped. Then she reached up and rubbed the side of the pony's neck.

Luke came forward and took the reins from John's hand. "I'll hold her."

John put a helmet on Daisy before setting her in the saddle.

On one side, Mark adjusted the stirrups to Daisy's foot. Then John did the same on his side. "How does that feel?"

"I'm riding a pony!" Without realizing what she had done, Daisy kicked Pickles' side and the pony whinnied and tried to take off.

Thankfully, Luke had a strong hold on her reins. "Shhh, it's alright Pickles." He rubbed her forelock and put a comforting hand on her neck. "Daisy, remember. You can't get too excited. And never kick a pony in her sides, it makes her want to run."

Eyes wide, Daisy nodded. "I'm sorry, Pickles." She rubbed the pony's neck.

After a few more lessons, Luke led her around the enclosed paddock a few times. None of them were ready to let Daisy ride on her own; she was still too young for that. But Daisy didn't even realize she wasn't riding on her own.

When they finally took her off, she ran away yelling that she was a real cowgirl now.

Luke offered to take Pickles back in the barn and brush her down.

"Just be sure to give her an extra treat and some grain. I want Pickles to learn to love having Daisy ride her daily." John rubbed the little pony's neck and thanked her for being so well behaved.

Chapter 15

Daisy's nap time was just about over. The little girl had worn herself out with her excitement over Pickles and went down for her nap very easily. She was out before anyone even had a chance to kiss her cheek.

John and River sat in the kitchen, drinking iced tea together.

"I don't want to take Daisy in to see Andrew today." River looked at her hands. Water from the condensation ran down in rivulets and stopped at her hands where they clutched the glass.

"Do you want me to go with you?" He'd be there no matter what. Rosie's was a public place, so Andrew couldn't bar him from coming. But that didn't mean John would be welcomed to sit with them.

"I do, but I doubt Andrew will allow it. This is his time."

"I can't believe he got a judge to allow this. I thought the paternity test showed he wasn't the father?" Frustration bubbled up inside of John and was about ready to spill over.

She held up a hand. "Don't, John." River sighed. "I'm guessing his father pulled some strings somehow. They are very well connected in Wyoming. I think that's why Donna liked him to begin with."

John bristled at the mention of Donna liking Andrew. But as he considered his emotions, he realized he was no longer jealous of Andrew, or any man. What he felt was anger and betrayal toward the woman whom he thought loved him and only him. "Can I take a look at those court documents?"

"How about I take a look, too?" Georgia joined them at the kitchen table. "I used to work for lawyers. I wasn't a legal aid, just an office assistant. But I did read a lot of contracts and legal documents. So I might be able to help out."

"Really?" Relief washed over River's face. "I could really use your help."

"Why don't you read the documents first, Georgia, then I'll read them later?" John asked. "Wait, do you have time to read them this afternoon?"

With a laugh, Georgia agreed. "Of course I'll read them right away. It's really important to understand what is going on now so you can plan your course of action. I do highly recommend getting an attorney if you don't already have one."

"I don't have one." River bit her lip. "And I can't afford one."

"Social services might be able to help you, but I doubt their attorneys are very good. Most of them are overworked just like the social workers." As she stood up, Georgia put a hand on River's shoulder. Then she went and got herself a glass of iced tea.

"I'll help you with an attorney," John offered.

"No, you've already done so much for us."

"River, if Daisy is my little girl, I'm not going to let Andrew take her from you."

"And what about you taking her from me?" River's lower lip quivered.

This was it. John knew this was what had River so frightened. She wanted him to help her, but she also feared he'd steal Daisy away.

"I've already decided that if you want to be a part of Daisy's life, then you will always have a place here. I don't know what the future holds, but I would never rip Daisy away from you. That much I can promise." He took River's hand and squeezed it.

Georgia cleared her throat. "The first thing to do is find out what Andrew's up to and what rights he has. Then we need to prove that John is Daisy's father."

"Um, I'm already working on part two." John took his phone out of his pocket and sent a text to Stu, checking to see if there was any word yet. He knew it was too soon, but it would be nice to know for sure. Either way, he was going to help River.

Thirty minutes later, they were guiding a sleepy Daisy out the door and into John's truck. He still hadn't heard back from Stu. However, God was with John. Before lunch with Andrew was over, John had a short text message from his friend.

Congratulations, it's a girl.

It was all he needed to move forward. He said a quick prayer of thanks to God for getting the results back so quickly and set about thinking out how he would make his move.

Andrew hadn't allowed John to sit with them, but he couldn't stop the cowboy from sitting in the booth next to theirs.

Not able to hide his smirk, John stood when Andrew did and followed him outside. When River made to get out of the booth with Daisy, he held a hand up to stop her. "Be right back."

"Andrew, can I have a moment?" John caught up to the man before he could get into his luxurious vehicle. This guy was most certainly not a rancher. While the Hummer was nice, there wasn't anywhere to put hay or other large supplies ranchers needed on a regular basis. Plus, the thing was in pristine condition. It probably hadn't even been taken off-road yet.

The intruder rolled his eyes. "What do you want?"

"I wanted to ask why, after all this time, you finally decided to come after Daisy." That one piece has been bugging him since the sheriff first mentioned the man. Why would a court give him visitation rights when he wasn't the father?

"What's it to you?" Andrew looked John up and down and sneered. It was obvious the rich guy didn't think John was going to be any competition, or trouble.

"I'm close friends with River and Daisy. And from what I heard, you aren't even Daisy's biological father." Everything in John wanted to scream from the rooftops that he was Daisy's pa, but he was going to play it cool. It was best to keep his ace in the hole a secret. At least for now.

"Well, whoever told you that was lying. I am Daisy's father."

"That's not what the original paternity test said." John crossed his arms and stared daggers at the man in front of him.

Andrew's ego began to deflate. "Yeah, well, I was young and stupid. I fessed up to having the test altered and my dad has decided that Daisy needs to be raised by us, not some foster mom. She's a Ryan." He stood up taller when he said his last name, as though it should mean something to John.

It didn't.

"I see. So, you paid off the original lab tech to say you *weren't* the baby's father?"

Andrew's nostrils flared. "Something like that."

Without a word, John smirked and walked away. He realized that if the judge didn't have a current paternity test showing proof, then River could easily, and legally, demand one. And the judge would have to agree. If he didn't, then that would be grounds for filing an appeal. And then not only would Andrew have some answering to do, but so would the original judge who'd sided with him without any real proof.

"I think we have a lot on our side," John said when he joined River and Daisy in the diner.

"Uncle John, can I go see Pickles when we get home?"

The fact that Daisy had called the ranch her home softened John's heart. "Of course. In fact, why don't we bring Pickles a treat when we get home?" John leaned over and mussed her hair.

"Hey!" Daisy reached up to grab his hand, but he pulled it back too fast for her. "Weave my hair alone. It was perfect."

"It's still perfect." John grinned at his little girl. *His little girl*. This was the first chance he'd had to let it settle. There was proof now. While he wanted Daisy to call him pa, he knew it was best to wait to share the news with her. First thing he needed to do was to get rid of Andrew.

Chapter 16

Once John got home that day, he called a family meeting. This time, Callie was invited. But since Leah had to close, Mark stayed back with her to help her get everything done. They agreed to come out for dessert and coffee after closing the store early.

Of course, Judith kept a warm plate of her chicken enchilada casserole for them so they wouldn't have to worry about grabbing a quick bite before coming out.

River agreed to let Daisy have her dessert early and get her ready for bed early. With the excitement of the day, Daisy didn't complain much. Especially after John told her she could ride Pickles again the next day if she was a good girl.

After Daisy was ready for bed and tucked in, John came in and read her a short story from one of the many books he and his siblings had growing up. "You know, I think my dad used to read this story to me all the time." He held up a small book with two ponies on the cover.

Daisy yawned. "I love ponies. Will you read it to me?"

"Of course." He sat on the bed next to Daisy, who cuddled up next to him. As he read her the story of two ponies who became the best of friends, the little girl's eyes began to droop. Before John even finished the story, she was out like a light.

Mark and Leah were finishing their dinner when John and River walked in.

"Perfect timing." John took his seat, where a giant piece of apple pie and a hot mug of coffee awaited him. "Mmm, one of my favorites."

River sat next to him with the same dessert in front of her.

"I've called this meeting because a lot of information came to light today." John looked to Georgia, who nodded. "Georgia has read through all of the court documents Andrew gave River." He motioned for her to take the lead.

She pulled out the file and her notes. "Now, I have to start by saying that I'm not an attorney, and this isn't legal advice. I'm not qualified to give legal advice. So even after I say my piece, I highly suggest you get an attorney, cuz you're gonna need one."

"I've got that covered." Caleb sat down at the head of the table. "I've made a few calls to some friends in Wyoming."

"But Caleb, that's too much to ask of you," River complained.

"You didn't ask," Judith stated. "We want to help."

John could tell that River really wanted to accept the help from his family. This was more for Daisy than it was for her, but her pride looked to be getting in the way. "Why don't you wait until all of the facts are stated tonight, then decide?"

River nodded. She looked to Georgia and waited for the quiet woman to tell her the bad news. Since moving in temporarily with the Manning family, River hadn't had much of a chance to talk with Georgia, but from what she could tell the woman was very nice and intelligent. Which was why River couldn't understand why the woman had been living on the streets when she met the Mannings.

"From what I can tell, Andrew Ryan has a sworn affidavit from a former lab tech who claims that Andrew approached him almost four years ago, right after Daisy was born. He paid off the lab tech to falsify the report stating that Andrew Ryan wasn't the biological father of Daisy Myers." Georgia took a drink of her decaf coffee.

Murmurs went up around the table. River wasn't surprised to hear that Andrew had paid off the guy, but she was surprised that the lab tech owned up to it. Andrew's dad must have paid him a lot of money to come clean.

"That document is the basis for his claim to Daisy. And with the support of his father, he wants full custody of Daisy and to change her name to Daisy Ryan." Georgia shuffled some papers around, then continued, "I did some digging. This judge, an Honorable Myron Smith, plays golf on a regular basis with Mr. Ryan." She made a funny face.

"Isn't that a little dishonorable?" River asked.

Nodding, Georgia agreed. "This judge should have recused himself since he's friends with the plaintiff's father. But this also gives us great reason to file a counter-suit, at the very least." She looked to John. "And if there is other proof out there that someone else is the child's father..."

John wasn't sure if he wanted everyone to know yet or not. He certainly didn't want the facts getting back to Andrew. And when he looked to Callie to see what she thought of it all, he noticed her small smile and the slight nod of her head.

Taking in a deep breath, he let it out slowly. "It's probably best if this stays here, in this room only. I don't even want Daisy to know yet."

Everyone in the room nodded, even Callie.

"Alright." John nodded more for himself than anyone else. "I have proof that I'm her biological father. The results came in today." He puffed his chest out. He was a father and darn tootin' proud of that fact. No one was going to take his little girl away from him.

Caleb stood up. "That settles it. Daisy is a Manning. And you know what that means."

Matthew stood. "We fight tooth and nail for her." His stern face and raised fist only bolstered John's resolve.

River shrank back into herself, not saying a word.

No one seemed to notice her. Instead, they all spoke about how they fought for their family and how proud they were of John for taking responsibility and fathering such an adorable little girl.

Judith wiped tears from her eyes. "I'm a grandma."

Elizabeth turned tear-filled eyes to her mom. "And here I thought I would be the first one to parent a child." She laughed with her mother as a few tears made their way down her face. Then she sat up straight. "I'm an auntie!"

She was so loud, the rest of the room quieted. Then in turn, each of John's siblings and their spouses realized they were aunts and uncles as well.

"I guess this means we should call Chloe and tell her the good news, too." Elizabeth pulled her cellphone out.

John held up his hands. "Wait. Remember, we said it wouldn't leave this room."

"But, you want to keep this from your sister?" Matthew asked.

With a quick shake of his head, John said no. "I don't want to keep it from her. I think we should invite her for a weekend visit, longer if she has the time, and tell her then. But we must explain to her the importance of keeping this quiet."

Georgia held up a hand. "I have to agree with John."

"What? But he has proof that Andrew's lying." Incredulity covered Luke's face, and he hunched his shoulders.

Georgia cleared her throat as she waited for everyone to quiet down. "Andrew lied. And he got someone to lie with him. And the biggest part, the judge is good friends with his dad. Doesn't anyone else find it odd that after four years Andrew is coming back with a lie that his dad is helping him with? *Why* does Andrew want Daisy so badly? I think we need to keep our cards close to our chest and figure out the why. Then we can use it all to get him to go away."

Red-rimmed eyes looked at everyone around the table. "Does anyone care what I think or want?" River stood up and ran from the room. When she entered the room she shared with Daisy, she closed and locked the door.

John followed closely on her trail. He tried to open the door and found it locked. Not wanting to wake Daisy, he whispered, "Come on, River. You're a part of this family now, too. I told you that before. I'm not taking Daisy away from you."

"You say that now, but I see how your family was in there," she whispered back through the door, cognizant of the little girl lying not too far from her. "Not once did they mention me. It was all about the Mannings this, the Mannings that. I'm not a Manning."

Nothing but quiet came through the locked door. Then, a throat cleared. "But you are a Manning, by proxy. You may not have been born a Manning, but we have adopted you into our family. It may not be like the Hansons, but you are a part of our family... That is, if you want to be."

He prayed that she did want to be a part of their family. While he didn't feel as though she were a sister, she definitely did belong there. There was no way he could imagine life without River included. That thought brought him up short. Why was he imagining the rest of his life with River in it? How was she a part of his future? She couldn't be Daisy's foster mom. He would one day marry, and the woman he married would be Daisy's stepmom. Aunt didn't seem right, either.

Lord, please give me the wisdom to do what's right here. Daisy loves River. I know it would tear my little girl apart if we kicked River out of her life. I won't do it. But how do I make this work?

John was so happy that church was the next day. He'd have to ask the pastor if he had some time to help him figure this out. Which reminded him—so far, River hadn't wanted to attend church with the family. Maybe now she would?

"River, tomorrow is Sunday. Would you and Daisy go to church with me and m...the family?" He almost said "my," but caught himself at the last moment. It was her family now, too. And he needed to ensure that she felt the familial bonds.

It took a moment, but River finally answered in a small voice, "Okay. What time should we be ready?"

He couldn't help but smile. He was going to take his little girl to church for the first time, and River would be there, too. Maybe God would work a miracle in River's heart. Or at least open a door to talk to her about God and His love for her. "Be ready to go by nine-fifteen." He started to walk away, then turned back around. "And you can wear whatever you want. But Daisy will probably want to wear one of her new dresses. The other little girls seem to wear frilly stuff, but most moms are in jeans. Some will wear a dress, so just wear what you're comfortable with."

"Thanks."

"Good night." John turned and went to join his family. He doubted he'd see River again for the rest of the night, even though it was only about eight o'clock.

When he walked back into the kitchen, his mother came over to him. "Dear, what did she say?"

John sighed. "Ma, I tried to explain to her that she would always have a place here in our family, that she was now basically adopted into the Manning bunch. But I don't think she believes me."

"Then we'll just have to show her that she's now part of the family," Callie stated boldly.

"I do have some good news." John waggled his brows.

"What's that?" Elizabeth asked.

"She and Daisy are going to church with us tomorrow." John beamed. He knew he wouldn't be able to tell his church family the truth about Daisy, but at least they would be in church and Daisy could start meeting some friends from the area. He knew that growing up with lots of playmates was really important for her stability. Especially after everything she'd already gone through.

"*Oh!*" Judith put her hand to her heart. "I'm so happy for you, and for River. I get the feeling she doesn't yet know about the love of Jesus."

"I think you might be right, Ma." John had wondered about River's soul. The few comments she had made sounded as though River might believe God was real, but he didn't think she'd ever prayed the Sinner's Prayer and asked Jesus to come into her heart.

When River and Daisy came out of their room for breakfast, John just about did a double-take. Daisy was so cute in the pink-and-purple sundress he had bought her in Idaho. And it went so well with her roper boots. The little girl was the spittin' image of a little cowgirl model. Her hair was up in a ponytail and it hung down her back in curly tendrils.

But River—whoa, Nelly! John had never seen her in a dress, or with much makeup on. Today, she was wearing a spring dress with green-and-blue accents. It went down to just below her knees, and she had on a light-green sweater. Her hair was curly and pulled back out of her face. And she wore makeup. Not a lot, but enough to make the green in her eyes pop. And his stomach began to feel like he was on a roller coaster.

She was beautiful.

No, she was breathtaking.

And he couldn't get a word to form on his tongue.

"I...ah... Wow." John licked his lips and stared.

River giggled. "Thank you. I only have this one dress, so I hope it fits for church."

"Oh, River. Aren't you pretty," Judith gushed over her and her dress. Then bent down to Daisy's level. "And you, my little chickadee, are just adorable." She pinched one of Daisy's cheeks before standing up to get breakfast on the table for everyone.

"Judith, can I help?" River had thought long and hard last night about what she was going to do. Helping out around the ranch seemed like a good start. This family had done so much for her and Daisy already. They'd promised to do more. She wasn't sure if they'd keep their promise about her, but she knew without a shadow of a doubt that they'd do whatever it took to help Daisy. And this was exactly where she wanted to raise Daisy.

"Hm?" Judith looked over her shoulder. "Oh, not today. I have it all under control. But maybe tomorrow morning you can?"

River smiled and filled a mug with coffee. When she joined Daisy at the table, the little girl was talking animatedly to Callie about her pony, Pickles.

"You should see her, she's perfwect." The little girl took a drink from her sippy cup of milk, then began explaining what the pony looked like and how she rode it and would ride again after church. "I'mma gonna ride Pickles every day." She nodded her head as though what she said was the absolute truth and nothing was going to change her mind.

Chapter 17

Walking into the small country church, River shivered. She'd only been inside of churches for weddings, funerals, and the occasional special service, like Christmas. Otherwise, she'd never accepted the invitations to attend with the Hansons. Mostly because she never had the inclination to attend. Today was different. A small piece of her wanted to be there, and not just for Daisy but for herself as well. River had heard that it was always better for kids to grow up in church. But since she hadn't, she saw no reason to raise Daisy in church. Now that the decision was no longer hers alone, she figured she'd give it a try.

What was the worst that could happen?

Chasing a screaming little cowgirl down the parking lot after church was not what she had expected when she agreed to take Daisy to church.

The morning stared out as she had expected. Taking Daisy to the little Sunday school classroom seemed normal. In fact, it all felt normal as she took a seat next to John on the pew. The first sermon was about God's love for his children. River liked how it all sounded. But she knew she wasn't good enough to be called one of God's children, so she filed it all away in her brain as a sweet story.

Then, when she thought it was all done, they stayed in their seats and spoke for a few minutes as John introduced her to those sitting around them. When a choir began to sing, her ears perked up and she recognized the song.

Our God is an awesome God
He reigns from heaven above
With wisdom, power, and love
Our God is an awesome God...

A zing passed through her entire body, beginning in her heart and moving down to her toes just as it went up and filled her head. She automatically closed her eyes and felt the music permeate her entire being. Something was happening, but she didn't understand it. Someone was speaking to her, but there was a block. She *knew* there was someone there, but their words just wouldn't break through the barrier that had been erected between her and the speaker.

Her spirit wanted to reach out and break that barrier. A message was there, she knew it. Something she needed more than air to hear. Mentally she reached out, but she couldn't break through. When the song ended, her eyes flew open and she felt John holding her hand.

"Do you feel that?" he whispered in her ear.

She couldn't speak, so she nodded.

"Don't fight it. Feel it and listen."

River wanted to listen. She wanted more than anything to hear what was being said. She knew she hadn't gone deaf because she could hear John and everyone around her singing. No, the voice she was straining to hear was more...ethereal. Otherworldly, was it? No, He couldn't be trying to speak to her. She did not deserve to hear from Him.

But...could it be? The more she focused, the more it felt like maybe it was God. Then the music ended and a man came to the podium to speak. The moment was lost, but only for a few minutes. Once the preacher came up and began his sermon, she felt the pull toward the altar.

John continued to hold her hand during the sermon, and she paid more attention to the speaker than she ever did to a teacher in class, even with John so close. The message must have been just for her. He spoke about how no one deserved God's grace and mercy. None of us deserved to have a personal relationship with Jesus, and there was nothing we could do on our own to get that relationship. We couldn't even buy it.

That made her think of Andrew and how his dad was trying to *buy* Daisy, in a way. Humans might be able to buy a lot of things, including people, but they couldn't buy a relationship with Jesus.

Then the pastor looked right at her and said, "God sent his Son down here to die on a cross to bear your sins for you. He wants so desperately to have a relationship with you"—then he turned and looked at someone else—"and you, that he gave His only begotten Son that you might have eternal life."

It felt like a knife had pierced her heart.

Was God trying to get her attention? Was that Him trying to speak to her during the songs? Could she have a relationship with God even when she'd never gone to church? Or after all the bad things she had done growing up?

Why would He want anything to do with her? She hadn't done a single thing to make Him want a relationship with her. River knew she wasn't worthy, and yet...

Once the sermon was over, she sat there thinking about what she had learned that day. John sat quietly next to her, still holding her hand.

After half of the congregation had exited the room, he spoke softly, "We should go get Daisy. She'll be waiting for us."

"Huh?" She turned glassy, wide eyes to him and blinked. "Oh, yes." She shook herself out of her thoughts. "Of course, let's go get our girl."

They stood up, and she dropped his hand before exiting the pew. The moment his warmth left her, a chill ran up her spine and she wished she still had his hand. But she wanted to be the one who let go. There was no way he would want to walk through the church still holding her hand. Everyone would look.

In order to get to the smaller Sunday school classroom, they had to walk out of the church and then off
to the side of the building. The moment she walked
outside, she heard a shrill cry that sounded familiar.
"Daisy!" Her heartbeat soared, and she ran to where she
thought she had heard her little girl screaming.

John followed, close on her heels.

"Daisy, what's wrong?" When River caught up to the
little cowgirl, tears were streaming down her cheeks and
her mouth was open in what appeared to be preparation
for another shriek.

"Oh, Daisy. Come here my little girl." John soothed as
he put his arms out for her. She'd chosen him over River.
He couldn't believe she would come to him for comfort
and not River.

"They...they..." She sniffled a few times and buried her
head in John's shoulder.

John rubbed her back and looked around to see
what might have happened. His eyes narrowed when
he caught sight of three rapscallions who needed a turn
behind the woodshed.

The boys were laughing and pointing at Daisy, but the
moment they caught sight of John glaring at them, they
shut up, turned tail, and ran away.

"Sweetie"—John leaned back just enough to get a look
at Daisy's tear-streaked face—"did they touch you?"

She shook her head. "No, but the worm did." Daisy
shivered again.

River tried very hard not to laugh. "Did they put a
worm down your dress?"

She shook her head again. "On my head!" Her little lip protruded, and John couldn't figure out how she had mastered the pout so early. It must have been a genetic trait her mom had passed down to her.

Mark walked over with a scowl on his face. "Were those the Murphy boys I saw running away? What'd they do this time?"

John held his little girl closer. "They put a worm on Daisy's head."

"Why those little..." Mark held his tongue, and John could see the wheels turning in his head. It looked like there was going to be payback.

Normally John wouldn't bother with local boys, but those boys were the town's terrors. Even Mark never did half the stuff those three juvenile delinquents did.

After a few more sniffles, River took Daisy out of John's arms and held her tight. "I was so frightened when I heard you screaming, and then saw you running through the parking lot. Don't do that again. A car could have hit you."

"Sorry," Daisy mumbled, and stuck her thumb in her mouth.

River sighed over the top of the little girl's head. "She doesn't normally suck her thumb, but things have been so strange and scary for her lately. Can we go home? Maybe once we've eaten she can go see Pickles?"

"Of course." John motioned for them to follow him to his truck.

Daisy fell asleep on the way home, and John didn't have the heart to wake her. Instead, he carefully removed her from her car seat, took her in the house, and gently laid her on the bed she shared with River.

Keeping his voice low, John asked, "Would you like to join us for Sunday supper, or stay with Daisy? She should sleep for a while, right?"

River nodded. "Yes, she'll sleep for a while after her morning." A yawn escaped her mouth. "I might want to nap as well. It's been an emotional day so far."

"I can understand. I'll ask my mom to save you and Daisy some food." He kissed Daisy's forehead and quietly closed the door behind him.

In the hallway, he leaned against the wall and sighed. The morning had started so well. Daisy was excited to make some friends, and River seemed to really enjoy the service. He looked down at his hand and flexed it. He could still feel the warmth of her hand in his. If only she hadn't let go.

Chapter 18

Monday morning came bright and early. River hadn't experienced the family rooster waking her up before, but she had heard about it. She had thought it was a cute story when John told her how their rooster loved to wake people up before the sun shone, and he had the uncanny ability to know when someone needed to be up early.

She didn't actually believe the bird knew who needed to get up when—until now.

The sun had barely risen and a cock-a-doodle-doo was screeching outside her window. If that bird didn't shut up, it would wake Daisy. The last thing she needed was a grumpy Daisy.

After her nap Sunday afternoon, she was in a foul mood all day and night. Even seeing Pickles and going for a quick ride around the paddock didn't help. River and John both hoped a good night's sleep would help the little girl.

But if that darned rooster didn't move its ugly beak, she was going to wring its neck and fry it up for dinner.

"Fine, fine. I'm up. Geesh," River grumped as she looked out the window and shook her hand at the fowl staring at her.

Once he was happy she was up, he began pecking at the ground and moved around the corner of the house where she could not see, or hear, the blasted beast.

River looked back at the bed when she heard the covers moving. Holding her breath, she waited to see if Daisy would wake up. When she was confident the little girl was still asleep, she chanced a look at the clock. "What?" She put a hand over her mouth. It was quickly approaching seven in the morning. She needed to be ready to go before eight if she wanted to be on the call Caleb had set up with an attorney on her behalf.

She made it to Caleb's office with only five minutes to spare.

With coffee mug in hand, she wiped the crumbs from her shirt before sitting down. Judith had made a full breakfast of eggs, hash browns, bacon, sausage, and toast. But River only had time for a piece of toast and two slices of crispy bacon. When the meeting was over, she'd see what was left and fill up then.

"So, how do you know this attorney?" River knew that Caleb Manning and the man she was going to speak with today were friends, but she wasn't sure how close they were, or why he'd even agree to take her case.

"Jackson Strauss and I go way back. His family runs a ranch just outside of Cheyenne, and when he was younger he and his family came up here a few times for the rodeo, where we met. They ended up buying cattle from us on a regular basis for the next few years." Caleb took a seat behind his desk after motioning for River to sit across from him.

"So, you're old family friends. Is that why he's agreed to take my case before even talking to me?" This made more sense to River. Jackson wasn't doing this to help her and Daisy, he was doing it as a favor to an old friend.

Caleb shrugged. "I suppose that's part of it. But when I told him the situation, he got upset and offered to represent you at no charge. I think there might be an old rivalry or something going on here. Which just might be to your benefit."

"A rivalry with the judge? That wouldn't work well for me. Especially since the judge is buddies with Andrew's dad." River cringed. Maybe accepting his help wasn't a good idea. Was it too late to find another attorney?

"Something tells me it's more about the Ryan family." Before Caleb could say any more, his desk phone rang. He answered it and put it on speaker phone. "Jackson, thank you for calling."

After they got the niceties and introductions out of the way, Jackson asked a few questions about Andrew and Daisy. Once she explained that Andrew had never wanted anything to do with them until just recently, the attorney was quiet.

Jackson asked, "Do you have any idea why Andrew would suddenly perjure himself, and the lab tech, just to get custody of Daisy?"

She shook her head, then realized that he couldn't see her, so she answered, "No, no idea at all. It's weird really, someone came in and bought out the apartment complex I lived in and evicted me right away. They even locked me out of my apartment, and I paid on time every month."

"That's probably the Ryan family. They're under-handed in their dealings." Jackson paused. "Is that why you ran to Montana?"

River bristled. "I didn't run anywhere. I had no job and no apartment. Once I knew I was going to lose my job at the diner, I began searching for John Manning. I already had his address, so I decided to finish Donna's list and came here. It seemed like the right move at the time."

"Did you know that Andrew had filed for custody?"

"I had no clue; the guy didn't even reach out to me before I left. Although, I had seen him skulking around for the past few weeks. It unnerved me. When the sheriff showed up, that was my first inkling he wanted something." River rubbed her forearms.

John walked into the room before River finished what she was saying. When he noticed she was cold, he went to a chest under the window. After getting a blanket out, he walked over and put it around her shoulders.

She smiled up at him in gratitude.

"Is there any sort of trust fund or inheritance for Daisy?"

When the attorney asked that question, something sparked in her memory. "Oh." She put a hand over her mouth. "I was supposed to contact someone a few weeks back about the Hansons. I got a message that they left me something."

"Who are the Hansons?" The attorney's voice sounded excited.

"They were mine and Donna's foster parents. She was much closer to them since she lived with them for close to five years. I only lived with them my last two years of high school. Lately we hadn't spoke as much as I would have liked. It was my fault. I'd been taking care of Daisy and working full time." River slumped in her chair and put her head in her hands. "They passed away a couple months ago."

"Were they wealthy?" This time it was Caleb who asked the question.

"Not that I knew. They had a ranch, but always lived so frugally Donna and I both thought they were barely making it. They never spent much on themselves, but they took very good care of us. We never went without." River bit her lower lip. "They even gave Donna a horse when she showed such promise as a barrel racer. When Donna died, they took the horse back."

"Hmm, maybe they wanted to give Daisy the horse?" the attorney asked. "Either way, it sounds promising. Why don't you give me the name of the attorney you were supposed to call and I'll reach out to him. See if maybe he knows something about Andrew."

"Ah, I don't know what I did with his contact information." Sheepishly, River shrugged and looked to John.

"Do you remember anything about him? Like where he was from? Did he call your cellphone?" The questions coming from the attorney prompted River to remember something.

"Yes, he did call my cell. I'll check my call logs. But, there's something I do remember. He had a weird name. It reminded me of a computer. Dell? No, that wasn't it."

"Could it be Ausus?" the voice over the phone asked.

River perked up and pointed to the phone. "Yes! That's it. Some weird first name with Ausus at the end."

"Sounds like a probate attorney I know, Strom Ausus. Pronounced a bit differently from the computer." Jackson chuckled. "But since I know this attorney, I'll give him a call when we're done and see if he's the one. If he is, may I tell him where you are so he can get you any paperwork needed for whatever you might have inherited?"

"If it's a horse, I can't afford to keep it." River bit her lip and thought about Daisy. She'd probably want her momma's horse.

Caleb interrupted. "If it's any sort of animal, we can help out and care for the animal. Especially if it was something Daisy's mom might have owned at one time."

She hesitated. They had already done so much for her and Daisy. But, they were Daisy's family now. They should have any animals that might have belonged to Donna at one time. She'd want Daisy to have them.

Especially Midnight, her horse. "Alright, that might be best."

Daisy was getting further and further away from her. River could only hope that John would keep his word and let her see Daisy as much as she wanted.

"Alright, now about paternity..." The attorney went on to discuss how he would petition the court for a new test to be done. He agreed that keeping John's paternity a secret would be best.

For the moment the Ryan family didn't suspect anything about John, and it would be best to keep it that way. At least until they understood what the Ryans were up to. "If it were a simple case of Andrew really thinking he was the father, we'd get John tested again and discuss it with the court. But there's something else going on here. We need to find out why they want Daisy so we can fight them."

"I agree." John sat up straight in his chair and looked across the desk at his father.

"If River agrees, I say we move forward as you suggest, Jackson." Caleb looked back at River.

She worried at her bottom lip for a few moments. "Yes, I think this is the best course of action. Thank you so much for your help, Jackson. Please, call me any time." River gave him her cell number and then they hung up.

"Well, I think that went extremely well." With eyes on River, John continued, "Do you think there's anything of real value that the Hansons might have left Daisy?"

She appeared to be looking off into the distance. "I don't think they owned anything of value. They had old trucks that were always breaking down. Their tractors weren't much better. The ranch was in great shape that last time I was there, but like I said, I don't think they made much from it. My guess is all their money went back just into living and working the ranch. Other than what they spent on the foster kids they had."

"Did they know Daisy?" John asked.

River nodded. "Of course. We spent most holidays with them. And on occasion I would get a few days off in a row and we'd go stay with them. But now that they're gone, I realize we should have visited much more often."

John looked to his dad and River noticed something passing between them, but she couldn't decipher it.

Chapter 19

After River left to check on Daisy, John and his father sat in the study talking about what went down in that phone conversation.

"Are you thinking what I'm thinking?" John asked.

"Yes. If they could give Donna a horse good enough for her to enter barrel racing competitions on a professional level, then they just might have had more than River realized."

"What do you think their property might be worth?" John wondered if River, and possibly Daisy, were listed as the sole beneficiaries of the ranch. "And do you know if the Hansons had any kids of their own?"

Caleb rubbed his chin. "I really couldn't say. It all depends on how big the ranch is, how many buildings they have. It does sound as though they kept the place in good shape, so that will help the value. But if they only have a hundred acres, it won't be worth much. And

I didn't know them, so don't know if they had other kids or not."

"Yeah, we should probably check into the ranch and any other family." Would John be able to find time to head down to Wyoming and look into it without the Ryans finding out?

"We should wait to hear back. It might be a moot point. If they have natural-born children, they would most likely inherit the whole thing. My guess is that Donna's horse was bequeathed to River or Daisy." Always so reasonable, Caleb made a good point.

"If there is a large inheritance, maybe we could get Hank Walton to check into the ranch? The Ryans probably won't even know our connection to the Waltons. If it's just a horse, I doubt Andrew would be so interested in it." If there was something there, Hank would know. And John knew just who could get Hank to help—Matthew.

It seemed the Mannings had an uncanny way of making friends in lots of places that was turning out to be very helpful now.

Matthew was more than happy to call up Hank. They hadn't spoken in a while, and he missed his friend. Both of them were very happily married and running ranches, which kept them busy. By the end of the call, Hank invited Matthew and his wife to come for a visit.

"Matthew, I think it might be a good idea if you and Claire took a trip to see Hank's cattle. And Claire might appreciate his horses." If anything could get Claire's attention, it would be talk about horses. Not only did she train them, but she had also recently started a breeding program.

"Does he breed horses?" Claire had been in the room, looking over some paperwork on her breeding business. Even though she had a nice office in her barn, built especially for her, she did tend to bring work inside the house when Matthew was there. If for no other reason than to be near her husband. He would do the same, bring work into her office on occasion to be near her.

John hadn't understood their need to be close to one another, especially when they were working. That was until recently. Now, he wanted to be closer to Daisy. He would find himself looking for an excuse to go inside and check on the little girl.

And the past few days he had finagled his schedule to be near River as much as he could. Something he hadn't even realized he was doing until just now.

John rolled his eyes. "Of course he does. And he also raises cattle. That's how we met him."

"I've been to his ranch; he's got a sweet setup. We should go and visit him. Plus, he told me there's a ranch near Cheyenne we might be interested in seeing. Our new friends spent some time right next door." Matthew raised his brows and waited for his wife to catch on.

He knew she had when her eyes widened and her mouth formed an *O*. "Let me check my schedule. I'll see about moving some things around so we can go. One of my horses will need to go back to her owner's ranch, and maybe we can make a delivery to Cody on the way?"

Matthew rubbed his hands together as though he were cleaning them. "Sounds like we have a plan. One that shouldn't attract any unwanted attention."

While Matthew and Claire prepared to head out in two days' time, John spent more and more time with River and Daisy.

The same day Matthew and Claire left, John planned a picnic with Daisy and River. It would be Daisy's first time leaving the paddock and barn area on horseback. John knew she was ready to ride Pickles farther than the barn. River, however? She wasn't so sure.

"John, I don't know about this. Isn't she too small to ride that far?" River worried her lower lip.

"We'll both be with her. Don't worry, she's got this. If ever there was a girl born to ride, it's Daisy." With pride evident, he beamed at his daughter who watched the two discussing her.

"I'm good, Aunt River. You'll see." Daisy bounced up and down on the balls of her feet.

John took River's hand. "Trust me, she's got this." Warmth spread through John when he took her hand. Then he stared longingly into her eyes.

River's breath hitched, and she held it in. His hand felt so good in hers. She couldn't understand what was going on with her lately. Her emotions were all over the place. At first she'd thought John was rude and maybe even a monster. But she quickly changed her mind when she put herself in his shoes. His original gruffness made sense. He'd missed out all this time on his daughter, and a possible marriage to Donna.

Then, she went to church and felt...a presence. It was warm and inviting. She still didn't understand why an all-powerful God would want a relationship with her.

And now, with John looking at her the way he was, did he too want a relationship with her? That thought sent a zing down her spine and her toes tingled. Did she want a relationship with the man who was working to take Daisy away from her?

Well, to be fair, Andrew was working to take Daisy away. John? He was helping her fight Andrew, but in doing so he would end up with custody of his daughter. Where exactly would that leave River? Sure, he said she would always have a place with Daisy, but what about work? She couldn't keep living on the charity of the Manning family. River needed a job.

Right then, she decided that the moment this stupid case with Andrew was thrown out of court, she would do whatever job she could find in town. The idea of working at Rosie's Diner sounded really good. She had enjoyed their food and the environment when she was in there. And the people of Beacon Creek seemed really nice so far.

Releasing that breath she'd held, she made her choice. "Alright, let's do this."

John's gut tightened. Had she known what he was thinking and responded to that? Or to his request to trust him?

While River considered the ride and Daisy's ability to stay on Pickles, John had been thinking about River. She was beautiful in her own right. Not like Donna. Instead, her beauty flowed from within. River was sweet and loving. Intelligent and thoughtful. She also put Daisy's needs above her own, something that John really appreciated.

She didn't have high cheekbones or soft features like Donna did. Instead, she had a sweetheart face with eyes that drew him in. Every time he looked into her eyes, he felt like he was floating on cloud nine. He loved the specks of gold and how her eyes could be green one day and brown the next. She kept him on his toes, and not just because he couldn't figure out why her eyes changed from one day to the next. No, he just couldn't understand why she was still single. And why she made him feel things he hadn't felt since Donna left him.

There was something magnetic about River. She pulled him in. In fact, he felt a physical pull right then. When he paid more attention, he realized it wasn't River pulling him, but Daisy yanking on his sleeve. He looked down at his little princess.

"Uncle John, when are we gonna ride?" She stomped her little boot, and that cute lower lip of hers protruded and tugged at his heartstrings. Man, he couldn't wait for the day she began calling him *Pa*.

"Oh, I'm sorry, sweetheart. We'll go now." He tousled her hair and led them to the horses that had already been saddled and stood waiting for them.

He'd even packed the lunch and a blanket on his horse before he went back inside to get River and Daisy. Everything was waiting for them. All they had to do was mount the horses and ride.

John gave Daisy a few more reminders, and once he was confident his little girl was ready to ride, he led them out of the paddock into the first pasture. Today they wouldn't go far, just to the little creek running through their ranch. They had a picnic table there and the trees would be full of leaves, changing colors and readying for winter.

Every time John looked to Daisy, she had a huge grin on her face. And every time he looked to River, she had worry etched across hers.

Chapter 20

The day was beautiful and warm. The water in the creek was low, but it was also fall. Most of the water flowing in that particular creek was runoff from the mountains, which had long ago shed their white winter coat. Now, all that ran along the side was the little bit bubbling up from the natural underground springs or wells.

Daisy had ridden like a pro. Anyone watching the little girl who wasn't quite four would have thought she had been riding since she was born. Even River did well, for someone who'd never quite warmed up to horses. Part of that must have been that Whiskers was a calm and loveable mare.

Whiskers started out as Chloe Manning's horse. Then when she moved to Frenchtown, the poor mare didn't get any regular riders until... John's heart stopped. He couldn't believe it. How had he missed it?

It was no wonder Mark had snickered last night when John said he was going to saddle up Whiskers for River to ride. His brothers knew it but chose to not tell him. He'd get Mark back for this.

Until then, he had a new name for Whiskers—The Cursed Mare.

Every woman who'd come to the ranch and ridden Whiskers ended up marrying into the family. Sure, he liked River. But marriage? He was nowhere near ready to even utter the word, let alone think about it with one woman in particular.

He grabbed his chest when his breathing became labored. Then he leaned against a tree and tried to clear his mind.

"John? Are you alright?" River put a hand on his shoulder, and he pulled away.

"Yeah, yeah. I'm fine. Just needed to take a few breaths, that's all." He looked to Daisy, who was oblivious to his fear.

The little girl was chasing a butterfly over the grassy area next to the little creek.

"Be careful, you don't want to accidentally fall in. That water is cold," John chided.

Daisy stopped in her tracks and turned wide eyes to John and River. The color drained from the little girl's face and she stood stock still.

"What? What happened?" River ran to Daisy's side and looked around her, checking to make sure she hadn't stepped in an ant hill or on anything else that might have hurt her.

John turned around and saw what had frightened the little cowgirl. Coming toward them were about a dozen cows lazily eating grass as they moved closer to the picnic spot. He looked around to make sure the ol' Johnson bull wasn't anywhere near them. The last thing he needed was to have that cantankerous old devil coming after his girls.

His girls?

When did River become *his girl*?

John slowly walked toward Daisy. "Daisy, it's alright. They won't hurt you." He leaned down and picked her up. When he walked toward the cows, she put her head into his neck and tightened her grip on him. "Shhh, it's alright."

"Wait, what are you doing?" River reached out to stop them, but John pulled away.

"It's time you both learn how to get along with cows. If you're gonna live on a ranch, this is important." He smiled over Daisy's head at River, then turned back to the approaching cows.

"First thing to remember is check their heads. Make sure you aren't approaching a bull with horns. None of our cows have horns, only the bulls do. If there is horns, stay away. Not all cows or bulls have horns. The best way to tell if the cattle is a bull or a cow is to look at their neck. Most of the ranchers around here keep a form of collar on their bulls. It's really more like a rope, so we can grab them and move them easier if they refuse to be herded." John chuckled. "I keep trying to get Mr. Johnson to put a bell on his ol' bull, but he refuses.

"But never, ever run. That only makes a bull want to chase you. If a bull is nearby, climb up a tree or get back on your horse and head home." John hoped his girls would never get near a bull. The Manning bulls were cared for properly and kept far away from the house and this picnic spot, so they shouldn't be an issue. But you never knew.

Usually the cows weren't near their picnic spot, either. John guessed Mark and Luke had lost a few as they were moving them to a better pasture for grazing. Instead of mowing their pastures, the cows would be moved from one fenced-in area to another. They would eat the grass and then they wouldn't have to worry about overgrowth on the pastures or spending money on feed. And this was truly the best food for their cattle; range-fed and grass-fed beef was always the best and garnered the highest prices at auction.

"Okay, but what about the cows? Won't they try to run us down?" River kept a close eye on the cows, but they were lazily grazing and seemed to ignore the humans in their path.

"They won't run you down unless something scares them. So, no running around them and no loud noises. It's best to stay away from them, but I want you to feel confident if you do find yourself in a situation like this without me or one of my brothers around."

John walked up next to a cow who was munching on the grass at his feet. "Stay calm, Daisy." He reached out one of his hands and patted the cow's back. "See, it's fine."

In a small voice, Daisy asked, "Do cows like to be pet?"

"You mean like a dog or horse?" John asked.

Daisy nodded and stuck a thumb in her mouth.

Whenever she did that, John realized how young she still was. And how insecure she was in her environment.

"Yes, they do. Our cows don't get too much personal attention since we have so many. But in general, cows like to be groomed just like Pickles does. Do you want to pet this one?" John took Daisy's hand and began to bring it closer to the cow in front of them.

She started to squeal, and the cow lifted its head and mooed.

John stepped back. "Shh. Remember, they don't like loud noises."

When Daisy quieted down, he moved back in and she reached her hand out.

Daisy scrunched her nose. "It's not swoft like Pickles."

John stifled his laugh. He didn't want to spook the cow. "No, cows aren't generally soft. But they do like it when you scratch behind their ears." He demonstrated, and the cow lifted its head and sniffled them both.

"I heard about cow cuddling. Is that really a thing?" River scrunched her nose.

"Yes, it is." John had done it a few times. It wasn't really his cup of coffee, but he knew people who really enjoyed it. He had also read an article that spoke about this very thing. Quit a few people with emotional issues, anxiety, and even physical issues found comfort in cuddling a one-thousand-pound animal. Of course, most used for cuddling programs were mixed breeds with softer fur. One ranch even employed Scottish Highland cows, which were known for their long hair, and cross-bred them with Angus. It resulted in a smaller cow with no horns, but it still had the long fur of a Highland cow that everyone loved.

"Want to try?" He pointed to the cow next to them. "She won't bite as long as you don't get in the way of her eating. Start out by petting her back, then move to her head, and when you're comfortable, hug her."

"You're joshin' me, right?" Unsure eyes looked between John and the cow.

He shook his head and looked solemnly at River. "I'm as serious as a heart attack. This is a real form of treatment for some people. And for some, it's just fun."

She seemed to consider his words for a moment as her head tilted and she examined the cow in front of her. "Hug a cow?" She chuckled. "It sounds like something you'd do at a carnival for points or a prize."

A grin spread across John's face. "Go ahead, it won't hurt you."

John hadn't paid much attention to Daisy, but she had been listening to their conversation. She leaned over and put her arms around the cow's neck. Well, as much as her little arms would fit. "See, Aunt River. The cow don't hurt." She nuzzled the cow's neck.

John chuckled and watched his daughter show no fear. That little girl was a ball of sunshine all wrapped up in a daredevil costume. She might shy away from something new or different at first, but once she warmed up to a subject, she went full bore. Just like a bull rider. If he wasn't careful, she'd grow up to ride bulls.

Now *that* was something to fear. He shuddered at the thought of her falling from a bull and getting trampled like he did. John wasn't trampled, but he did fall from a bull during a rodeo performance and injure his knee. Thankfully, the rodeo clowns had distracted the bull. They'd most likely saved his life.

He'd be forever grateful to Rowdy Ron and Crazy Chase.

The dulcet tones of a tinkling laugh yanked him out of his reverie. River was hugging a cow and Daisy was laughing.

"You're right, it does feel good to hug a cow." The cow she was hugging seemed to be hugging her in return. Her nose nuzzled River's hair and she looked to be enjoying herself.

"But it would feel better if its fur was softer. If you brushed them regularly, would their fur soften?" River pulled back with a grin and a glint in her eye.

"Well, most cuddling cows do have softer and longer fur. Have you ever seen a picture of a Scottish Highland cow?" He brought his cellphone out of his saddlebag and pulled up a picture of the breed from an internet search. "Here." He handed his phone to River.

Her eyes widened, and she looked at John. A small chuckle escaped her lips. "I've seen pictures of these cows and always thought they were photoshopped, or painted. I had no idea cows could have such long hair."

"I've always wanted one of these type of cows, but Pa said their meat isn't very good." He raised his index finger. "But, I did some research. Did you know that the Queen of England will only eat beef from a Highland cow? She even has her own herd!"

"Seriously? Wow, that's crazy." Without realizing it, River ran her hands down the side of the cow next to her.

John watched the rhythmic motion of River's hands and then noticed the tension leaving her face. Even her shoulders relaxed a bit.

"And the Highland cow beef has less fat and cholesterol than a chicken! So, it's actually better to eat than chicken." He put his thumbs through his belt loops and puffed out his chest. "Matthew agrees with me. I think we might have Pa convinced. He's ordered a side of beef from a ranch in Wyoming that sells Highland beef. He said that if it tastes just as good or better than any of our cuts of beef, he would invest in a small herd and see how it goes."

"Do they like to cuddle?" River seemed very interested in cow cuddling now, even though she was leery to start.

"I like cuddle cows," Daisy announced. The little girl must have felt she'd been left out of their attention for too long, as she turned around in John's arms and put her hands on his cheeks and turned his head to look right at her. "Can we picnic now?"

John kissed her hands and walked her back to the picnic table. "Of course we can. Just don't go near the cows without River or me holding you. You're too small, and they may not notice you."

She nodded and gave John a peck on his cheek.

He turned back to River. "And yes, the Highland cows do like to cuddle." He winked at her. John wasn't sure why he did it, but it felt good, and right, to flirt a little with River. They were friends, after all. What could a little bit of flirt between friends hurt?

He didn't think he'd forget this day any time soon. Not only did he get closer to his girls, but they also grew closer to his ranch. And he wanted them to fall in love with ranch life. He *needed* them both to love the ranching life.

Chapter 21

Pure joy radiated from John. The picnic couldn't have gone any better. On the way home, River and Daisy both talked animatedly about the picnic, the cows, and riding their horses. River's attitude had done a total one-eighty. He could tell she finally enjoyed something on the ranch. If she stayed, he'd have to make sure to get her a cow to cuddle. And probably one for Daisy, too.

When they arrived, the look on Caleb's face and the fact that Matthew stood behind their father with a scowl stopped him short. "What's wrong?"

River picked up Daisy and held her close to her chest. "Is everything alright?"

Judith walked to them and put her arms out for Daisy. "Why don't I take Daisy in for a snack and let her tell me about your adventure?"

John didn't like this. Not one bit. However, he recognized the need to get Daisy out of earshot, so he nodded to River, who handed Daisy over to Judith.

The moment Daisy and Judith were in the other room, John narrowed his brows and looked to his dad. "What happened?" But he couldn't hear anything over the sounds of a river gushing through his head. His body was tense and the muscles in his jaw twitched.

River scooted closer to John and grabbed ahold of his arm.

John felt tingles up and down his arm, and he relaxed enough that the river rushing through his head slowed down and he could hear his father speaking.

"The attorney called. It's as we feared—the judge presiding over the case is good friends with the Ryans. While he should have recused himself from this case, he's refusing to let another judge hear it, even after Jackson requested a new judge." Caleb winced.

This was a setback. If the judge had taken himself off, then they would have had a chance at a fair hearing. But with a judge who was so biased, John wasn't sure what was going to happen. They still had a few aces up their sleeve. And if this went to a full-blown trial, he'd have a jury of his peers. That would make it harder for the Ryans to rig. Or at least it should. But it also meant a long, drawn out battle.

"So, this means that River and Daisy have to show up next week in Wyoming?" John asked.

Caleb nodded. "But don't worry, we have some good news as well."

A pregnant pause held the attention of the entire room. Everyone was waiting on Caleb to share the good news since so far it had all been bad news.

"We found out why Andrew wants Daisy." Caleb tried to finish the story, but everyone began asking questions all at once. He held his hands up, palms out. "Hold yer horses, give me a chance to speak." Caleb chuckled and shook his head.

Once the room quieted down, he continued, "Jackson checked with the probate attorney for the Hanson ranch. He wants to see both River and Daisy before the hearing next week. But, they did inherit the ranch."

"What's it worth?" John asked. "The only reason Andrew could want it is if it was worth a lot of money. But if the land has a large mortgage on it, then it wouldn't do him any good, would it?"

Caleb shook his head. "The probate attorney wouldn't say. He needs to speak with River first. So, Jackson thinks we should drive down right after church on Sunday and come in on Monday to see him, then Monday afternoon he's going to set up an appointment for River and Daisy to meet the probate attorney."

"With the hearing on Wednesday, that doesn't give us much time." River sucked in a breath and held on tighter to John.

"It's alright, we've got this. But more importantly, God's got this." He put a comforting hand on top of hers. "Trust in God and He'll take care of everything."

River sighed. "But I'm not a Christian."

"You can be." A lightness overtook John's entire being as he followed the Spirit's lead. Everyone else left the room, and John continued with River. "All you have to do is confess your sins and ask God to forgive you and live in your heart."

River looked down at her hands. "But, I'm not good enough for God to want to save."

John hugged her. She wasn't ready yet, but she was on her way. "River, you'll never be good enough to be saved. No one is—or will be. That's why salvation is the *gift* of God. It's not something to be worked for, it's something to accept."

She stood awkwardly in his arms, not moving and not talking. River didn't even return his hug.

It wasn't a romantic hug, John knew this. He was trying to comfort her. But still, he had hoped she'd return his affection, even if it was a friendly gesture. He felt his heart expanding and wanted nothing more than to help her understand about salvation.

He would have to pray more about this and be open to any questions she had.

River wanted to return his hug. She also wanted to kiss the cowboy. There was one thing she knew: the moment he figured out how she felt about him would be the moment she was booted off this ranch.

Not only was she not good enough for God to love and forgive, she wasn't good enough for a man like John.

She wasn't beautiful like Donna had been. She might be pretty, but no one had ever called her beautiful.

And she was poor, dirt poor. What did she have to offer anyone? A foster kid, a mountain of problems, and possibly a ranch with a ton of debt. No man would want that ranch if it was as bad as River expected. She had overheard conversations between the Hansons before about how tight money was. So she knew that if she or Daisy inherited the ranch, there wouldn't be much after she sold it. For she would have to sell it. She couldn't run the place on her own.

However, it did mean that she might have a place to go until the sale went through. That was of course if *she* inherited the ranch and not Daisy. The probate attorney wanted to speak with her about it, but that didn't mean she'd gotten the entire place. Maybe it was left to all of the Hansons' foster kids. Did they have other foster kids?

As far as River knew, the Hansons had only fostered her and Donna. But that didn't mean they hadn't left a portion of the ranch to other people, like the foreman. He lived on the property with his family, and they could have left him part of the property. If so, she might not have control over selling the place. And she couldn't afford to keep it. Maybe her inheritance was family photos, or a few other mementos?

Daisy's inheritance would most likely be Donna's horse. And River hoped that any pictures of Donna still at the Hanson ranch would go to the little girl as well. She'd need those as reminders of who her mother really was as she grew up.

"River, do you have a Bible to read?" John's question came out of nowhere. Of course she didn't. She hadn't even been to church in the past decade, except for special services. At least not until she came to Beacon Creek.

She shook her head.

"I'd like to give you one. And ask that you read the book of John in the mornings when you first wake up." He rubbed the back of his neck, looking unsure of himself. "Then maybe we can talk about what you've read."

Did she even want to read the Bible? A still small voice told her she did. But another part of her scoffed at the idea. She almost chuckled. The back and forth in her head right then reminded her of an old Sunday comic she'd once seen in the paper. A little angel and a devil were on the shoulders of a woman who was trying to make the right decision about keeping something that wasn't hers. Of course, the angel said she needed to find the owner, and the devil told her it was hers—*finders keepers*.

River felt like she was in the same boat. But this time, the lost item was her soul. Did God really own it? Or was she a lost soul that could be picked up by the devil and not returned to its rightful owner? The little devil on her shoulder was singing in a deep baritone—*finders keepers, loser weepers*. She remembered singing that song as a kid when she found a candy bar at one of the many group homes she had been stuck in.

The angel drew her attention back to him. It seemed to be asking her if she believed God was real. If this back and forth in her head was real, then there most likely was a God. She hadn't really seen much proof that He existed, except for when she watched the sunset on a lightly clouded day.

How could a sky with colors of white, light blue, dark blue, orange, and red just be something created by chance? Then add in the rare days when purple showed up at the end of the sunset; that was just too weird to be happenstance.

River had a lot to think about. But first, she wanted to see Daisy and make sure the little girl was alright.

Chapter 22

After church on Sunday, two members of the Manning clan were packed and ready to join John, River, and Daisy on their trip. Matthew and Claire were already there and had planned on waiting for them to arrive before they headed back.

John was glad Caleb was going with them. As was Mark, even though Leah couldn't get away from the store that long. Logan and Elizabeth stayed home as well. And of course Judith needed to stay home to take care of the ranch in place of her husband.

They couldn't take their entire family with them; they did still have a ranch to run, after all. So Luke stayed home. John did wish his little brother, Roman, could have come home, but he was a football player in college. The fall was their busiest season with games and classes. In fact, they wouldn't see Roman until Thanksgiving, and that was only if his college team wasn't playing in a bowl game.

After the pastor said a prayer for them, the five took off on their road trip. They had a horse in the trailer attached to Caleb's Ford F-250 quad cab that needed to go to Cody, Wyoming. It slowed them down, but not by much. They were still able to pull into the Walton ranch before ten that night.

When their lights shone into Hank Walton's front window, he came out to the driveway with Mimi next to him. "Howdy." Hank held a hand up and smiled at his guests.

River got out and John helped her get Daisy out of her car seat. The little girl had fallen asleep and wasn't the least bit interested in waking up. He walked up to the porch with Daisy in his arms, her little head resting on his shoulder. He would have thought she'd wake up from all the jostling, but she didn't.

After everyone greeted each other with hugs, handshakes, and congratulations, Hank herded the group into his house. John looked around at the ranch-style home and made note of the various styles he liked.

Mimi led him down the hallway to the guest room where River and Daisy would sleep for the duration of their stay. Still, the little girl slept. John and River worked together to get her changed into a nightgown and tucked into bed.

Then they all went back out to the living room where the rest were waiting.

Hank's home had a great room instead of a separate kitchen, living room, and dining room. Which was something he liked, a lot. Hank's house felt large but welcoming. People could sit at the kitchen table and still talk to those sitting in the family room. And whoever was in the kitchen could still be somewhat involved in the conversation. The kitchen island was the only real barrier to anything, and that was only waist-high.

"So, what's the plan for this week?" Hank motioned for everyone to sit while Mimi went to the kitchen to prepare hot tea.

River joined her. "Thank you for letting us stay here while we sort this mess out."

Mimi smiled at River and handed her a tray to use for the coffee mugs that she pulled down next. "I'm so happy to have friends come by. And I'm glad I get to meet you and Daisy. I've heard a lot about you two recently."

"Oh, no." River lowered her head and hoped the gossip mill around Cheyenne wasn't working overtime about her. Gossips never got things right and she hated that.

Mimi giggled. "It's all good. I've just heard about you from my sister, Harper. And also Leah, Elizabeth, and well, most of the women in the Manning family."

"Then y'all must be pretty close since I haven't been around that long."

"We are. And you'll find that you're gonna be just as close to all of us very soon." Mimi winked.

If only that were true. River felt her cheeks heat with embarrassment.

While River and Mimi prepared tea, Caleb talked with the rest of the group at the kitchen table, which made it possible for River to listen in and be a part of the conversation.

"Tomorrow's going to be a long day with the attorneys." River glanced at John over her shoulder. "I'm not looking forward to this."

John got up and went to her side. "Don't worry, I'll be with you the whole time. You don't have to do any of this by yourself."

"We'll be here for you and Daisy," Caleb added.

"Speaking of Daisy," Mimi suggested, "I could watch her tomorrow if you like."

"Thank you so much. That's very generous. But she has to attend the meeting in the afternoon with the probate attorney." For the life of her, River couldn't understand why an attorney insisted that a three-year-old come to the reading of the will.

"She'll be able to nap in her car seat and any of us can stay in the truck with her. That is until we see the probate attorney," John added. He helped them bring the tray of mugs with hot water in to the living area, and River brought over the milk and sugar while Mimi brought a tray with a large selection of various teas.

John wasn't much for tea, but since it was so late he opted for the SleepyTime tea. He needed to make sure he got to sleep as quickly as possible. Even if he wasn't going to help with morning chores, his body wouldn't let him sleep in. He was too accustomed to getting up before the sun rose to feed the animals.

With a plan in place for the next day, everyone went to bed exhausted. John, however, had a difficult time sleeping. Even after drinking all of his SleepyTime tea, he laid there thinking about River and Daisy and how his life had changed for the better. He wished he would have had the chance to be a husband to Donna and a father to Daisy from birth, but he wasn't going to look a gift horse in the mouth. He had his little girl now—well, almost had her. She was at least in his home, even if she did call him Uncle John.

When he finally fell asleep, it was to a dreamless night. Instead of having a rooster wake him early, he heard a knock on the door.

"Come on, sleepyhead. You're gonna miss breakfast if you don't get up." Matthew rapped on the door again.

"I'm comin'. Keep your boots on." John pulled the covers back and slid his legs around. When his feet hit the cold floor, he yelped. Back home he had a rug next to his bed. In this guest room, it was a cold hardwood floor. Made for easier cleaning, but was awful on the feet first thing on a cold fall morning.

When he looked at the clock, he got the lead out; it was already seven in the morning. John had thought he'd wake up early enough to go out and help with the morning feeding before breakfast. The late-night thinking must have done him in.

"Here, looks like you need a cup o' joe to get going." Mimi put a full, hot mug of black coffee in front of John when he sat at the kitchen table.

After a few sips, he noticed River's t-shirt that morning and chuckled. It said: *A morning without coffee is like... Never mind, I've got no idea.* John didn't doubt that statement one bit. His entire family was the same way. No one got going without at least two cups of coffee. And if their morning took them out into the field, they always brought a thermos full of hot java with them.

"Mornin', River." He grinned at her over the rim of his coffee mug. "Did you and Daisy sleep well?"

Pink tinged her cheeks. "We sure did. Well, as good as anyone sharing a bed with a cover hog can sleep." She looked to Daisy and ruffled her hair. "I woke up with a heel jammed into my lower back, so I'm probably going to need some more coffee."

John thought she might need a back massage, but he wasn't going to say it out loud. He didn't want to give anyone the wrong impression, even if he would gladly volunteer for the job.

That image popped into his head, and he stopped short just before he put bacon in his mouth. He hadn't thought that way about anyone in years. Was he truly attracted to River? Or was this just a transference of emotions from Donna to her, since River had cared for his little girl all this time?

She was so beautiful. In fact, her inner beauty caused her to shine like Donna never did. Looking back, John realized that Donna was nice, but she was self-centered and a bit vapid at times. River was never like that. She put Daisy before her one hundred percent of the time. It had to have been tough coming to a man so far away that she'd never met before when she lost her job and her apartment. She was much tougher than Donna ever would have been.

When he looked at River, he pictured a halo above her head, the sun shining down on her and glowing all around her. He shook his head and told himself to knock it off; he wasn't a newbie rider. He'd been on this ride before, and it wouldn't lead anywhere good. Especially this week.

This was not the time to think about her. Today was going to be a crazy busy day, and he needed to keep his focus on the task at hand. In fact, this entire week he was going to have to control his emotions. He quickly prayed that God would help him in this area. He needed strength to keep on track.

Daisy needed him to be strong.

Before John could finish his breakfast, Caleb's voice broke through his reverie. "Alright, it's time we head out. I'll drive my truck. Matthew, you wanna take yours?"

Once everyone agreed on where to meet, they headed out with John, River, Daisy, and Mark riding with Caleb. The rest piled into Matthew's truck.

"Well"—John looked up at the single-story building that held a sign with Jackson Strauss's name—"I guess this is it." Anticipation and anxiety filled his body and he picked up Daisy, who had been walking at his side.

He held her tight as they walked through the door, with River right on his trail.

He hoped this guy was more of a legal eagle than a shyster. But he'd have no way of knowing until he met with the probate attorney and heard what he had to say. The fact that his dad was friends with this man spoke volumes for him. And he guessed the man was a pretty good attorney.

"Caleb! I'm so glad you could come with your family. It's good to see you again." Jackson smiled as he walked out into the reception area of his office to meet them. He motioned for them to follow him to the back conference room.

Once everyone was seated and had water, coffee, or tea, Jackson began by introducing himself to everyone. Then he opened up a file and pulled out a document. "I've spoken with the counsel for the plaintiff, and he's given me a copy of the original paternity test along with a statement from the lab tech. I'm rather shocked that the judge hasn't ordered a new test. I've filed a petition with the court to get a new test done at a different facility, but the judge turned it down."

"If that doesn't smell like horse manure, I'm in the wrong business." Mark slapped his hand on top of the table and sat back in his chair before crossing his arms over his chest.

"Yes, yes. I agree." Jackson pushed his glasses back up on his nose and pulled out some more forms. "I've also requested some information from Andrew, but his attorney has yet to respond."

"What information?" River asked.

"I want to know why he all of a sudden wants Daisy. And I specifically asked if he knew about any inheritance Daisy might have coming to her." His spectacles slid down his nose again, and he pushed them back up with his forefinger.

Hank raised a hand. "I might be able to help with this one."

"How so?" The attorney looked to Hank and waited.

"We've got a friend who lives adjacent to the Hanson ranch. Last week, after Matthew and Claire arrived, we all took a drive to see an old friend." Hank smirked.

Jackson tented his fingers under his chin and nodded for Hank to continue.

"It seems that Andrew Ryan has been out with his father trying to buy the ranches in the area. My friend heard that a big developer wants to put in a large shopping mall when the state widens the local highway. It could mean some pretty big bucks for landowners." Hank gave a knowing look to John and Matthew.

"Wait, are the other ranchers selling out?" John asked. If the other ranchers were selling, then it made sense to go after this land. But if any of them held out, then this would be a bad move on the part of the Ryan family.

Hank shrugged. "It's still such a new proposal, my friend didn't know. But if it's being considered now, then even if the current developers don't do it, someone will once the highway is done. If for no other reason than to build more homes. Those big-city folks are now moving into Wyoming thanks to the prices going so high in Montana."

Jackson took off his glasses and opened his laptop. "Does anyone know the name of the development company?"

Hank pulled out his cellphone and looked at the notes he'd written down. "Yeah, it's called 'Wyoming Consortium, Inc.'"

"Uh-huh. It's just as I thought, Andrew's dad owns a stake in Wyoming Consortium. That's what this is all about. They don't want the ranch, they want the land." The attorney closed his laptop and put his glasses back on.

River jumped up. "But they can't get the land, can they?"

"Only as long as Daisy is the sole beneficiary. Then her parent or legal guardian would be able to sell the land on her behalf."

"Jackson, you can't be serious. Is that why Daisy has to be in the meeting this afternoon?" John looked from Jackson to the little girl who sat in the corner of the office playing with toys they had brought with them.

Until that time, she had ignored the adults. But when she looked up and noticed all eyes on her, she jumped up and ran into River's legs. She buried her head into River and wrapped her little arms around the backs of River's legs.

"Honey, it's alright. You're just fine." River leaned down and picked Daisy up.

Once everyone looked away, Daisy relaxed. "Why is evewrywon lookin' at me?" She kept a wary eye on the occupants of the room while she occasionally twisted her head to look back at her toys.

"It's alright, nothing to worry about, sweetheart." John ran a comforting hand across her back. "They're all jealous that you get to play and they don't."

"Oh, well they can play wiff me. I don't mind." Daisy pointed to her chest and then to the corner where her toys were.

Claire stood up. "I'd love to play with you, Daisy. Care to show me your toys?"

The little girl squirmed out of River's arms and ran to her toys.

Claire sat cross-legged on the floor, distracting Daisy while the rest of the room continued to speak about her and the situation.

Chapter 23

"Shhh..." John put a finger to his lips as he settled a sleeping Daisy in her car seat.

Once they closed the door, John and River stepped away so they wouldn't disturb the little girl, but were still close enough to keep an eye on her.

"I don't like this. Something seems off. Why would the Hansons give the entire estate to Daisy?" John rubbed his face and sighed.

They had just gotten out of the probate attorney's office, where everyone was shocked.

"I don't know." River shook her head. "But my guess is they wanted me to run the ranch for Daisy until she grew up and could run it herself. I'd be taken care of as long as I cared for Daisy on the ranch."

"Well, they did leave you some money as well. Enough to make a clean start if need be." John eyed her warily. He hoped and prayed she didn't leave Daisy, or him, when this court case was all over with.

"Actually, I think it's just enough to pay for a new truck." River chuckled and looked around at the trucks in the parking lot. Most were four-wheel-drive monsters that could make it through just about any snowstorm the state could throw at them. "My little car wouldn't make it on a ranch in a Wyoming winter."

"Yeah, or a Montana winter." John was thinking ahead. If everything went the way he wanted, both Daisy and River would be with him in Montana.

He just had to hold his horses and get through the hearing. Then he could think about dating River. Until then, he'd stay focused and on task, just like when he rode bulls. He was cognizant of the rodeos still to come, but he always focused on the one he was at, or the one that was next. He never counted his chickens before they hatched. His buddy, Rick Reagan, taught him that lesson early on.

"So, what's next? Do we tell the judge who you are?" River wanted Daisy to be with her dad, but she also wanted to make sure that little gem was dropped at the right time.

John shook his head. "No. I think we need to see how this hearing goes and what the judge does. If he's totally against us, then we hold it until the end. We want him to hear this at the right time. Especially if he's considering sending this to an actual trial. He'd look really bad if we told him Andrew wasn't the biological father, and we had proof, but he refused to order another DNA test. This is just family court, and this judge wouldn't be able to do a thing if we had DNA evidence."

"So, we try to persuade him to find for us, or at least order a new DNA test and then find for us instead of going to trial?" River nodded, seeming to understand where John was going with this.

"If the judge wasn't already biased against us, we would just open with the fact that I'm Daisy's biological father. But if he's truly against us and wants to give Daisy to Andrew, then we need to let him know that we have some real ammunition." He took River's hand and brought it close to his heart. "I'm going to do whatever it takes to keep us all together. We're family now."

River stared into John's eyes, wondering what he meant. Did he see her as a sister or cousin? Or was he starting to feel more for her, like she was for him? All she wanted was to go back to Montana and spend time getting to know this cowboy better. The hearing was going to drive her crazy. Especially since she didn't know how long this was going to take.

It was a sham, a scam, a farce, and any other word that meant that this was nothing more than the rich getting their way and rubbing in the noses of those who followed the law.

The *hearing*, or sham as John was going to refer to it, only lasted an hour. There was only time for each side to present its opinions and for Andrew to submit his falsified documents about him being Daisy's father. John had no clue how this could be legal.

"I've seen enough. I find for the plaintiff, Andrew Ryan. He's the child's father and should have full custody as the only living parent." Judge Singleton pounded his gavel.

The courtroom erupted in people yelling that this was illegal, unjustified, a lie. And Andrew sat in his chair, smirking.

The judge banged his gavel again. "Be quiet! I've made my ruling. I want the child, Daisy Myers, to be delivered to Andrew Ryan by ten tomorrow morning." He looked at River. "Or you'll be in contempt of court."

AndrewRiver stood. "But he's not even Daisy's father. I have proof! If you'd just let us show you our evidence, you'd see Andrew is lying."

"Young lady, I've about had enough out of you and your friends." The judge pointed his gavel at River, then at everyone behind her. "You should be grateful I'm giving you the rest of today to say your goodbyes to Daisy." He stood and left the room.

"But, but..." Tears fell in large rivulets down River's face, and she sank into the chair. "How can this be? Will I ever get to see Daisy again?"

The sound of a throat clearing caught her attention, and she looked up through bleary eyes.

"I'm sorry, River. But I'm Daisy's father..."

"No!" River interrupted Andrew.

Andrew put his hands up in front of him in a placating gesture. "Wait. I have a solution."

River crossed her arms over her chest.

John walked up and stood next to River without saying a word and put a hand on her shoulder.

"I know you love Daisy, I can see it," Andrew said. "And I could tell when I saw Daisy with you that she adores you. I don't want to separate you two. I just want my daughter. But if you want, you could join us at my family ranch." He smiled warmly at River.

"What, as her babysitter?" River scoffed.

"No, as her future mother."

She stood up and turned unsure eyes on Andrew Ryan. "Are you proposing marriage?"

He chuckled. "Not yet. We need time to get to know each other first. I figure that if you move in with us..."

Again, River made to interrupt.

He held his hands up again. "It would be all on the up and up. You'd get your own room. You could even have the one next to Daisy. We could all be together daily, and you and I, well, we could get to know each other better with the understanding of possibly marrying in the future."

She was so confused. Andrew had taken away the only person left in this world she loved, and who loved her. Now he was offering her a home and a way to be Daisy's mother?

"This is a lot to take in," River started.

"Wait, you can't be seriously considering this." John's brows furrowed and he lightly touched River's arm.

She looked at him and gulped. "I think I have to consider it. Daisy needs me."

"But, what about..." He stopped short, then turned cold eyes to Andrew. "This isn't over. Don't go thinking you've won. This was just a hearing. It can easily be overturned."

Andrew smirked. "You're in my state. You'd best move on. I'm Daisy's legal dad now."

River was so confused. It had all happened way too fast. She heard her attorney talking to Caleb, but she couldn't make out what they were saying. And to be honest, she really couldn't process anything at that moment. "Um, Andrew. Can I give you my answer tomorrow when I bring Daisy to you?"

Andrew's expression turned to one of compassion. He took both of her hands in his and kissed the back of her right hand. "Of course, River. Take your time tonight and let me know tomorrow. I'll make sure the housekeeper has the room next to Daisy's all ready for you, just in case."

Everything felt off, but she knew she had to do what was best for Daisy. So she only nodded, her head in a fog.

When her attorney took her arm, she didn't say anything, just followed him out of the courthouse and into his car. She knew that Claire had Daisy, but she couldn't focus. Then all of a sudden tears fell again, and she sobbed into her hands.

Everyone followed Jackson back to his office. The moment they were all inside the conference room, they erupted into shouts and complaints.

John was livid. He couldn't understand how a judge could do something so callous. It had to be illegal what he'd done. The man didn't even let River give her evidence. "Jackson, what do we do now?"

The attorney stood at the head of the conference room table and motioned for everyone to be quiet. Once they were all seated and looking at him, he asked, "Where's Daisy?"

Matthew answered, "Claire has her. They're in the breakroom getting a snack. I didn't think you'd want her in here." He turned to River.

She nodded her agreement. "Thank you. That was the right thing to do."

John wasn't happy about it, but he knew that Daisy didn't need to see everyone so upset or hear the yelling. But boy did he want nothing more than to go and hug his little girl.

His little girl. What was he to do now? "Jackson, this has to be illegal, right?"

The attorney took a deep breath. "Not precisely, but it is highly irregular. He used the statements from Andrew and the lab tech and nothing else to make his decision. Which actually gives us a chance to file a petition for a trial by jury."

Without waiting for Jackson to continue, John interrupted, "How long before we can get a trial?"

Jackson pushed his glasses back up his nose. "It can take a long time. I'm afraid they'll have a chance to sell the ranch and pocket that money before we can be heard."

"I don't care about the ranch or the money they'll get. I just want my little girl. She's all I care about."

River's heart broke when he confessed. She had been wondering what to do—should she fight alongside John, or follow Daisy? But he'd just made her decision for her. He didn't care about her, only about Daisy. If John had cared in the least bit about her, he would have asked her about their next steps. He would have made some sort of move to work with her, and not leave her out of the decisions...again.

She knew Andrew only cared for Daisy, but at least she'd be near Daisy and would be able to protect the little girl from whatever Andrew had planned.

She wasn't naïve enough to think he was going to marry her. River knew he only wanted her to take care of Daisy. But the little girl did need someone in her court. And if following Andrew meant she could protect her little girl from harm, she would. Even if it was a short-lived option. Staying close to Daisy was the most important thing for River to do.

River knew that Andrew had won. He had the judge in his pocket, and there was no way the Manning family would be able to fight this.

Andrew was right, this was *his* state.

Chapter 24

After Jackson outlined exactly what he would do to get a trial and to petition the court to seek a new DNA test, they all headed back to Hank and Mimi's ranch.

Mimi didn't even need to ask how it went when everyone walked into the ranch house with downcast faces. "I take it things went bad?"

Hank walked up to his wife and held her tight. "As bad as it could go."

"I'm so sorry, River and John. But there's still a way to fight, right?" Mimi, still holding her husband, looked to the two who weren't standing anywhere near each other.

River had decided she wanted nothing more to do with John. She had stuff at his house, including her car, but she figured Andrew would help her get it all after she moved in with him.

John had broken her heart and she couldn't stand being near him. She really thought he was coming to care for her. But when he said all he cared about was Daisy, that told her all she needed to know. He could have at least asked her what she thought about it all. Instead, he was selfish and only considered his feelings. The least he could have done was asked her what she wanted to do next.

She was Daisy's sole caretaker for almost four years. No one else helped her get this far. And if Andrew hadn't come along, then they would have been just fine. John came riding in on his horse, literally, and bought Daisy all sorts of stuff, but that didn't mean that he knew what was best for *her* little girl. How could he not see this? What made him think that he knew what was best for a little girl that he barely knew?

Of course, she told herself, this was what she deserved. The Hansons had told her to search out Daisy's real father and to stop taking her time with it. Had she found John sooner, before the Hansons passed away, he could have taken custody of Daisy and Andrew wouldn't have been able to do anything about it. He wouldn't have wanted to back then.

She still would have never attracted a man like John, but maybe she could have moved to Beacon Creek and gotten a job in town and still been a part of Daisy's life that way. Daisy deserved to have a real father. One that would love and cherish her. She hoped John would keep fighting, but she knew how the system worked. And nice people like the Mannings always lost. All she could hope for now would be that Andrew would fall in love with Daisy and treat her like she was his own.

This would be John's last night with Daisy. And River was going to let him have the time to say goodbye. "I'm not feeling too well. I think I'll skip dinner and head to my room." She turned to John. "Why don't you spend some time with Daisy and bring her to my room when she's ready for bed?" A lone tear streaked down her cheek, and she let it.

John watched as River walked away, defeat evident in her posture. He knew what her decision was, and he couldn't blame her. Part of him was glad she would choose to follow Daisy wherever she went. His little girl was going to need her Aunt River. But part of him was sad that she would no longer be in his life.

Jackson said it could take years for him to get custody of Daisy. He wasn't going to stop trying, but that meant if Andrew was serious about marrying River, then they would be married before John would even have a chance with the pretty young woman. Was that what he wanted, to give up before he even had a chance to try?

If giving up on River meant Daisy would have River as her mother, at least until John got custody of his daughter, then he would give up the chance to get to know River better. But what did that mean for the future? With Daisy and River? If—no, *when*—John got custody of his daughter, for he would only think that way, would River hate him? She'd be married to Andrew and he would never want her to divorce the man just to follow Daisy. Would he be able to share custody with River? Or maybe

River could come for visits? And then when Daisy got older, she could go spend time with River on the ranch with Andrew?

The biggest question was: would Andrew be good to Daisy? John knew he only wanted her for the money. As he went round and round in his mind about River, he realized that Daisy's safety and happiness was the most important thing. It was more important right now for River to stick with Daisy, to ensure her safety. And for no other reason than to make sure that someone in her life loved her. John would have to let go of any thoughts of getting to know River better.

It hurt, but he couldn't imagine how much it would have hurt if they had started dating and he had fallen in love with her before this happened. All he could do was put his trust in God. God would work all things out to His glory. This was going to be a total test of his faith and trust in God, but he had no choice. Daisy was his daughter.

Once he got his head on straight, he went looking for Daisy. It was time he made sure she knew how much he loved her. Even though he wanted her to know he was her real father, John knew he couldn't do that to her. It would be too confusing for such a little girl. And only a week before she turned four.

"Daisy, hey there." John picked up his adorable cowgirl who had been playing dolls with Claire. "How's my little girl?" He hugged her tight.

"Uncle Joohhn." She rolled her eyes and tried to get out of his grip. "I'm playing dollies with Aunt Claire." Daisy spoke as though nothing was wrong at all.

"I'm sorry, baby." He put her down and sniffed back his emotions. "I just wanted to spend some time with you, that's all."

"You wanna play wiff us?" The little girl looked at him with wide, expectant eyes.

He grinned. "Of course I do. How do I play dollies?" Since John only had sisters who were much older than him, he'd never had occasion to play with dolls. Well, unless you counted his GI Joe action figures. But no one called GI Joe a doll.

When Mimi called them all to dinner less than thirty minutes later, he was grateful. He had no idea how dads played dolly with their little girls. Claire was going to make a great mom someday—he hoped soon. She was a trooper, and she seemed to be an expert dolly player.

When she suggested a tea party, John got a little excited. That was until he realized it was pretend tea and cakes, not real food or drink. His stomach grumbled its misery with the realization that it wasn't getting any food yet.

Then came the chow bell, and his stomach did a somersault of happiness. At least one part of his body was happy with the day. His heart ached for his little girl.

And he wasn't the only one who had a tough time getting through dinner without crying, or talking about what would happen the next day. They had all agreed not to talk about it in front of Daisy. John wanted his little girl to have a nice final night with him. He decided to wait until morning to tell Daisy what was going on. Until then, he'd soldier on.

"Uncle John, where's Aunt River?" Daisy asked after grace had been said.

"She's not feeling well, so she went to bed early." John kissed the top of Daisy's head and began to put food on her plate. "I get to have you all to myself for the rest of the night." He grinned at his little girl for what would probably be the last time.

Hank turned a furrowed brow on the pair. "Why does she call you uncle?"

Daisy took her fork out of her mouth and said with a mouthful of macaroni and cheese, "Because he's gonna marry my Aunt River." She looked to John and grinned with a string of cheese hanging from one side of her mouth.

"We don't talk with our mouth full," John gently chided. He took a napkin and wiped her face.

"What makes you say he's going to marry River?" Caleb asked.

John furrowed his brow and looked away.

"God told me." Daisy went back to eating, oblivious to the looks around the table.

"Out of the mouths of babes," Mimi said with a smile for John.

And with that, John lost what was left of his appetite.

Chapter 25

River cried herself to sleep after packing up what little she had brought for her and Daisy. Not in a million years had any of them thought this week would end this way. How could they? What that judge did was criminal, and she hoped he'd pay just as badly as Andrew and his father were going to.

In the meantime, she needed to find a way to keep her feelings in check. She couldn't let them, or anyone, know how she truly felt. If Andrew knew she despised him and blamed him for this nightmare, then he'd kick her out. She would have no recourse, no rights to see Daisy if he told her she couldn't. So, she'd be strong and do whatever was best for Daisy.

That little girl needed a protector. It would have been one thing if John got custody and cut her out of Daisy's life. Although, she doubted he would have ever done something so horrible. No, she was confident that if John had custody, he would let her be a part of Daisy's life, and not as only her babysitter.

She also doubted he would use Daisy as a means to get her to marry him. Or was Andrew using marriage as means to get a full custody of Daisy since he really wasn't her bio-dad? A back-up of sorts in case the judge changed his mind? That was probably more like it. Andrew didn't need to bribe any woman to be with him. He was good looking, rich, and charismatic, he could have almost anyone he wanted. If River hadn't known what a rotten man he was, she might have fallen for him.

The morning came too soon, and she missed the rooster that crowed outside her bedroom window when she slept too late. River and Daisy had shared a bed in the room they shared at Hank's ranch, so she turned over to see if her little girl was still asleep.

Most of the covers had been pulled away from her; that was Daisy's doing on a nightly basis. But this morning she didn't feel little feet pushing against her back like she normally did. Her heart dropped when she saw an empty space next to her. She felt it to see if maybe Daisy had just gotten up, but it was cold.

"Daisy?" River called out as she got up. She put on her robe and slippers before leaving the room to look for the little girl.

She wasn't two feet away from her bedroom door when she heard crying.

Daisy was crying.

"Daisy!" River took off at a run toward the sound she'd know anywhere. "Daisy, what's wrong?"

John looked up from where he sat on the couch holding his little girl. His eyes were rimmed in red with tears streaking down them. "I just told her about Andrew."

"No, why?" River had planned to do this with John. Why would he do it without her? Just one more reason she made the right decision to follow Daisy and not stay with John. He just never seemed to consider her place in Daisy's life.

"I'm sorry, she overheard us talking about it in the kitchen and asked who Andrew was." John wiped at his face with one hand.

Rubbing her forehead, River sat down next to Daisy and John on the couch. She blew out a long breath. "I'm so sorry, hunny. I was going to tell you this morning."

Daisy hit John's chest. "No! You can't weave me. You gonna marry Aunt River!"

Tears began to stream down John's cheeks again.

And River couldn't hold back the floodgates, either. It was what she had hoped might happen one day. If it took years for this case to get to court, she knew that John wouldn't wait for her.

"Honey, I'm going to fight to get to see you again." John pulled her closer and held her little hand in his. "And your Aunt River will never leave you."

"That's right, honey. I'll never leave you. I'm going with you to live on Andrew's ranch." River ran her hand down Daisy's back to comfort the little girl.

"But...but...I don't wike Andrew. I want John to be my daddy and you to be my mommy." Daisy tucked in farther to John's arms and cried some more.

"Oh, sweetie. I'd like that, too. But the judge said Andrew is your daddy for now." John looked to River over Daisy's head, defeat evident in his eyes.

River's heart broke for the cowboy, as well as for her and Daisy. They would have made the perfect family. But there was nothing they could do.

She didn't know how long the three of them huddled together, but eventually Mimi came into the room.

"I'm sorry to interrupt, but if we're gonna leave on time you'll need to finish getting ready, River. And I think it would be good to make sure Daisy eats something for breakfast, even if it's only some toast and juice." Without waiting for a response, Mimi left them alone.

"She's right—I can't deliver Daisy to Andrew hungry. He'll use that against me in my claim... I mean suit." John looked pointedly at Daisy.

River wiped her nose on the sleeve of her pink fuzzy robe. "You're right. I'll go get dressed."

"Do you want anything to eat?" John asked.

She shook her head. "No, just some coffee."

"I'm going to miss your snarky coffee shirts." John was going to miss more than her shirts, but he didn't feel it was appropriate to tell a woman who was moving in with another man, even if she did have her own bedroom, that he would miss her. That would be taking it too far.

By ten that morning, they were all at Andrew's family ranch. He lived more than an hour from Hank's ranch and close to two hours from the Hanson ranch. John still hadn't said anything about the ranch to Andrew. If he did, the guy would probably work even harder to sell it before John had a chance to get Daisy back.

Even though John wasn't interested in the Hanson ranch for himself, he did want Daisy to be able to have it one day. The Hansons obviously wanted her to run it. He would have liked to have helped that final wish come true.

When they got out of the truck, John got down on a knee in front of Daisy. "Hey there, don't cry." He wiped a tear from Daisy's face. "Maybe Andrew will let us come visit once in a while. And I bet if you ask nicely, River will let you call me on her cellphone." At least, he hoped she would.

"That's a great idea, Daisy. Maybe we can set up video calls after church on Sundays to see John and his whole family." River tried to smile, but couldn't quite get herself to show any level of happiness.

"I wuv you, Uncle John." Daisy hugged his neck.

John returned her hug. "I'll always love you. Never forget that, Daisy Myers." He pulled back and looked into her eyes. "I love you very much. And I'll never stop loving you."

Andrew walked outside and toward the little group as they were all saying their goodbyes.

John noticed the smirk on his face right before he changed it to an obviously fake smile. "Daisy, it's so good to finally have you home with your pa." When he walked up to the little girl, she shied away from him.

"You're not my pa." She hid behind John's legs.

An emotional storm crossed Andrew's face, and John noticed the twitch in the man's jaw. "What did you tell her?" he demanded.

River stepped between the two men. "Andrew, Daisy is watching. She doesn't need to see you angry. Especially today. This is very hard on her." She put a hand to his chest.

Andrew took her hand and pulled her to his side, a bit roughly for John's taste, but River worked hard not to show how uncomfortable she was.

John noticed and clenched his jaw but said nothing. Once Andrew settled himself down, John said, "I told her the judge said you were her pa now. It's too much of a shock for her. Give her time, let her get to know you."

He knew that if Andrew was a good man, Daisy would warm up to him. But if Andrew wasn't a good man, Daisy would pick up on that. Kids were smart. Smarter than anyone ever gave them credit for. They had this uncanny knack for picking up on a person's true nature.

Where most adults looked at a person's exterior and listened to their words, kids saw what a person's heart was like and watched and judged based on their actions, not their words. John would be praying constantly for God's hand of protection to stay on both Daisy and River during this trying time.

"Of course. That makes sense." Andrew again smiled at Daisy, but it never even came close to reaching his eyes.

Even John knew it was fake.

River noticed Andrew eyeing her suitcase. "Does this mean you've chosen to live with me?"

River took a deep breath. "I've chosen to stay with Daisy. And I'm open to getting to know you better." She looked down at Daisy's confused little face. "I can't make any promises, but Daisy is the most important person to me and I'm not giving her up." She wanted to add – *at least not without a fight*, but thought she'd better keep that to herself.

A glimmer of respect shone in Andrew's eyes. "Let's go in and I'll show you both around your new home." Andrew reached for River's suitcase. "Oh, I almost forgot. Daisy, I have a surprise for you."

River didn't say goodbye. How could she? It was the last thing she wanted to say. Instead, she waved at John and his family and gave them all a tightlipped smile. All the while in her heart, she tried to believe she would see them again.

Other than the Hansons, they were the only ones who'd ever showed her kindness and love. They were the first family to demonstrate what a loving family should be like.

Before she made it to the house, John called out her name. She stopped and turned back.

"I have something for you." He handed her a pretty purple Bible with her name engraved on the cover. "I thought you might want to be able to read about God and His love. And if you were able to attend church here, it might be nice for you to bring your own Bible."

"Thank you. It's beautiful." No one had ever given her a Bible before. "Where do I start? On page one like a novel?"

John's lips curved up in a lopsided smile. "Start with the book of John. Then call me."

River watched as the man who had shown her so much compassion walked out of her life. Probably for good.

Later that night, after Daisy had gone to bed, River opened the Bible and found the book of John.

Chapter 26

Thanksgiving was only a few days away. While Daisy had warmed up a little to Andrew, it was tough going. Mostly because he was hardly around. River had no clue how she and he were supposed to get to know each other and eventually get married if he was never around. They'd not even had one date in the month she'd lived there.

"Aunt River, can we call Uncle John today?" It wasn't Sunday, but lately Daisy had been asking more and more to see John. They had started FaceTiming each other on a regular basis. It seemed to help Daisy, and if she were honest with herself, it helped her, too.

"Okay, we can call him tonight before bed. How does that sound?" River tapped the little girl's nose and she giggled. It was only the second time she'd done so since moving to the Ryan ranch. River missed the girl's sweet giggles.

River was getting anxious. Andrew hadn't wanted her to go and get her car from the Triple J Ranch yet, so she and Daisy had been stuck on the Ryan ranch for the past month, only allowed out to attend Sunday morning services. Alone, of course, but after church on Sundays the two of them went out to lunch and FaceTimed John. They had agreed to keep it quiet.

"When can we go visit Uncle John, and Pickles?" Almost daily Daisy asked to go visit.

She even asked Andrew one night. He had said something vague, but River knew he was just putting her off. Tonight, she'd ask him about getting the rest of their stuff from John just as soon as she saw Andrew again.

Unlike the Manning family, the Ryan family rarely ate meals together. That was something she really missed. Even if it was the Ryans, she still wanted to have dinner with them. It would have helped them all to get better acquainted.

"Laura, do you know when Andrew will be home?" River asked as their cook began to serve them dinner—something River didn't like. She had tried on many occasions to help the cook prepare and serve their meals, but the woman refused, stating she'd lose her job if Mr. Ryan caught River or Daisy in the kitchen cooking, or serving, a meal.

"Mr. Andrew should be home soon. He said he would eat dinner here tonight," she said as she laid a plate of mac 'n' cheese in front of Daisy and a plate of lasagna with garlic bread and a side salad in front of River.

"Mmmm, is that your lasagna, Laura? It smells wonderful." Andrew sauntered into the formal dining room.

One more thing River missed about the Manning family: they all ate in a dining room, but there wasn't anything formal about it. Theirs was warm and inviting. It welcomed people to talk to one another.

The Ryan family dining room was designed for large dinner parties; the table easily sat twenty. On the few occasions when Mr. Ryan and Andrew joined them for a meal, Mr. Ryan sat at the head of the table, Andrew at the foot, while River and Daisy sat in the middle. It made it difficult to hold any sort of conversation with the Ryans. River was sure that was the point. They rarely spoke to her.

"Andrew, what a surprise. I didn't know you were planning on having dinner with us tonight." River smiled tentatively at Andrew.

"I wasn't sure when I'd be home, but my meeting ended early so here I am." He spread his arms wide and smiled from ear to ear as though his coming home for dinner was the greatest thing since sliced bread.

Daisy continued to eat her dinner, not paying any attention to Andrew.

"Well, I'm glad you're here. I wanted to ask you about heading up to Montana after Thanksgiving so I can get the rest of our stuff, including my car. Can you go with us?" River hoped he would just let them take a bus up and drive back, but if Andrew wanted to go with them, that might be good for Daisy to spent time with her...uh...well, with Andrew.

She still couldn't bring herself to calling Andrew Daisy's daddy. And neither could Daisy. After the first week, Andrew stopped asking her to call him daddy, or pa.

In fact, now that she thought about it, Andrew had hardly paid her any attention since their first week in the house.

Andrew shook his head. "I'm afraid not. I've got a business deal closing next week and I have to be here. But if you want to go up after December fifth, that should be fine. I'll get you a plane ticket and then you can drive your car back." He smiled up at Laura when she set a plate in front of him with an even larger piece of lasagna and garlic bread on it. Unlike River, Andrew didn't care for salad so he didn't have any on his plate.

"We can go up while you're working hard to close your deal. Then be back to celebrate with you once it's closed." River knew if he was closing a deal the following week, he wouldn't even be around to miss them. Shoot, even if he was around he wouldn't miss them.

His fork clattered to the table. "I said no. I don't want you leaving until after I've closed my deal, and that's the end of it."

Daisy turned wide eyes to River, who patted the girl's hand. When her lower lip protruded, River knew Daisy was about to cry. Andrew didn't do well with kids crying.

"Daisy, why don't we go riding tomorrow? I bet your new pony will be happy to see you." River and Daisy rode most days, but talking about the pony usually put Daisy in a good mood. While it did force that little lip of hers back into place, it didn't make the little girl smile.

Daisy nodded. "Okay."

The rest of dinner was quiet, except for the sounds of forks and knives scraping against the plates.

Something was going on, and River wanted to get to the bottom of it. Only problem was she didn't really know how to do it. So far, the only time she had spoken to John was to connect him and Daisy, but maybe after Daisy's next call with John she could ask him if he knew anything yet.

After dinner, River hoped Andrew would want to spend some time with Daisy, but he went straight to his office without a word. It rankled River that he'd worked so hard to get Daisy and now wanted nothing to do with her. He only wanted to keep her and River as prisoners on his ranch.

Daisy, however, didn't seem to care about Andrew. Instead of being upset about his lack of attention, her eyes lit up when he left and she whispered, "Can we call Uncle John now?"

With a full heart, River smiled at her little charge and nodded. "Let's head up to your room and then we can call from there."

River turned on some kids bop music to help cover up their sounds, just in case Andrew was anywhere near them. They had been put in a different wing of the ranch, which made it easier for the Ryans to ignore them. But it also made it easier for them to make phone calls. On a few occasions she'd even spoken to Judith Manning after Daisy went to bed. She missed Judith and all of the Mannings.

"Hi, Daisy!" John's face shone through on the phone's screen when he accepted their FaceTime request. "I'm so happy you called."

"Uncle John!" Daisy squealed.

"Shh. Remember, we have to be quiet," River admonished.

John's brow furrowed. "Are you not allowed to call me?"

River got in the picture and quietly said, "He hasn't exactly forbidden it, but he has said we aren't to see you again. And he won't allow us to come and get our stuff and my car. If we don't go soon, I won't be able to get my car until the spring. The weather will be too bad to risk driving my car in the winter."

"I wondered about that. We have all of your stuff packed up in your room." John's eyes widened. "I have a great idea! Why don't we bring your car and your stuff to you? We'll just show up one day during the daytime, and hopefully Andrew and his dad won't be around."

"If you can do it next week, that would be perfect. They're closing some big business deal and they won't be around much." River's excitement was starting to bubble over, and she couldn't contain her smile. If this worked, she might even get a few hours with John.

"I'll see who can come with me. We'll stay the night at Hank's place and then come over in the morning, after when the Ryans usually leave for work."

"That would be perfect. They usually leave before eight in the morning when they plan to spend the day in the office, which is most days. It's very rare they work from the ranch." She was actually grateful they didn't work from home very often. It was always so uncomfortable when she was around them. If they weren't ignoring her and Daisy, they were giving them strange looks.

On multiple occasions she had walked into a room only to have them stop talking, and they got up without a word to her and left the room. Her second week on the ranch, Andrew had a TV installed in her bedroom and told her they could watch whatever they wanted in her room. He hadn't come out and said they weren't welcome in the media room, but he'd implied it.

Every day that went by, she felt more and more like a nanny or governess and less like a potential wife.

While she was grateful for choosing Daisy, she wished she didn't have to make that choice at all. But, at least the staff were nice to both of them. And Daisy had the cook wrapped around her little finger.

"I'll text you with the details." John pursed his lips. "But River, I highly suggest you and Daisy keep this between yourselves. And delete my messages and your call logs. I don't think it would be good if Andrew knew we were talking."

"Great minds." River chuckled. "We have kept these talks quiet. And I've deleted my call logs after every one of our calls."

"And Daisy, can you keep this a secret?" John turned his eyes to the little girl, who sat there quietly smiling at her Uncle John.

She nodded. "I'm a good secret-keeper."

River hated that she was teaching Daisy to keep secrets, but she knew it was the safest thing for them.

Before she could ask John her questions about the case, a knock on the door startled her. She froze. No one ever came to her room at night.

"Daisy? River? Are you in there?" Andrew's voice came through the door.

John must have heard because his eyes widened like saucers and he whispered, "Gotta go. Remember to erase." Then he hung up the call.

River, not knowing what to do, put her phone under her legs before calling out, "Come in."

Andrew walked in and looked between the two girls. 'What are you two up to?"

River's heart was beating hard, and she felt a drop of perspiration on her forehead. There was no way Andrew could know about the plan for next week. She must have been reading too many fairy tales to Daisy, for all she could think of was that Andrew would lock them away in a tower or a dungeon.

"Nothing, just trying to decide which fairy tale to read tonight." River mentally tried to calm her heart and put a hand on Daisy. "She really likes them, and the stories about princesses."

"Will you read me Rapun...Rapanuzal? No, that's not it." Daisy looked to Aunt River. "What's the princess locked in the tower?"

River almost burst out laughing. Either she and Daisy were sharing one brain, or they were spending too much time together. "Do you mean Rapunzel?"

Daisy nodded. "Yes, Punzel has pretty long hair." She scrambled off the bed and ran to her bookshelf. The one good thing Andrew had done was ensuring that they had plenty of kids' books. "Here, Andrew. Read me." She handed him a picture book with a giant stone tower and a princess leaning out the top window with her hair reaching all the way to the ground.

Andrew took the book and looked at River. "Uh, can we talk?"

River's brows rose and she looked to Daisy. "Sure."

"I mean, out in the hallway?" He handed Daisy back her book.

"Okaaay?" Not sure what was going on, she got up and put her phone in her back pocket and then followed Andrew to the hallway. "What's up?"

Chapter 27

Andrew ran a ragged hand through his hair and walked down the hallway a few feet from Daisy's room. "I understand you spent some time with the Hansons growing up?"

River nodded. "What's up?"

"Well, I don't know if you knew this, but Daisy inherited their ranch."

This was it. This was the moment Andrew was going to fess up to what he'd done. Or at least she hoped he would tell the truth. He seemed nervous enough.

"Yes, I was made aware of that fact." River eyed him cautiously. "What are you going to do with the ranch?"

"We've just sold it. And as I understand it, there are some items of yours still on the property. Tomorrow we need to go there and remove any personal items before the auction next week."

That was not what River expected to hear. She deflated like a balloon and had to lean against the wall to keep herself upright. "You sold the ranch? Already?" How could it have happened so quickly? She would have thought that the paperwork alone would have taken months.

He cleared his throat. "It was a cash offer, so it went very easy. Escrow is going to close next week only a day or two after the auction. We need to take what we want before the auction house comes and puts the larger items up on the docket."

"So, tomorrow morning?"

He nodded. "Yes. I'll need you both ready by six so we can get going. Breakfast will be ready at five-thirty."

To say River was shocked was an understatement. She was so thrown by this she didn't know what to say. Daisy's future was gone. "Are you putting the money from the sale into a trust for Daisy? It is her money."

"Of course. Daisy will always be taken care of. She is my daughter, after all." Andrew arched an imperious brow.

"Really? You could have fooled me." She scoffed. This was it. After the escrow closed and he had the money, River bet they'd both be thrown out on their butts, and he wouldn't even care if she had her car or not.

Thankfully, he didn't seem to know about her inheritance. She'd keep that little tidbit to herself. And she'd forgo buying that sweet truck she wanted; her car would be enough to get her and Daisy somewhere safe. She knew John would take Daisy without question, but would he still be willing to help River? She would need a job in order to afford a small apartment near Daisy.

Or should she and Daisy go somewhere new, like maybe to California? Get as far away from Andrew and his reach as possible. Her inheritance would be enough to at least get them a place and keep them going until she could get a job waitressing. River had always wanted to live by the beach, but could they afford a small bungalow in a beach town?

So many things to think about and plans to make.

"River? Did you hear me?" Andrew interrupted her thoughts.

She looked at him. "What?"

"I asked what you meant by that snarky comment of yours." He put his fisted hands on his hips and glared at her.

She narrowed her eyes and put her fisted hands on her hips. "You never spent any time with Daisy. You fought tooth and nail to get her, and the moment"—she pointed a finger in his face—"the very moment you get custody, you sell her ranch. How'd you know about it before you got custody? Huh, Andrew? Is that why you forged that document? And you probably paid off that judge too, didn't you?" River was on a roll. She was so angry she could spit. It no longer mattered what he thought, she knew these were their last days at the ranch.

"How dare you!" Andrew pointed a finger at River. "You have no right. In fact, I want you out of my house, tonight!"

"Fine, Daisy and I will pack up our things and be gone." River was glad to be leaving.

"No, not Daisy. Just you." He motioned for her to leave right then and there.

"What? How are you going to take care of a four-year-old? You didn't even know you had to buy her birthday presents. And you couldn't even arrange a small family party for her. You go days without seeing her and now all of a sudden you think you can take care of her?" She scoffed.

"I'll hire a real nanny. Not some"—he scrunched his nose and looked down on River—"uneducated trash who thinks she knows best."

River slapped his face. "That's it. I'm not going to allow you to raise Daisy. You'll turn her into a rotten person, just like you!" She turned around and ran back into her room and locked the door behind her.

"Aunt River? Don't leave me." Daisy ran into River's legs, and both girls cried.

Through the door, River could hear Andrew cussing and throwing a fit. "Not crying. Anything but tears." Then he slapped the wall.

Both River and Daisy jumped at the sound of the wall being pounded upon.

A ding sounded on River's phone, and she gasped. When she pulled the phone from her pocket, she could have wept all over again. She took Daisy's hand and moved as far from the door as she could. Then she dialed.

"John, we're in trouble. Andrew just kicked me out of the house and won't let me take Daisy. And he's already sold the ranch." She continued on rambling and crying.

Chapter 28

After he finished FaceTiming with River and Daisy, John went to speak with his father about when he could leave to head back out to Wyoming. They had been in constant contact with Jackson, and other things were starting to move into place for them. If all went as he hoped, he'd have both Daisy and River back in Beacon Creek by Christmas.

He just had to keep cool and not get anyone's hopes up.

When they'd returned over a month ago from Wyoming downcast and devastated by the ruling, Mark had called his friend Stu. Stu had an uncle who was a Wyoming congressman. Turned out Congressman Watson Mason was golf buddies with the governor, and Judge Singleton was already under investigation. If River and Daisy could keep cool and not make waves for a couple more weeks, then this could all be over and done with. Hopefully they'd even be able to keep the ranch in Wyoming for Daisy when she grew up.

John wouldn't mind running the Hanson ranch and raising Daisy there. But would River want to join them? Was he ready to make such a move with River, let alone any woman?

"Pa, I need to head to Wyoming next week. But I'll need help getting River's car down there to her." John sat down in the chair next to Caleb where he was reading a Bible commentary on the book of Revelation. "You wouldn't believe how Andrew is treating the girls. They're basically prisoners on that ranch." He shook his head.

Caleb set aside his book and closed his eyes for a moment. When he opened them, he looked directly into his son's face. "John, we have to tread lightly here. If you go down there with River's car and things, you can't demand anything."

John held his hands up. "I know, Pa. I know. I may not even be able to see Daisy. But here's the thing, Andrew and his dad are going to be very busy next week on some business deal. River thinks it's the best time to come for a day visit. Andrew can't really say anything if I'm bringing their stuff to them, right? I mean, Southern hospitality and all that says they have to at least invite me in for refreshments." He grinned.

His dad chuckled. "You should have been a lawyer."

"Nah, I love the ranch too much. And besides, all that back-biting and sneaking around isn't really for me. I'm doing it now because it's for my daughter."

"True enough." Caleb rubbed the day's stubble on his chin. "See if Matthew can go with you, since he's such good friends with Hank. But I want you both back here in time for Thanksgiving dinner or your mother will tan my hide." He winked.

"Oh"—John chuckled—"don't I know it. She'll have ours, too." No one missed Thanksgiving dinner with the family if they could help it. Chloe had a couple of times, but she didn't live in town. She lived a few hours away and was building a life in Frenchtown.

The fact that Roman was going to miss Thanksgiving this year because he was playing in a college bowl football game had his mother proud, but also sad. There would be no living with her if he missed this year in particular.

When Caleb picked up his book again, John took that as his cue to leave the room. He headed toward where Matthew and Claire's ranch home sat on the Triple J land. He could have called them, but he was too antsy to sit still. John needed a walk to clear his head and calm down.

For some reason he didn't understand, he was beginning to feel a sense of dread. He had a very strong need to run to Matthew's house. A still small voice was urging him on. As he ran, he wondered if something was wrong with Matthew or Claire.

When he reached their house, he stopped in his tracks as he realized it wasn't Matthew or Claire, but someone else.

River.

His mind was filled with images of her and thoughts of needing to help her.

Matthew smiled and called a greeting to his little brother. "Hey, come and join us by the fire." They were sitting in their front yard by a firepit Matthew had made. They were both sitting in Adirondack chairs with quilts over their legs, and a small radio was playing the local country station.

Instead of answering his brother, John sat down in a chair, took out his cellphone, and sent River a text message. Nothing revealing, just a simple, *Hey, how are you doing* sort of message. That way, in case Andrew was around it wouldn't look as though they were planning anything.

He may have been overreacting. It was possible nothing was wrong with River, but his spirit was telling him otherwise and his gut knew to trust his spirit. Once he sent the message, he started to tell Matthew and Claire what was going on, but his phone rang.

"River..." John was cut off by the panicked voice on the other line.

"John, I need your help." River kept going, telling him how much trouble she was in.

He stood up, terror filling his entire being. He put his phone on speaker and looked to his brother, pleading with his eyes for help.

Both Matthew and Claire stood up abruptly when they heard River speaking.

Claire came right over and put a comforting arm around John, who stood there taking in everything River was saying.

He stood stock still, waiting for River to take a breath. When she did, he went into action. "River, are you safe where you are right now?"

"Daisy and I are locked in my room, but Andrew most likely has a key." Terror filled River's voice.

Matthew pulled out his phone. "I'm calling Hank. He can get there and help her before we can."

"I'll go pack us an overnight bag so we can head out right away." Claire took off and headed inside their house.

"What is he going to do with Daisy?" John's mind was working a mile a minute. The worst things possible were going through his head.

"Andrew has a cook and housekeeper who lives on-site. She'll probably have to watch Daisy. But he did say he was going to hire a nanny."

"Matthew's calling Hank right now. Is there any way you can hold still for two hours? That's about how long it will take Hank to get to you." John clenched his jaw and waited to hear what River said.

He was going to kill Andrew.

You didn't throw a woman out of your house at night. If he no longer wanted River around, he should have given her time to get a new living situation. This was unacceptable. And Daisy? He couldn't take care of her. From what River had said this past month, the man barely even saw her as it was. John wished he wasn't an almost nine-hour drive away.

"I don't know if he'll let me stay here that long. He said I had to pack my bags and leave right away. And Daisy couldn't go with me. But he never said how I was to leave. Since I don't have a car here, someone would have to come and get me." River's voice cracked, and John could tell she was about to cry some more.

"Do whatever you can to stay in that house until Hank arrives. But keep me posted. We're gonna head out now—I'll be there as fast as I can." John turned from his brother and back to his house. He needed to tell his dad what was going on and grab a few things. He prayed Andrew wouldn't make her walk to town at night.

River couldn't remember when she'd been so frightened—not for herself, but for Daisy. She knew she could deal with whatever came her way. She always had. But Daisy? She was such a little girl. How could Andrew do this to Daisy?

There was no doubt in her mind that he only wanted the little girl for the money. She just hoped he would make sure she got a good nanny to care for Daisy.

Even though River had been going to church and reading her Bible, she just couldn't understand why God would do this to such a little girl. Didn't God hold kids in higher regard than adults? Why didn't he do something to protect her?

First Daisy had lost her mother, then she missed out on having a father, and now that she was so close to getting one, he'd been stolen from her and replaced with an imposter who only wanted to steal her inheritance for himself. That was some kind of evil. How could a loving God allow that?

River looked up and shook her fist at God. "If you're real, why aren't you doing anything to protect Daisy? I don't care about myself, just this beautiful, innocent little child that you're supposed to love and protect. Why can't anyone ever protect kids?" Tears ran down her face as she held Daisy close to her.

"Please God, if you're really there, help Daisy. She's still so innocent and needs someone to protect her."

She expected Andrew to break down the door, or maybe even use a key, any minute now and drag her out of there. But after an hour of holding Daisy and going back and forth between pleading with God to protect Daisy and railing after Him for not protecting her, she and Daisy both fell asleep on the ground in the corner where they sat.

So when kind hands lightly shook her awake, she was startled to see a friendly face.

"Hank? Am I dreaming?" River rubbed her eyes, but he was still there.

"River, Matthew sent me to help you out." Hank held out a hand to help her and Daisy up from the floor.

When River stood, she still held Daisy in one arm.

The housekeeper came over, and with downcast eyes she took Daisy without a word.

"Wait! Where are you taking her?" River followed Laura as she carried the still sleeping Daisy to her own room. "Will you watch out for her?" The words barely made it past her clogged throat.

"Yes." Laura settled Daisy in bed and took her shoes off before covering her up while still dressed in her clothes from that day. "I'll watch her as though she were my own granddaughter." She stood up and looked at River. "I'm so sorry, River."

River put a hand on the older woman's arm. "I know. Please, don't do anything to get yourself booted as well. Someone in this house needs to look out for Daisy."

A lone tear streaked down Laura's cheek. "I will do everything I can to keep her safe."

River wanted to say more, but she couldn't. She looked down at Daisy sleeping peacefully. One thing about this little girl that River always loved was how hard she slept. A Mack truck could come rumbling through the house and Daisy wouldn't even stir. "I love you, my little girl. Don't you ever forget that."

Hank came up behind her. "This isn't the end. Don't worry."

River whirled around. "What do you mean?"

He looked around and put a finger to his lips. "Shh, not here."

She nodded.

"Let's get your stuff packed and get going. Mimi's got a room all ready for you. And Andrew did say that you needed to go to the Hanson ranch tomorrow and get the last of your personal items. At least he's still going to let you take your stuff away." Hank winced.

River couldn't remember what she'd left there, but there were a few family heirlooms that Daisy might want one day. She knew Donna had left a few things there, and the Christmas tree topper the Hansons used every year was something she knew had to be saved for Daisy.

The Hansons had handed that topper down from generation to generation. The fact that they didn't have any kids of their own meant it needed to go to Daisy. It was beautiful. Handcrafted by a German metal and glassworker back in the 1800s, River knew Mrs. Hanson would expect River to save it from the auction.

There were probably a few other things Daisy would want one day, things that Andrew wouldn't even look twice at. She would take everything she could for Daisy.

Chapter 29

Caleb insisted on going with Matthew and John, and neither man would let John drive. Not with how angry and upset the cowboy was.

"John, your mind isn't here. It's in Wyoming with your girls. If we let you drive, I doubt we'll make it safely there." Caleb took his keys off the peg and insisted they take his truck.

"I can't just sit there in the truck for nine hours," John scoffed.

"We're heading straight to Hank's place. He's going to get River now, and they'll be safely back at his ranch by the time we get there. So it's only about seven and a half hours." Matthew put his overnight bag in the back of the truck and climbed into the quad cab.

John's nostrils flared. "What about Daisy? Who's going to look after my little girl?" If John could, he'd go and take her right out of Andrew's hands.

When he suggested kidnapping the girl, his dad rightly explained to him that it would hurt his court case and he'd probably not get custody of Daisy if he did that. John quieted down after that, but he still wanted to find a way to get Daisy to safety.

Once they were on the road, Hank called to inform them that he had River, and Daisy was safe with the housekeeper.

At least that calmed John down a little bit. River and Daisy both had spoken kindly about the housekeeper who doubled as a cook. She liked Daisy and always had some sort of sweet treat for the little girl. At least there was one person in the house to look after her.

"Do you think this action will help us to get custody faster?" While John knew River had zero legal claim to Daisy, he hoped that this type of brash action would reflect poorly on Andrew in the eyes of the court, and maybe even get social services to remove Daisy from his care. And since River had already been the girl's foster mother, he prayed she could get her again.

Caleb shook his head. "Sorry, son. Until we get there and speak with Jackson, I can't rightly say anything. But I doubt it will hurt Andrew. He has a good housekeeper looking after her, and if he does hire a respectable nanny soon, then the courts will keep her there."

"At least until we prove your claim, John," Matthew added. "I know that once a decent judge looks at the case files, Andrew will go to jail and you'll get your little girl."

"From your lips to God's ears." John spent the next hour in silent prayer, petitioning God to protect both River and Daisy.

He couldn't imagine how River was doing. Since it was so late, he didn't want to call her in case she was able to get to sleep. Even though he doubted she'd sleep a wink that night. But just in case, he wouldn't want to be the one to disturb her sleep.

Caleb and Matthew took turns driving and sleeping, but John couldn't even close his eyes, except when he prayed. His mind was mulling over all of the possible scenarios, none of which helped him to feel any better.

So when they finally pulled into Hank's drive before sunrise, he was grateful to finally be there and see for himself how River was doing.

She ran out of the house before he could get up the steps and stopped in front of him. John wanted to pull her into his arms and comfort her, but she held herself back. He could sense a wall between them, and he didn't know if he should attempt to breach it.

But first thing's first. "How are you doing, River?" John licked his lips and waited anxiously for her to reply.

A storm of emotions passed over her face. "How do you think I'm doing? I was kicked out of the house last night and couldn't bring Daisy with me."

John shook his head. "I'm sorry, that was a stupid question. Have you heard from Daisy or Laura?"

She shook her head. "No, it's still too early. I thought I should give them a couple more hours before I call Laura and see how Daisy's doing."

His hands itched to hold her and let her know it would all be alright. But she still held herself away from him.

God was in control. John didn't know what God had planned, but the one thing he did know what that his Lord was in control, and he was going to trust in God.

"Oh, thank goodness." River sighed and hung up her cellphone. She was in the truck with Caleb and Hank as they drove to the Hanson ranch. "Laura said Daisy was doing good, all things considered. She refused to eat her breakfast until we spoke. She promised she would eat now that she's heard from me. But I bet Andrew gets an earful tonight from her. Well"—she rolled her eyes—"that is if he even sees Daisy tonight. She's very angry with him for giving me the boot."

John couldn't have been happier. Well, he would have been happier if Daisy were with him. "Good, he deserves it. I hope she kicks him in the shin." Guilt flowed through his body. He knew he shouldn't want Daisy to be upset with anyone, but...well...the last thing he wanted was for Daisy and Andrew to bond. Especially not now that he was so close to getting her back.

"Do you think Andrew will be at the ranch today?" River bit her lower lip.

John could tell that thought freaked her out. Part of him wanted to see Andrew to give him a piece of his mind, but he also knew that would be wrong.

Even though Andrew had done something awful, Jesus wouldn't want him to pay evil for evil.

In fact, 1 Peter 3:9 came to mind at that very moment:

Not rendering evil for evil, or railing for railing: but contrariwise blessing; knowing that ye are thereunto called, that ye should inherit a blessing.

John was called to be kind, even to those who were evil. The Bible was full of examples where Jesus didn't repay evil with evil. In fact, he was kind to those people. If he were to do what Jesus would do, then he would be considerate if he saw Andrew again.

He nodded. "Probably. But we'll be there with you. Just stick with one of us the entire time and you'll be safe."

She worried her hands in front of her. "You don't think he'll bring Daisy with him." The way she said it sounded as though she was resigned to not seeing Daisy that day, or any day soon.

John hadn't had a chance to inform her yet of what was going down with the corrupt judge. He would, but he wanted to wait until after they left the Hanson ranch. He couldn't take the chance that someone would talk about it and Andrew would overhear and then run off with Daisy. For now, he needed Andrew to think he'd won. That was why his attorney hadn't even filed a petition yet for John's claim of custody.

The congressman had said they should wait for the investigation—it was almost complete. And if he was found to be guilty of taking bribes, then all of his recent cases would be nullified. Daisy would go back to River until a real trial could be held and all of the evidence supplied. John could live with River having custody, as long as they stayed in Beacon Creek. He never wanted to be separated from his girl again.

Before John could say anything to help alleviate her anxiety, they were pulling into the Hanson ranch. A big black Hummer sat in the drive.

"He's here already." River's voice hitched, and she sighed.

John took her hand in his and squeezed. "Remember, we're here to help you. Let us." He let go of her hand and got out once the truck stopped in front of the large ranch home.

Andrew furrowed his brow. "John? What are you doing here?"

It took every bit of strength John had to be civil. "I'm here to help River." He had no more strength or patience, and he knew it. So he walked past Andrew and into the house with River trailing him.

Andrew's mouth opened and closed almost like a fish sucking for air. Then he jogged up to River. "Hey, just remember to only take your stuff."

She bit back a retort. But boy howdy did she want to say the same thing to him. "What about Donna's stuff? Can I take that? And family photos?"

Andrew scrunched his nose. "Yeah, go ahead and take family stuff. The auction house won't want any of that."

River thought he probably didn't want to have to hire anyone to come and clean out all of the "family stuff."

So she should be safe to take whatever she wanted from inside.

When lunchtime came around, they were still packing up personal items. Hank went out to get them lunch. John and River were in the attic going through Christmas boxes.

"You know, if Andrew doesn't say anything we could take all of these Christmas boxes home and you can go through them later. We have a Christmas fair in Beacon Creek. What you don't want could probably be sold there." John picked up a large brown box that had seen better days and held it out for River to inspect.

"You don't mind?" She wasn't sure how much she wanted to keep, but certainly didn't want any of it to go in the trash. So far she had only managed to put aside four boxes for trash, and had at least thirty she still wanted to keep. Not to mention the row of boxes still to go through. The one good thing was that she had found the tree topper and ornaments. So if she couldn't take more, she would deal with it.

But the idea that she and Daisy wouldn't get to find the ancient collection of snowmen did sadden her. At least until John suggested they take the rest of the boxes with them.

"Hey, what about these?" As River made her way out of the attic, she noticed a few boxes marked *personal.*

"I think we most definitely need those. They might be important down the road."

Once they had all of the boxes out of the attic and into the trucks, River took one more look around the only home she'd ever felt loved in as a kid. Sadness overtook her, and she regretted not coming back to visit more often after Donna passed away.

"Do you know what happened to Donna's horse?" River asked as they walked out back.

"River, sweetie. It's so good to see you." Juanita, the foreman's wife, walked up and gave her a hug.

"Juanita? You're still here?" River thought for sure Andrew had fired them the moment he got the place. They had been there for close to forty years working the land and the animals alongside the Hanson family.

She chuckled. "We're leaving once the last of the animals are gone. Manny and I have decided to retire to Florida." She waggled her brows. "Sunshine, beaches, and our grandkids are there now."

River put a hand on the nice lady's arm. "I'm really happy for you. Family is so important. I wish you the best, and I'm very glad that you're able to stay to care for the animals until they're gone."

"Thank you. You're right, family is muy importante. Don't forget that." Juanita smiled at John and looked back to River and winked.

River felt her cheeks warm and she looked down at her feet. "Ah, do you know what happened to Donna's horse?"

"Oh, that was so sad. Mr. Hanson sold her mare last year. He said that no one was going to barrel ride anytime soon, so someone should be able to use that poor horse. One of the neighbor girls had just started barrel riding and needed a good horse."

"I'm glad that Knickers will get to keep riding. Donna would have wanted that." She looked out over the stables and wished there was a way to save this all for Daisy.

Juanita leaned in. "Trust in God. He will take care of everything."

River scoffed. "Where was He when Donna died? Where was he when Daisy..." She couldn't finish and started to walk away.

"River"—Juanita put a gentle hand on her shoulder—"we don't always understand God's ways, especially when we are in the middle of chaos. But in the end it will all make sense."

River shook her head. "There is no way a young, beautiful woman with a brand-new baby dying so young makes sense. If she had suffered from some disease since birth, maybe, but she was in the prime of her life."

"Everyone has a time, and it was obviously Donna's time to go." Juanita hugged River to her. "Listen, you need to keep it together for Daisy. She's gonna need you as she grows up."

"You haven't heard? I'm no longer welcome in her life."

"Pft. That boy has no idea what he's doing. Mark my words, Daisy will be back in your life." The nod from Juanita was of finality.

River didn't want to argue with the woman. She had this annoying knack of always being right. Although in this case, River hoped she was.

Chapter 30

Hank invited everyone to stay as long as they needed.

"Thanks, but we'll be heading back home in the morning. There's a lot to do this time of year, as you well know." Caleb thanked Hank for his help and then turned to River. "Young lady, you are always welcome at our ranch. If you want to come home with us, we would love to have you."

She shook her head. "No, I want to be close to Daisy in case Andrew changes his mind."

"You're welcome to stay here with us as long as you like." Hank handed River a mug of coffee.

"Thank you, I appreciate that." She looked to John.

"I think staying here is smart. Daisy is going to need you soon." John had explained to River what the Wyoming governor was up to. If all went well, Daisy would be back with River in the next two weeks or so.

"I agree." River bit her lip. "But when I get her back, what do you want?"

John grinned. "I want you both to come back home. You belong in Beacon Creek, with us."

Did that mean he wanted her to come back as Daisy's nanny? Like what she was doing with Andrew before she lost her cool? If so, she'd probably be able to deal with that. At least John and his family were a real family and loved Daisy, and even welcomed her into their home. It wouldn't be difficult taking care of Daisy. "What about my car? You left it in Montana."

A sheepish look crossed John's face. "Yeah, about that." He scratched his head. "Your car is a piece of junk. I was afraid it wouldn't make it here, or at least not in a timely manner. But when you get Daisy back, I'll come back down here and get you both and bring you back. Then you can go buy that truck you wanted."

Matthew added, "And send that heap of junk to the scrap pile." He laughed and it helped break up the tension in the room.

"Ha, ha. You wish you had a car as awesome as mine," River retorted. "What about all of the boxes? There's too many to go back with you right now." She hadn't thought about what she'd do with everything before. She was more worried about getting what she wanted.

"You're more than welcome to leave as much here as needed," Hank offered.

"Thanks." She considered his offer. "I think I should at least keep those boxes marked as personal and go through them."

In fact, that very night she began going through the boxes and stopped with a slow smile spreading across her face. In the middle of one box was a letter with her name on it. No address, just her name. She wondered when the Hansons had written it.

My Dearest River,

If you're reading this then we are both gone and you know that Daisy has inherited the ranch. We lived a frugal lifestyle as much as we could. And we insured the ranch so that it would be paid off in the event of our deaths. I know Donna would have wanted Daisy to have the ranch, so we left it all to her. You never were much for the ranch or horses. Which is why we left you money. I hope you don't mind. And I hope Daisy is all grown by the time you read this.

Don't cry for us. We are in a much better place now. I know you were never one for church, or God, but you should know that He exists, and we are with Him now. I know this for a fact because I believe the Bible. Roger and I have known Jesus as our Lord and Savior since we were both young. We taught Donna about Jesus as well, but I'm not sure about her salvation. We do hope to see her in heaven, and we have prayed every day that you would accept God and meet up with us in heaven down the road after you've lived a very long and happy life.

I hope you will take Daisy to church and teach her about the love of Jesus. She needs to know her Heavenly Father loves her so much that he sent his Son to die on the cross for your sins, and for hers. God spared her life for a reason, keep that in mind.

I know you're feeling guilty for not spending as much time with us as you should have. We did the same thing after Donna passed. It's normal. Forgive yourself. We never thought anything bad about you or Donna for not coming home very often. We loved all the time we had with you girls and wouldn't trade it for anything.

Tell Daisy about us. Show her the tree topper and tell her about its family history. Make sure she always sees pictures of her mother, and us. And let her know that we loved her very much. And I'm 100% positive that her mother loved her as well.

Donna sent us letters while she was pregnant telling us how excited she was to be a momma. Those letters are in the boxes with this letter. Share them with Daisy when you think she's ready.

Just know that your time on Earth is limited. We all have a time to live and a time to die. This was our time. One day, yours will come and I hope you are as prepared as Roger and I were to meet our maker.

Please, go to church, read your Bible, pray, and learn about God. Know that we will be looking for you to join one day, way down the road.

We love you very much, River, don't you ever forget that. It didn't matter that we only had you in our family since you were sixteen, you are our daughter, and we love you so very much.

Do with the ranch as you see fit, Juanita and Manny will help you as long as they are able to. Please, go to them with any questions you have about the ranch, but more importantly, about God.

Tears streamed down River's face and she wiped her messy nose on her shirt sleeves. She kept digging through the box where she found that letter and discovered the envelopes with the letters Martha mentioned. She pulled them out and hugged them to her chest. She wasn't ready to read them. Not yet. But she would one day. And then when Daisy was ready, she'd share them with Donna's little girl.

As she sat there on the bed in the Hanson's guest room, she wondered if God hadn't put it in her heart to bring these boxes back with her. She didn't take everything, but she did get all of the boxes that were marked as personal. There was too much to sort through in one day and since Andrew wouldn't let her go back to the ranch, she just grabbed as much as she could.

The idea of seeing Martha and Roger again in the afterlife warmed her heart.

The coming days were a test. She knew they were. River checked her phone multiple times every day looking for messages from John letting her know he was about to go and get Daisy now. And at the end of the day when none came, she asked Hank, "Any word yet?"

After two weeks of doing the same thing, Mimi stepped in. At dinner that night she suggested they attend the Christmas carnival. "Trust me, you'll like it. And the best part is that it will take your mind off of everything else."

River scrunched her nose. "I don't know. What if I get the call to go and get Daisy?"

Mimi smiled and her pretty face lit up. "That's the best part. The carnival is only thirty minutes from Andrew's ranch."

River perked up. "Really? Why didn't you say so before?" When a smile spread across her face, a calculating gleam entered her eyes. "Do you think we could drive by their ranch and stop in? You know, ask if we can take Daisy to the carnival? Maybe Andrew won't care since the sale has closed escrow and he probably had the money now."

The thought of Andrew stealing from Daisy put a damper on her joy, but if she could get Daisy back, she'd be so happy. Even if it was for just one night. Laura had been great about calling her when Andrew wasn't home so that she could talk to Daisy. The poor little girl missed her and John both something awful.

She was even able to do a three-way call once with John, and that seemed to brighten the little girl's day. Or at least that's what Laura said before they hung up.

Hank looked to his wife, who shrugged. "Let's see what John has to say. I don't want to mess anything up with the case and for you to lose out on your chance to get Daisy back while they sort it all out."

River had thought that if the judge was brought up on charges and his cases dismissed, John would just get custody. But Jackson explained that custody would automatically revert back to River, if she wanted, while they investigated John's claim of paternity. Eventually, John would get his case heard and he'd win if another DNA test proved he was Daisy's father. But until then, River would have custody restored to her. That meant she needed to keep out of trouble, which was the only thing keeping her from running over to the Ryan ranch and grabbing Daisy. She couldn't kidnap the girl and then get custody. No judge would allow that.

"I promise I'll be on my best behavior. I won't kidnap Daisy, even though it's what I want to do. I'll just be her auntie if Andrew lets me see her." She started to wonder if maybe Andrew would be out of town. If so, then Laura might let her take Daisy for a few hours. Next time they talked, she'd have to ask the housekeeper and cook.

"I guess there's no harm in dropping by, as long as you're on your best behavior," Hank said.

"Momma?" A little girl who was the spittin' image of Mimi toddled into the dining room and climbed into her mother's lap. Maribelle Walton wasn't quite two. She'd celebrate her birthday come January ninth.

"Hey, baby. I thought you were getting a bath?" Mimi loved to care for her own daughter, but since she was expecting another little one, she had hired help.

One of the high school girls on a neighboring farm was interested in becoming a nanny after college. So, a few nights a week she came over and helped Mimi with her daughter, Maribelle. Ruth James was going to study early childhood development in college and hoped to one day run her own daycare center in town.

Right behind her ran a ragged, and wet, teenager with a sheepish grin. "Sorry, Mrs. Walton, I turned around for one second and she took off. I think your daughter is going to become a sprinter."

Everyone at the table chuckled.

"I don't doubt it." Mimi kissed the top of Maribelle's head and handed her back to Ruth. "Maribelle, you know the rules. You have to take your bath and then I'll come in and read to you."

River watched and felt tears prick the backs of her eyes. Daisy was the same way when she was that age, preferring to skip the bath and go straight to storytelling. She wondered how the little girl was doing and hoped she would be back home where she belonged soon. This waiting was driving her crazy.

Two days later, River couldn't stop bouncing in her seat as they drove to the Ryan ranch. You would have thought she was a kid with how excited and antsy she was.

"I hope Andrew really is gone when we get there. Laura said he planned to be out of town for a few days. What luck." River beamed as she replayed the conversation for the umpteenth time.

Mimi and Hank didn't mind. They understood how important this was to River. And Maribelle just loved to chatter.

But what they saw when they arrived sent chills down River's spine. "Hurry up, Hank!"

Chapter 31

John didn't know what to think. Jackson had left him a cryptic message on his cell telling him to get down to Cheyenne right away. So when he came in from the barn after checking the cows, he quickly showered and told his parents where he was heading.

"Son, did you try calling him back?" Caleb asked.

He nodded. "Yup, but no answer. It went straight to voicemail. I'm not sure what's going on, but I gotta get down there now."

"Let's call Hank or River and see if they know anything first. And if there is something really big going down, I'll drive you there myself," Caleb offered.

"It's too bad we don't have a small plane, what with all this back and forth," Judith joked.

For the first time since he'd received that disheartening message, John cracked a smile and almost chuckled.

Then he pulled his phone out of his pocket and dialed his Wyoming friend.

"Hank, it's John. Is something goin' on?" He waited for Hank to respond. And when he did, he turned saucer-shaped eyes on his pa and his mouth hung open wide. "Are you sure?"

"What? What's going on?" Judith Manning asked.

"It's happening. It's really happening, Ma." John fist-punched the air after he hung up his phone. "We've gotta get there now." He kissed his mom's cheek. "You weren't too far off with that plane joke—we really could use it right about now."

"Should we fly down and rent a car?" Caleb asked.

"No, it wouldn't be any faster. I've checked the flight schedules, and the next one isn't until later today." John left to pack a larger bag. After what he'd heard, he figured he'd be in Cheyenne for a while.

"Judith, will you be fine here for a week or so without us?" Caleb turned worried eyes to his wife.

"Dear, you know I'll be fine. However"—she reached up to kiss him—"I will miss you somethin' terrible."

"I'll miss you, too. Stay safe and don't do anything I wouldn't do." He arched a brow at his adventurous wife.

"You know I only do those things when you're around." She winked and pushed him toward their bedroom to pack a bag.

John was ready before his pa, so as he waited he kept trying to call River, Hank, and Jackson. He only left one message for each, but in his impatience, he did end up leaving multiple text messages for each, to no avail.

"Alright, son. Have you called any of your brothers?" Caleb grabbed his Stetson off the peg by the door and his lined denim jacket.

"I thought I'd call them once we were on the road." John followed his pa outside, then hopped in Caleb's truck.

While on the road to Wyoming, John called each of his brothers and apprised them of the current situation as he knew it.

Hank pulled up the drive of the Ryan ranch, but he was stopped by troopers when they were only a few hundred yards away from the front door.

The trooper motioned for Hank to roll down his window. "Sorry sir, but this ranch is off limits right now."

"Officer?" River stuck her head between the seats in an effort to see the lawman's face. "I'm River Cassidy. I'm here to see Daisy. Is she alright?"

He put his hand out, palm up, and reached for his radio. All River could hear was the squawk of the radio and the man whispering once he turned his back toward them.

Nervous energy filled her, and she tapped her hand on her leg as she waited.

When he turned around, he pointed to the front door. "Drive up there and someone will help you."

"Thank ya, sir," Hank said before rolling his window up.

"But, how's Daisy?" What had been excitement turned to panic as she stared at all of the police vehicles. Half the cop cars still had their lights flashing. Her worst fears were starting to play out, and she reached for her phone.

Noticing she had missed multiple calls and texts from John, she called him right away. "John? Do you know what's going on?"

"River, oh thank the good Lord! Where are you?" His panicked voice only worked to cause her level of panic to rise.

"I'm at the Ryan ranch. There's something going on here, but no one will tell me."

"How's Daisy?"

Tears pooled in her eyes. "I don't know! We're just now pulling up to the front door. I'll find out and call you back." She hung up.

But as she did, she heard John's voice telling her to wait, he had good news. It was too late—before she could stop herself, her finger had pushed the hang up button. Although, she was now at the source so she could find out from the trooper coming her way.

River jumped out of the truck before Hank had it in park. "Officer, what's going on? Is Daisy alright?" She ran up to him pleading for answers.

"Miss, calm down. The little girl is just fine. She's in the kitchen with the cook."

"Oh, thank God. I was so worried when we saw all these flashing lights." After she caught a breath, her brain kicked in. "Then what's going on?"

"Are you the River Cassidy who had custody of Daisy Myers?" the trooper asked.

She nodded.

"Please, come inside and I'll explain everything." He held the door open for her, and Hank, Mimi, and their little girl followed them inside to the formal living room.

As they walked inside, they passed the office, where officers and others were tearing it apart. River wondered what could have happened to cause them to be in such trouble.

Once they were seated, the officer started, "First of all, are you willing to take custody of Daisy once again until everything is situated? I'd hate to see her go into the system while waiting for a hearing."

River's eyes widened and her jaw slackened. "What? I can get custody of my little girl back?"

He nodded. "it would be temporary. There's a social worker on her way her now, and she was going to call you. I guess she already reached you?"

River shook her head. "No, I haven't heard from any-one in social services today." She pulled her phone out to look at her call log in case she'd missed the notifica-tion. Nothing there, and no missed messages, either.

Hank, who'd been quiet so far, asked, "What's go-ing on here? Why are officers going through the Ryan house? What are they searching for?"

Mimi asked, "Where are the Ryans?"

"They've been arrested." The trooper didn't expound on what was going on, even when River asked. "I'm sorry, but I can't say any more, other than to say that

Andrew Ryan has lost custody of his daughter for the time being."

"His daughter?" River asked. "You mean, all of this has nothing to do with the fact that he isn't really her father and he forged documents to say otherwise?"

The trooper arched a brow. "Are you saying Andrew Ryan isn't the biological father of Daisy Myers? Do you have proof?"

'Yes, and yes. But the proof won't hold up in court. If I have custody again, I'd like to request a new DNA test of Daisy and the man I know to be her biological father." River knew that as soon as the courts got to the truth, she'd lose custody. But it was the right thing to do. If God really was up there watching out for them all, maybe He'd see to it that she could still be near Daisy and be involved in her life as she grew up.

"Stay here. I'll go get the detective in charge of this case." He left the room, and the remaining occupants stared after him.

"What is going here?" Mimi whispered.

"I wish I knew." River blinked and turned back to the Waltons. "What should I do?"

"First, get Daisy. Let's make sure she's alright and then see if anyone will tell us what happened here." Hank stood up and went to the edge of the room and looked out at the passel of people moving about the house. Some carried boxes of paperwork, and others spoke on their phones. But they all were law enforcement of some sort.

River joined him at the door and looked around the edge. "Is that woman from the IRS?" She pointed down the hall.

"Whoa, if the IRS is involved, then this is much bigger than Andrew lying about being Daisy's dad." Hank whistled and shook his head.

"You're right. This is much bigger." A man with a black leather jacket, blue jeans, dark-brown cowboy boots, and a notepad in hand walked up to them. "I'm Detective Russel. Who might y'all be?" His southern drawl was pronounced, almost like he wasn't from Wyoming but Texas instead.

"I'm Hank Walton." Hank pointed to himself, then to Mimi. "This is my wife Mimi Walton and our daughter, Maribelle."

"And I'm River Cassidy."

Hank and River backed up to make room for the detective to enter the living room.

"Please, take a seat. I've got some questions for y'all." The detective motioned for them to sit on the sofa and he took a leather armchair. "I'd like to start with Miss Cassidy. How do you know the Ryans?" He sat across from her with his notepad and pencil.

River noticed his black, curly hair that was in need of a trim, and his brown eyes staring at her intently. She felt as though she might be the one in trouble and not Andrew. She also noticed he was handsome in a strong, rugged way. He had a chiseled jaw and high cheekbones. When he was younger, he could have been a model. Not that he was old; she figured he was probably in his mid-to late-forties.

"I've known Andrew Ryan since he dated my foster sister Donna Myers, Daisy's mom."

"I see, and where is Donna?" He looked down at his notes and frowned.

"She died, four years ago." Pain still filled River whenever she told anyone about Donna's death.

"I see, and is that when you obtained custody of Daisy?"

She nodded, then went on to tell the detective about Andrew and how he wasn't the biological father, but John Manning was.

"And where is this John Manning?" He narrowed his eyes at River and watched her intently.

"He lives in Beacon Creek, Montana. But I spoke with him earlier, and he's on his way here. Should be here in about eight hours or so." She couldn't wait for John to arrive and help with all of this.

Hank was great. River had become fast friends with Hank and Mimi, but they didn't have a stake in all this. Not like John did.

"I'd like to speak with him when he arrives."

"Of course, Detective Russel."

"And what brought you to the ranch today?" The detective continued to question River, and she answered all of his questions.

When she felt he was done, she asked one of her own. "What happened with Andrew and his dad?"

Detective Russel looked to Hank and nodded. "You noticed the IRS agents here?"

They all nodded.

"The Ryans have committed tax fraud for the past six years, at least. And they have had some very questionable land deals lately."

"I knew it!" River jumped up. "They stole the Hanson ranch from Daisy and were probably forcing the other ranchers to sell, too."

The detective narrowed his eyes. "Tell me about the Hanson ranch and what it has to do with Daisy."

River went into the entire story, about how Andrew all of a sudden had a change of heart and confessed to forging the original DNA paternity test so he wouldn't have to marry Donna or take responsibility for Daisy. And then how he was a rotten dad to Daisy.

"But the worst part, he sold Daisy's inheritance the day he got custody of her. As though the deal was already set to go and he just needed his judge buddy to sign off on the custody papers. There's a suit already filed to nullify that illegal hearing." Vindication was close for River and Daisy, she could feel it.

"Will the money from the sale of the land be transferred to a trust for Daisy?" Hank's suggestion caught River off guard.

"Is there no way to get the ranch itself back?" River asked. After reading that letter from Martha, she wanted Daisy to have her ranch.

"I don't know about that land deal, but I will look into it. If there is an inheritance for Daisy, I'll do whatever I can to ensure that whatever is left goes to her." Detective Russel took time to write down what they had just spoken about.

"Can I see Daisy now?" They had been talking for a long time and she was anxious to see for herself that her little girl was alright. Everyone had said she was fine and with Laura in the kitchen, but until River could see her and hold her, she wouldn't believe it.

"Yes, I think that would be fine. I'd like to speak with Hank and Mimi for a little bit, but I'll have an officer escort you to the kitchen now." He got up and poked his head out of the room.

When a uniformed officer entered, Detective Russel asked him to escort River to Daisy. "She can't stop and look at anything. Take her straight to the kitchen."

"Yes, sir." The young officer motioned for River to follow him.

Chapter 32

They were finally nearing the Ryan ranch, and John couldn't believe what he'd discovered along the way. "Tax evasion. That's how the Ryans were taken down." He chuckled and shook his head.

"Well, I guess this will get the girls back to Montana sooner. We'll still have to work on getting my rights as Daisy's pa situated." John beamed with joy. "But there shouldn't be any issues with that now that River has Daisy and her custodial rights have been reinstated."

"I just hope we can take them both back home with us soon." Caleb slapped the steering wheel of his truck. "Who'd have thought it would be something like taxes?"

"Kinda like those mobsters. Al Capone, wasn't he brought down by the IRS?" John looked to his father. John hadn't ever really been into mobsters, but names like Capone or Scarface, as he was dubbed, weren't easy to ignore.

"How do you think this will all affect my case?" While John was ecstatic River was getting custody back, he still had to fight for his rights as father to Daisy. And if River didn't want to come back to Montana with them, he'd have no way of making her. Not that he wanted to force River to do anything. He hoped she'd *want* to be near him and his family. They all certainly wanted her nearby.

In fact, his mother even texted him that she had River's room all ready for when they returned. Ma was excited not just for Daisy to come home, but for River. They had gotten along quite well. She fit with his family—perfectly. But would she feel that way?

When they were in southern Wyoming, Hank called. "John, we're back at my ranch now with Daisy and River. Come on over here. We'll have supper for you both and rooms ready for you to stay as long as you need."

"Thanks, I really appreciate all your help, Hank. You have no idea how worried I've been since River lost custody. And today, during this drive, not being able to be there for my little girl and River, it just about tore my guts out." John wasn't joking, either. The first part of the drive was difficult, not knowing what was happening.

Then, when he heard bits and pieces from River and Hank both, he began to relax. But what really helped was finally hearing back from Jackson. "I can't wait to tell you all about what my attorney said this afternoon. When we arrive, I'll tell y'all about it."

And he did.

But first, he was reunited with his little girl.

The moment John entered the Walton ranch, he heard a scream he'd recognize anywhere.

"Uncle John!" the little girl yelled out, and ran so hard into his legs he almost fell back.

He reached down and untangled her arms and picked her up and held her tight to his chest. "Daisy." Emotions choked him up. Once he could speak again, he told her how much he missed and loved her.

"Uncle John, do we get to live with you again?" When Daisy pulled back, her face was smothered with her messy tears.

River picked up a few tissues and cleaned the girl's face off.

John looked to River, who refused to look him in the face. "That all depends on River." He waited, and when she said nothing, his heart stopped beating. "I would love to have you both at the ranch. River, the Triple J is your home now, if you'll have it."

River licked her lips and finally looked at John. "Are you sure you want me there, too? And not just Daisy?"

John's eyes softened when he looked at the pretty girl who had changed his life for the better. "River, even when Andrew had custody you were wanted at the Triple J. We've all missed you somethin' terrible."

Some emotion that John couldn't name passed over her face, and she nodded. "Alright, when we're allowed to leave, we'll move back in with you." Her eyes widened and she stammered, "I mean, um, not *with you*, but at the Triple J."

John chuckled. "I knew what you meant." And hope began to blossom in his heart that maybe, just maybe, things would be even better than before.

Mimi had asked Ruth to put a roast in their crockpot when she realized they would be home for dinner that night. The girl was happy to help and did a great job of cutting up the vegetables and adding in the right seasonings.

So, over a pot roast dinner with all the fixins, everyone updated the group on what was going on. After River told John and Caleb everything that had happened that day, John told them about Jackson's good news.

"The governor's case against Judge Singleton was heard this week, and he's been indicted by a grand jury. Which means that all of his cases are going to be called into question." John picked up a homemade biscuit, slathered it with butter and honey, and took a giant bite. "Mmm, these are fantastic."

Mimi blushed and lowered her head. "Thank you."

Hank grinned at his wife. "I don't think I could have married a better cook, or mother."

"Stop it." Mimi slapped his arm, and her cheeks grew even redder. "Please John, continue with your story."

"Yes, ma'am." John went on to tell them that Jackson already had documents prepared and ready to file for a new hearing about Daisy's paternity, and to request that

Andrew return to the court any all funds, animals, and possessions belonging to Daisy.

"When does Jackson think you'll get a hearing?" Hank took a bite of the pot roast and moaned, "This is so tender. This must be some of the best-quality beef out there." He winked at Caleb.

The older Manning laughed and shook his head. "That's only because you use the Manning method of raising your beef, young man."

"Touché." Hank raised his fork.

Chapter 33

I t only took three days before they were able to all go home to Beacon Creek, Montana with Daisy. The little girl jumped with joy and squealed so long and loud that the dogs on Hank's ranch howled when they told Daisy she was going back to the Triple J Ranch.

"Really? I get to go home wiff you? Furever 'n' ever?" Her pronunciation still needed a little work, especially when she got excited, but it only made her that much more endearing.

Unsure what to say, John looked to River for help.

"Yes, you'll never have to leave John again." River tweaked Daisy's nose.

The little girl giggled and then turned serious eyes to her aunt. "Will you come, too?"

"Of course she will." John wasn't about to exclude River from anything that had to do with Daisy. It didn't matter that River was still technically Daisy's legal guardian—Jackson was working on getting him custody. But River was such a huge part of Daisy's life. He wouldn't do anything to break either of their hearts.

Besides, he wanted River to live with them forever, as more than Daisy's nanny. But for now, he'd settle for having her on the ranch as Daisy's caregiver. Hopefully, in time, they could grow to become more than friends.

First, though, he needed to make sure they weren't unequally yoked. The Bible was very clear on that. "Daisy, why don't you go and tell Mimi and Maribelle the good news."

"Okay." The little girl ran out of the room, leaving River and John all alone.

"Well, I'd say that went over really well. She seems so excited to be going back to your ranch." River bit her lower lip and turned to look at John. "I have a few questions."

"I thought you might." What he wanted to do was talk about God, but if she needed to know about anything else, he'd be happy to discuss whatever she wanted.

"I've been reading the Bible you gave me and going to church on Sundays." She rubbed her hands together nervously in front of her.

"Let's sit down." He couldn't believe his luck. She wanted to ask him about God. Did this mean she was ready to accept His love? If so, they might have a chance after all.

"How can I go to heaven? I don't get it. From what I've read, I'll never be good enough for God to love." She kept her hands in her lap and sighed.

John hadn't led too many people to God before, so he hoped he didn't mess this up. *God, I can't do this without you. Please give me the words to say here.* With a deep sigh and a trust that God would provide, he explained what he knew.

"River, you *aren't* good enough."

"What? But then, why did you give me a Bible and tell me I could?" Outrage and confusion marred her beautiful face.

"Hold up." He held his hands up in a placating gesture. "None of us are good enough on our own. But God did make a way for us."

"How?"

"The Bible says in John 3:16, 'For God so loved the world, that he gave his only begotten Son, that whosoever believeth in him should not perish, but have everlasting life.'"

"I've heard that a lot, and read it in the book of John. But what does it mean?"

"It means that God loved you before you even had a path to heaven. He loved you so much that he sent his only Son to come here on Earth, as a human, and die a horrible death on the cross." John stopped for a moment to listen to God. "Do you know what that means?"

"Die on the cross?" River nodded. "Yes, I read about that in the Bible and have heard a lot about how Jesus was tortured and crucified."

"Before Jesus came, the Jews and anyone else who wanted to be called one of God's children had to do regular sacrifices at the Jewish temple in Jerusalem. It was a very difficult journey to make back then if you lived far away. And with the way the temple was repeatedly destroyed, it wasn't a sustainable way to heaven. But God didn't mean it to be the way forever."

"He sent his Son here?" River asked. "To be the perfect sacrifice once and for all?"

John's grin went from ear to ear. "Exactly! When the Jews sacrificed their animals, it had to be perfect and without blemish, but they had to do it repeatedly. Every time they committed a sin, they had to do a sin offering, or sacrifice. Then there were other sacrifices they had to make at certain times of the year. But when Jesus came, he did away with those Earthly sacrifices and He became the perfect sacrifice for all of the world, and for all time. All you have to do is believe that Jesus is your savior and confess that you are a sinner, then ask Him to cleanse you of your sins."

River scoffed. "It's that easy, huh?"

John solemnly nodded. "It is. Salvation is one of the easiest, yet hardest things you will ever do."

"How so?"

"You have to admit that you're a sinner and you can't make yourself perfect. There isn't a work or a thing you can buy that will get you to heaven. The only thing you can give up is your pride. Once you do that and accept His gift, you'll forever be His child. The penalties for all of your past, present, and future sins have been paid. You just need to accept the gift and ask Him to come into your heart forever." He prayed that he'd handled that right and God could use his words to speak to River's heart.

"Will you hold my hands while I pray?" She put both of her hands out for him, and he took them.

"Of course I will." He squeezed her hands and smiled at River as joy, pure as the driven snow, coursed through his body.

"What do I say?"

John had heard the sinner's prayer said many times—he'd said it as a kid—but right then he was so nervous, he couldn't remember the whole thing. Did it matter if he said it verbatim? No, he knew the words themselves weren't nearly as important as the heart and what was intended when the words were said.

A person who didn't mean them could pray the exact same prayer he did as a little boy, but unless the person saying them meant what they were saying and were truly asking from the heart to have God come into their life, then it meant nothing.

"Why don't you repeat after me?" John suggested.

She nodded.

He could feel the perspiration building in her hands, and he squeezed them again for support. "Dear heavenly Father..." He waited as she repeated each line after he said it. "I know in your Bible you said that if I confess with my mouth and believe in my heart that Jesus is Lord who died on the cross, and you raised him from the dead, then you would be faithful and just and forgive me of my sins. And I will be saved. So Father, I'm confessing right here and now that Jesus is Lord. I want Him to be my Lord, now and forever more. Please send Jesus to live in my heart and keep the enemy away from me. I admit that I am a sinner and need your forgiveness for my sins. Please cleanse me from them and help me to stay away from sin. I thank you very much for making the path known to me and forgiving me. Thank you, Jesus, for becoming my Lord and washing me white as snow. Amen."

John felt a wave of anxiety pass over him, and then he opened his eyes to the most beautiful tears he had ever seen.

River was looking at him, her eyes shining as she smiled from ear to ear. "That was all I had to do?"

"As long as you believe those words, then yes. You are now saved," John confirmed.

"Thank you!" She hugged him.

When he pulled back, he cleared his throat. No one had ever warned him that leading a woman whom you cared about to the Lord could be such an intimate experience. He had never felt closer to any woman before. Nor had he ever *felt* so much for a woman before.

He wondered if this euphoria was what his parents felt when they studied the Bible together. If so, he could understand how they were still so much in love after all these years.

<h1 style="text-align:center">Chapter 34</h1>

"Can I call you daddy now?" Daisy's earnest request stabbed at River's heart. They had been at the Triple J Ranch for almost two weeks now. Christmas was the following week, and they had just told Daisy that John was her real daddy.

'Yes, you can call me daddy." John kissed his little girl's cheeks, and she squealed with delight.

Everyone was at the ranch, including Elizabeth and Logan with their new infant. Even Chloe and her fiancé, Brandon, had come for the weekend celebration. The only one missing was Roman, but he'd be there in a few days, right after he finished his last final of the semester.

River knew this was coming, but she didn't think she'd take it so hard. The paperwork was in for John's claim for paternity, along with the new DNA test showing proof. In fact, they ran the test at three different labs just to make sure.

Even from jail, Andrew was still claiming Daisy was his. Everyone knew it was because the money from Daisy's inheritance couldn't be touched by the IRS and he wanted it. From the sounds of things, the IRS was going to take just about everything his dad had. And the rest would most likely go to the lawyers. When Andrew and his dad got out of jail, they'd be broke.

"When Jackson called yesterday, he said it was all but done. After the new year, the judge will make it official and I'll be Daisy's daddy, legally." John beamed at his little girl who looked so lovingly at her pa.

"But, what about her inheritance?" Elizabeth asked. Since she had given birth the day after Thanksgiving, she hadn't been around to hear all of the details. She and Logan had kept to their house in town with the new baby as much as they could. Not only did they want the time to bond with their baby girl, Noel, they also didn't like the idea of driving in the snow yet. They might have been acting a little bit too careful, but no one was going to fault them for loving their baby so much.

The family now had two new additions to the next generation of Mannings, both girls.

River and John exchanged looks.

"What's a harrytence?" The sweet, naïve little girl looked to her new daddy.

Her pronunciation of *inheritance* caused the entire family to laugh.

"The things little girls say." John kissed Daisy's nose. "It's an inheritance. And that is something that someone who died left to you. Do you remember Mr. and Mrs. Hanson?"

She nodded. "Gammy an' Poppy." She twisted her little lips. "They in heaven with Mommy now."

John hoped that was where they all were, but he wasn't sure about Donna. "Well, they wanted you to have their ranch."

River interrupted, "But Andrew sold it."

With a furrowed brow, Daisy shook her finger at River. "Andrew was a bad man."

It wasn't a funny situation, but John could barely keep himself from smiling over how Daisy said things. "You're right, he is. What he did was wrong. And since they bulldozed the house the day after it closed escrow, River and I agreed that Daisy would take the money and we'd put it in a trust for her. It was a rather large amount."

"Really?" Logan hadn't said much about the entire situation so far, but he was curious.

"Is that business background of yours perking up?" John teased.

"Actually, it is. I'm wondering what sort of trust you set up and how much interest the money will accrue."

River jumped in. "We don't have the money yet. But it is being held by the courts in a sort of trust account at the moment. Once they finish unraveling everything, then they'll send the money to Daisy's..." She bit her lip and couldn't continue.

John picked up for her. "Her guardian will take the money and set up a college fund along with a standard trust fund." Before saying anything else, he looked to River who nodded for him to continue.

"Logan, when that time comes, would you be able to help us?" John stressed the word "us" because he was going to ensure that River was involved the entire way. While she wasn't Daisy's mother, at least not yet, she was a mother figure.

As for the future, he hoped they could explore their feelings more.

Later that night, after Daisy had been put to bed and read three stories, John took River's hand and led her out into the hallway. "Care to take a walk with me?"

She raised her brows. "Outside?"

He nodded.

"But it's snowing." She hated pointing out the obvious, but didn't he realize how cold it was?

He laughed. "Yes, but we do have a nice patio cover and a firepit waiting for us."

"Oh, well. In that case, let me get my jacket."

Once they were settled outside in two Adirondack chairs with blankets and hot chocolate, John looked at River. He really took in her beauty. Her long, silky auburn hair, and her sparkling eyes that showed more green than brown that night, with little flecks of gold and chocolate.

"I've been wanting to talk to you for a while now, but with everything going on, I thought it best to wait until we knew more." He cleared his throat. "This"—he gestured between them—"is more than just a shared connection with Daisy."

Even with the chilly weather and the snow coming down around them, River felt her cheeks grow warm. She couldn't help but smile as her heart raced.

"I'm attracted to you, River, more than I ever thought possible with anyone."

"Even more than Donna?" Her insecurities were starting to come out.

He furrowed his brow. "Donna and I, that was nothing. Well, it wasn't nothing. But it wasn't anywhere near what I feel for you."

"Wait." She held up a hand. "I thought you were in love with Donna?"

He nodded. "I thought I was, too. But until I met you, I really didn't know what love was. I can see now why so many people marry at a young age only to divorce later on."

River twisted her lips and looked down at her gloved hands. "Are you saying you and Donna wouldn't have lasted if you had been the one she wanted to marry?"

"No, I don't believe in divorce. I would never have divorced her. But I don't think we would have had the best marriage if she lived. We weren't in love. I might have been able to learn to love her, but she was never going to love me." He shook his head. "That doesn't really matter now. What matters is that I finally understand what all of my brothers have been going on about. True love is putting the other person's needs above your own. It's being happy when they are, and sad when they are. It's working together to solve problems."

"Like we've done?" Her whisper was almost too low for John to hear over the crackling of the fire.

"Exactly. We put each other's needs, and Daisy's, above our own. When you took Andrew up on his offer so you could be with Daisy, I was hurt at first. Then I realized you weren't doing it for him or me, you were doing it for Daisy. Because you love her more than anything else. I think that's when I started falling in love with you." He reached over and took one of her hands.

"What? You're in love with me?" She blinked and shook her head. "No, you can't be. I'm not pretty like Donna is..."

John interrupted her. "You are more beautiful than Donna ever was. Please don't compare yourself to her. Who you are on the inside shines like a bright star on the outside. I know we've been through a lot, and it's not totally over yet. There are still more hurdles to jump. But I want to work with you by my side. I want to get to know you better, not as a possible nanny for Daisy, but as my girlfriend."

"Really?"

"Yes, and then when you're ready we could talk about marriage. And I don't mean a marriage of convenience for Daisy. I want you to know that no matter what, you will always have a place here and a place with Daisy. I want us to fall in love with each other for who we are. And not because of Daisy." He looked down and felt his own insecurities rise as River sat there staring at him, not saying a word.

After a few more moments of silence, he asked, "Do you think you could love me for who I am? And not just because I'm Daisy's father?"

A warm smile began to spread over her face, and she nodded. "Most definitely."

He stood abruptly, bringing her with him, and without saying a word he pulled her to him and kissed her. When she wrapped her arms around him, he took that as permission and deepened their kiss.

When they finally pulled apart, both sucking in air, River kissed his lips lightly and then each of his cheeks. "John, I've been in love with you for months now. I just never, ever thought you could care for me."

"Really? But you're gorgeous, generous, and one of the nicest people I've ever met. How could I not fall in love with you?"

She giggled. "Can we take this slow?"

"I'll go as slowly as you want. Just as long as you don't leave me." John kissed each of her temples, and River leaned into him and sighed. He knew then and there that theirs would be a true love match that lasted forever.

Epilogue

Roman Manning couldn't believe the events of the past few months. Not only was he a new uncle to a brand-new baby girl, but now he was an uncle to a four-year-old girl. What a wonderful Christmas present this was.

Seeing baby Noel on FaceTime wasn't the same thing as holding her in person. And seeing Daisy on Face-Time was nothing to trying to keep up with her at the Christmas fair. Roman had no idea what made him think he could take her to the kiddie Christmas fair booths and not have a problem keeping up with her. The girl had more energy than a two-hundred-pound linebacker chasing a quarterback. Something he would know plenty about, seeing as how that was exactly what he'd done for the past three seasons at college. One more year to go and he'd have his degree and come home.

Roman missed his family and their ranch. And now that they had two little girls in the family, he missed it even more. By the time he finished college John would be married, and he'd be the only one left to get married. Chloe was already planning her wedding to Brandon, her fiancé.

He wanted to be married and have kids. It was his dream to have his own ranch and populate it with at least a dozen kids, some of whom would be adopted. He'd never want his wife to have to go through so many births, or to have such a huge age gap between the oldest and youngest as his family had.

Roman was lucky. Even though he and Matthew were twelve years apart in age, Matthew always took time for him. Probably because the oldest Manning had only recently met the woman of his dreams and married. They'd probably be announcing they were pregnant soon, and he would be ecstatic for them. Although, he hoped they had some boys in this family soon. No way would he let girls take over the Manning family.

Daisy ran from him, again. And he followed, yelling, "Daisy, wait up. Where in the world do you get all this energy?" With a chuckle, he grabbed her hand and slowed her down.

"Ducks! Look, Uncle Roman, ducks!" Daisy yanked on his hand as she pulled him to the little pond with rubber duckies floating around.

Chuckling, he pulled out two dollars and handed it to the game operator. "One..." When he looked into the green eyes of the short, pretty game operator with

strawberry blonde hair, he lost all ability to think or
speak.

Author's Notes

Wow, I can't believe this series is almost over. All that's left is to tell Roman's story.

I have loved this series so much, that it won't truly be over. I have plans for a spin-off series down the road. But first up, is a couple of stories that just won't leave me alone. LOL And of course, Christmas. If you've read any of my Christmas books, you'll know that I have a special place in my heart for this very special season. And in case you haven't heard, Chloe's story is told in , book 1 of the Big Sky Christmas series. This series is also now completed with 4 books.

Let me know what you thought of this story by leaving a review on , or any other place you enjoy leaving reviews.

If you don't know Jesus as your Lord and personal savior, I highly suggest reading the book of John and looking for a Bible believing church in your neighborhood. If you have a lot, ask some of your friends where they go, I'm sure they'd be happy to take you with them on Sundays. And maybe they'll even take you out for Sunday Supper afterwards! Yummy!

I want to give a shout out to my Scotland Sprint Sisters for working so closely with me on this book. We sprinted 6 days a week while I wrote this one. And I wouldn't have been able to get in so many words each day if it weren't for Audrey and Amie supporting me and cheering me on so often! Thank you both so much for your love and support!

Don't miss out on the free copy of Finding Love in Montana. It's the story of how Mimi and Hank got to-gether. Join my newsletter to get your copy! See below.

Also, if you love pulled pork sandwiches, then scroll down to get your free recipe! I love these and it's soooo super easy to make!

Newsletter Sign-up

By signing up for my newsletter, you will get a free copy of the prequel to the Triple J Ranch series, Finding Love in Montana. As well as another free book from J.L. Hendricks.

If you want to make sure you hear about the latest and greatest, sign up for my newsletter at: https://jenn ahendricks.com/newsletter/. I will only send out a few e-mails a month. I'll do cover reveals, snippets of new books, and giveaways or promos in the newsletter, some of which will only be available to newsletter subscribers. You'll also get a heads-up when I'm running sales on my books!

JENNA HENDRICKS
Finding Love in Montana
A Triple J Ranch Prequel

Pulled Pork Sandwiches

1 – 5lb bone in pork shoulder, or any cut of pork that looks like a roast.

2 – bottles of your favorite BBQ sauce (I used no sugar added Sweet Baby Ray's original sauce.)

8 – hamburger buns, or large Sweet Hawaiian rolls.

Crock pot, or Instapot

In at least a 5-quart Crock pot, bigger depending on the size of your pork, put in the pork shoulder and empty 1.5 bottles of BBQ sauce over the meat. Turn on slow for a minimum of 12 hours. Overnight is best, just check the pork first thing in the morning and turn it over a couple of times. Add more sauce if you feel the pork is a little dry. You only need to save enough to add to your sandwiches.

Once the pork is done, take it out and put it on a cutting board. Then use 2 large forks and pull apart. It should easily shred into pieces without using a knife. But if needed, or desired, you can cut it like a roast.

Serve with a side of your favorite potato or macaroni salad. And feel free to add chips or fruit to your plate for a rounded meal. Your family will love this and think you've slaved over the meal. You will love making it since it's so easy.

Sneak Peek

Her Montana Christmas Cowboy

Chloe Manning's first Christmas in French-town was heartbreaking. Will Santa give her her heart's desire during her second?

Brandon Beck left behind a woman for the benefit of his family ranch last Christmas. Now that he's back, why can't he get her out of his heart and mind?

When Santa and Mrs. Claus play matchmaker, will Chloe and Brandon fall under their Christmas Magic? Or will past hurts and fears keep them apart?

Don't miss out on the first Christmas story of the heart-warming Christmas Cowboy romance series, Big Sky Christmas. Where the romance is clean, and Christmas takes center stage!

Prologue

"**O**h!" Chloe Manning yelled as her foot slipped where the driveway met wet grass. The water pooling on the concrete driveway wasn't something she'd planned on when scheduling her move. Since it had rained early that morning, she could not have foreseen the hazard and rescheduled. But, she also knew that her brothers and sister had scheduled their week to help on this one day. "Great, just what I ne—"

A strong, masculine hand reached down and offered to help her up.

"Thanks," she said without looking up.

"My pleasure." A husky voice that Chloe didn't recognize turned her face up just as she stood, and she yanked her hand out of his. "Ah!" Not looking where she was going, Chloe fell over the headboard she had dropped when she'd fallen the first time. This time she fell on the wooden headboard and smacked her knee good.

"I'm sorry, I shouldn't have let go until you were steady." The stranger furrowed his brow and bent down to help her get back up, again.

"No, no. It was all my fault." Chloe's face heated up, and she did her best to stand. She inhaled a quick breath when she put pressure on her right leg. While she knew enough medicine to know she hadn't broken anything, she was going to be sore.

In addition, she'd fallen flat on her face not once, but twice, in front of a very handsome cowboy. Her pride had also taken a huge hit. To make matters worse, Chloe hadn't dressed to impress; she was wearing an oversized, faded University of Montana sweatshirt and yoga pants. Her blonde hair was up in a messy ponytail, and she had zero makeup on. The only upside was that she doubted this handsome cowboy would recognize her again.

A bright, white smile greeted her when she stopped wobbling and took a step away from him. "Thank you. I don't know what's gotten into me today."

"Are you the one moving in?" The cowboy looked between her and the house.

Chloe nodded. "Yup."

"Well, welcome to Frenchtown. You must be the new medical billing manager everyone has been talking about." The cute cowboy put his hand out. "I'm Brandon Beck."

Well, there went that thought. He knew exactly who she was. No way was she going to be able to hide her embarrassment behind anonymity.

Standing taller, she straightened her sweatshirt and blew her bangs out of her eyes. When she took his hand, a jolt of electricity swept through her entire being. "Ah, I'm..." She cleared her throat. "I'm Chloe Manning." She shook his hand and noted the calluses, but also the strength in his warm touch.

"Nice to meet you, Miss Manning." When he ended the handshake, he touched the brim of his hat and nodded.

"This is my sister, Elizabeth, and our brothers." Chloe pointed to them all and introduced her five brothers to Brandon.

Elizabeth looked between Chloe and Brandon and gave her twin sister a sly smile. If Elizabeth didn't know better, she'd think Chloe already had an admirer. But really, who *wouldn't* be attracted to Chloe, even in moving clothes? The men of Beacon Creek had always admired her sister. The only reason Chloe wasn't already married was because she had made it known far and wide that she wanted to move away as soon as possible.

Brandon took a closer look at the newest resident to Frenchtown, and something in his gut told him to watch out for this little filly. She just might cause *him* to fall at *her* feet. He wondered if that would be so bad.

Once Brandon had moved on, the sisters went inside with the headboard and set it up in Chloe's new bedroom.

"Wow, sis. You did good. This is a rental?" Elizabeth Manning walked around the room checking out the wooden floor and blocked wainscoting on all the walls. "There's so much potential with this place."

Chloe Manning agreed. She couldn't wait until the day the owners let her buy it. This was exactly what she wanted. The deal she'd made was to rent for a year, and if everyone was happy then she would buy it. The owners wanted to make sure she stayed there with her job and didn't go home. Mr. and Mrs. Rice, who owned the quaint house, lived next door and felt it was important to like their neighbors. They worried if they sold her the house now, she would leave and sell to someone they may not like.

Chloe knew she was home and wouldn't be going anywhere. "Yes, I think I'm going to be very happy in this house, and in this town." She beamed at her sister as they unloaded their boxes into a spare room.

Chloe and Elizabeth were twins. While Chloe had always wanted to get out of Beacon Creek, Elizabeth was happy to live there for the rest of her life. When Chloe was offered the chance to move to Frenchtown and manage the local medical clinic's administrative side, she'd jumped at the chance to leave her small hometown. Not that Frenchtown was much bigger, but it did offer her a chance at new experiences and a promotion at work.

The plan was to work in the Frenchtown Clinic and manage it for the next five to seven years, and then she could start applying for jobs in the big cities, like

Bozeman or Helena. Then, she would be doing exactly what she had wanted her entire life—get out of Dodge, so to speak.

"What about the men? If they're all as handsome as that cowboy we just met, then I think I won't be the only one getting married next year," Elizabeth teased her sister.

Heat shot up Chloe's neck and face. She deserved the ribbing after everything she'd put Elizabeth through when her now fiancé came back to town last summer.

The man who had helped Chloe up from the ground was gorgeous. Too bad he'd met her when she was at her worst. No makeup, hair a mess, and then to fall flat on her backside? She knew he wouldn't be back.

Just thinking about slipping and falling in front of the handsome Brandon Beck caused her face to heat up again. She wasn't normally a klutz, but today seemed to be her day of making a fool out of herself.

Even after he'd helped her up, she'd still tripped over the headboard because she wasn't looking where she was going. Instead, she was focused on the very good-looking and tall cowboy with chocolate-brown eyes and medium-brown hair that looked as though it needed a cut. His hair curled around his ears and above the back of his collar, which only served to make Chloe even more attracted to the cowboy.

All she could think of was running her fingers through his soft hair. Where that thought came from, she couldn't say. But when she'd realized where her mind was, that was when she'd tripped over the headboard.

____

Does this sound like fun? If you enjoy reading about the faith and fun surrounding a small town at Christmas, then this book is for you! And it can be read year-round. So check out today! You'll be glad you did.